SNOW
ANGEL
JJ MARSH

TRISKELE BOOKS

Snow Angel

Copyright © 2018 by JJ Marsh

The moral rights of the author have been asserted.

Cover design: JD Smith

Published by Prewett Publishing.

All enquiries to admin@beatrice-stubbs.com

First printing, 2018

ISBN: 978-3-9524796-7-4

For my golden godgirls – Jessica, Caitlin and Emily

Get your free copy of prequel
Black Dogs, Yellow Butterflies when
you sign up for the mailing list.

See back of book for details.

Prologue

Upton St Nicholas is proud of its annual festival and rightly so. Villagers spend much of the year preparing costumes and decorating floats, crafting gifts and rehearsing music. Logistics preoccupy the council from September onwards and it attracts onlookers from as far as Barnstaple, Plymouth and Taunton. The village green is closed off for the day so pedestrians can wander amongst the mulled wine stalls, browse original paintings or patchwork quilts, sample homemade jams and pickles and enjoy the entertainment. Jugglers and fire-eaters wander the green displaying their skills, leaving children wide-eyed and agape. Morris dancers jump and caper, waving handkerchiefs and rapping their wooden sticks, each movement accompanied by the tinkle of bells around their knees. If it snows, as it often does in early December, the festive charm is complete.

At no particular signal, the crowds spread along the road, each spectator seeking an unimpeded vantage point to observe the main event; the procession.

Ask one of the locals what it is all about and you'll get a different story each time. The majority agree the old fella in the hat and purple cloak is Saint Nicholas, or Archie the wood merchant in a fake beard, if you want the truth. Yet no such consensus can be found on whose patron saint he might be. Children, say some. Sailors, argue others. Heads shake and insist he is the champion of the poor. Claims are made with some vehemence for prisoners, pawnbrokers and virgins.

Whoever he represents, the saint sits high on a golden throne atop a tractor decorated with painted canvas as a mediaeval vessel. He wears a bishop's red mitre and holds three golden bags into which he regularly dips and scatters gold (chocolate) coins to the accompanying children and watching crowd. The audience are at liberty to consume theirs immediately with steaming paper cups of coffee. St Nicholas's young escorts must wait, stuffing their pockets until they have completed the carol singing.

In the wake of the saint's disguised Massey-Fergusson capers a more alarming figure. Dressed in a brown monk's habit with hood and black beard, he has neither boat nor tractor. On foot, he has licence to run at passers-by as if to snatch their chocolate coins or even their children. Shrieks and squeals of pretend fear accompany the sinister creature, whose soot-smudged face is half hidden by folds of brown cloth.

That is where the Christian theme tails away, as the next section of the parade takes on a pagan feel. Forest folk wassail past wearing antlers or ivy head-dresses, carrying holly branches and mistletoe, and cups of spicy cider. Towering over them plods a handsome grey Percheron wearing a festive wreath as horse collar and wicker panniers over his withers. The horse bears a pretty red-headed girl in a white dress, silvery cloak and ornate crown. She reaches into the panniers and throws gifts to the smiling faces lining the pavement. Tied bundles of lavender or cinnamon sticks, ears of wheat or small apples. Catch her eye and she might gently bowl you an orange studded with cloves. The folk musicians following the mighty horse play jigs on flutes, fiddles, guitars and timpani, in a lively rhythm to get cold feet stamping.

For years, people have been telling you it's worth the trip. They're not wrong. You find yourself beaming at the carollers and bouncing on your heels, feeling right at home.

A young man to your right claps in time to the rhythm, nodding in approval as the auburn-haired nymph and her steed pass.

"What's she got to do with St Nicholas?" you ask, lifting your voice over the noise.

His gaze remains fixed ahead and for a moment you think he hasn't heard. Then he speaks, his voice accented with the Devon twang. "Nothin'. That's The Winter Queen. We honour her before the solstice, offer her gifts and ask her to be kind."

"She doesn't have a festival of her own?"

A woman replies, "She used to. A long time ago." Her features, an older version of the man's, identify her as his mother. But where his jaw is stern, her face is softened by a kind smile. "We've always had the St Nicholas parade on the sixth of December, or the first Saturday afterwards. The pagan festival of Yule would be on the twenty-first, but times have changed. Now everyone is in thrall to the commercialism of Christmas." She sighs. "So the village celebrates its name day by honouring St Nicholas and showing our respect for The Winter Queen together."

"I see. She's very pretty."

Under his thick black brow, the man's eyes assess the back of the white-clad figure on the horse. "The prettiest girl in the village plays The Winter Queen. We vote on it. First time in years it's gone to someone new." He flushes, as if he has said too much, and nudges his mother. Time to leave. She smiles a goodbye and follows him into the crowd, blending into green-grey-brown shades of country jackets and stone walls.

The procession continues out of the green, past the post office and turns into the main street, the music lilting through the brisk December air. You follow them as far as the pub then leave the villagers to their eclectic celebrations and head back to the green to browse the stalls and seek some hot chocolate.

You take a left and find yourself walking along a row of semi-detached cottages, many of whose windows are lit with festive lights and doors hung with holly wreaths. Deep in admiration for the picturesque nature of this place, it takes you a minute to realise you are walking away from the village green and further from your car. You stop to get your bearings. Clouds pass over the sun and the frosty blue sky of the afternoon turns gunmetal grey.

You turn around in the quiet street and a flicker of movement makes you look up. A gasp escapes you. There in the window, pressed up against the glass, is a face. Twisted and ugly as a gargoyle, it is contorted with rage, all directed at you. A bare-chested man is mouthing words you cannot hear, words that must be violent and filthy. He scratches at the window as if he wants to gouge out your eyes.

You hurry back to your car, shaken and chilled to your bones. The streets no longer seem charming and joyous, but slushy and grey. You remind yourself of how tourists are detested by many people living in beauty spots. Grockles, they call people like you. You are not welcome here. Time to go, far from this toxic place.

Hot chocolate forgotten, you drive away from Upton St Nicholas. You doubt you will ever return.

Chapter One

"Good God. Wallace Pryor is dead." Butter dripped from Matthew's crumpet onto the obituary section of *The Times*.

Beatrice poured the coffee. "Who?"

"Writer. You know, horror. Very successful series about humanity's inner demons taking over Earth. You read one. Loathed it, as I recall."

He continued to scan the column, shaking his head and reading salient points aloud as Beatrice added warm milk. "Sixty-seven. That's no age. Died a wealthy man, apparently. In Ecuador."

Beatrice sighed and set down her spoon. "Matthew, is this to be our daily routine? Get up, make breakfast, see who's dead? Your fascination with the recently deceased could be described as morbid."

He folded the paper with a grin. "Fair point. Don't want to put you off your crumpets. Oh, was that the lot?"

"No, there are two more in the toaster. Anyway, you've already had three." Beatrice sipped her coffee and opened *The Paris Review*.

"Yes, but I am preparing for a full morning of physical exercise. I have to shift all those slabs from the patio after my round of golf with the chaps."

"Why don't you ask the chaps round here to give you a hand? That way you get your gardening jobs done and spend some time together in the fresh air."

The toaster popped and Matthew reached behind him for the hot crumpets. He plopped them onto his plate and shook his head. "No, no, not a good idea. Midge will still have a hangover from the weekend and Mungo hates anything resembling manual labour. His catchphrase is 'I have a man for that'. Anyway, to return to my point, it's on my mind."

Beatrice looked up from a review of a Dorothea Lange exhibition at The Barbican. "What? The patio?"

"No. Death."

Watching him slather butter onto both crumpets, Beatrice saw no evidence of a preoccupation with The Other Side.

She frowned. "One of those is for me, actually. Why is death on your mind, or does this happen to everyone at your age?"

He handed over a crumpet, with evident reluctance. "You see, so many of the names I've grown up with have disappeared. Not just people I know, but the icons of academia and the arts seem to be dropping on a daily basis. Gilles D'Or died last week. Seventy-five. Tragic loss to the world of jazz. He was the hell-raising trailblazer of my generation. Every last one of us wanted to be just like him. Last week, an enormous stroke, over and out. Meanwhile, those who try to fill such shoes in the spheres of literature, music, fine art, cinema, philosophy and even politics are snot-nosed and still in short trousers. What have you done with the blackcurrant jam?"

Beatrice pushed across the jar. "It's called getting old. Perhaps we should try and appreciate contemporary culture a little more. How about tonight we order ourselves a 'fusion menu' from the takeaway, watch *The Pop Factor* and have our own poetry slam before bed?"

His expression, flared nostrils and retracted lips, reminded Beatrice of an expression she'd once seen on a cat when encountering a dead hedgehog.

"There are few fouler phrases on the planet than 'fusion menu'. My stomach riots at the thought. Let's stick with your original suggestion. Sticky venison with red cabbage and chestnut stuffed mushrooms. What are your plans whilst I don my overalls and perform rugged manly tasks in the garden?"

Beatrice wiped her fingers on a napkin. "This morning, I'm off to the city to meet Tanya. There's a book event we want to attend. After lunch, back to writing. I'm not happy with Friday's chapter. It needs work."

"Give Tanya my love. You do realise you say 'it needs work' every day?"

"That's because it's true. Right, I'm off to get changed. Enjoy your golf and mind yourself with heavy lifting on the patio. You can have this crumpet, after all."

The drive back from Exeter, usually an opportunity for reflection, sped by as Beatrice listened to her new purchase; Dr Henry Moffatt's *History of Europe*. If she had spent some moments examining her feelings, there would have been a frisson of excitement. On Sundays, she had some Me-Time, an indulgence she sometimes missed.

The chapter ended and Beatrice pressed stop. She would savour this audio book and ration herself to one chapter at a time. No point in starting another as she was nearly at the new cottage. She corrected herself. Nearly *home*. A small sigh escaped. She should be grateful. After so many years in his solitary bungalow, Matthew had sold up to buy a bigger cottage in the next village, all because of her. It was beautiful, with a large garden, light rooms and a glorious view across to the River Creedy. But when would it feel like home?

A memory of her counsellor's voice echoed through her mind. *What's the hurry? Look on it as an extended weekend. How many times have you wished for just another day together? One extra day to go somewhere, do something, cook a new recipe. Trying seeing each day as a bonus. A chance to do something you've always wanted.*

Bless James. She was looking forward to next month's appointment with unusual enthusiasm. She missed him. She missed London.

It was a shame there'd been such a poor show at the bookshop, but Devon's apathy had worked to Beatrice's advantage. She and Tanya had buttonholed the poor author, bulldozing him with enthusiasm and curiosity, but failed in their pre-planned strategy of taking him to lunch. He had to leave for St David's and catch a train to London. So armed with her signed stash, Beatrice hugged Tanya goodbye and headed back to the car, in the happy knowledge she had gained some hours alone. Matthew would still be at the golf course and more than likely to stop in at The Boat for a pie and a pint before returning for a light doze on the sofa. Patio postponed for another day.

Her relationship with Tanya was an odd one. Beatrice never thought of herself as a stepmother. Probably because she wasn't, as Beatrice had resolutely refused to marry Matthew. Could she be described as a common-law stepmother? Or stepmother-in-sin? Now that sounded much more like it. She must tell Tanya next time they met; she'd enjoy that. They always had such fun together, partly because Tanya had an insatiable curiosity for the unusual, the quirky and the downright odd. Her wide eyes and perennial smile, not to mention her delightful six-year-old son, Luke, were some of Beatrice's favourite things about Devon.

Her stomach growled as she parked in front of the house and bundled her packages into an awkward armful. As she walked across the drive, her mind on what to make for lunch, she saw Matthew standing in the doorway. The look on his face stopped her dead in her tracks. Something was wrong.

"Matthew? What is it?"

"It's Vaughan."

Beatrice's mind scrambled for a second. She was unused to Matthew calling the man by his real name. "Something's happened to Midge? What is it?"

"Midge, or Vaughan Mason, is dead."

At the kitchen table, Matthew ran his hands repeatedly through his hair, his attention distracted. Beatrice sensed he was trying to articulate events more for himself than for her.

"We knocked at his door just before ten. He's often late to answer, especially after a heavy night, so we waited a good few minutes before ringing again. Mungo and I were chatting and discussing the news, but there was a nip in the air so we rang again. After the third try, we unlocked the door. Both Mungo and I have a key, after so many nights bringing him home drunk. We called him over and over again to no avail and searched each room in the house. Eventually we went upstairs and found him on his bed. In a bit of a mess, tell the truth. I'll spare you the detail. Stone cold and judging by the colour of him, he'd been gone a while. I called the police and while we waited, Mungo and I checked the house for some explanation for what had happened. Don't worry, we didn't touch a thing. Empty wine bottles, full ashtrays, dirty plates and discarded clothes are nothing unusual. A typical weekend chez Midge. Seems the old bugger choked on his own vomit."

Beatrice reached for Matthew's hand. His skin against hers was dry and cold, his grip limp, his eyes bleak.

"You poor thing. That must have been quite horrible for you. I'm so sorry, my love. What a dreadful way to lose a friend of over thirty years."

"Thirty-two. He joined the faculty thirty-two years ago although we didn't become friends until a good while later. In fact, I used to hate the sight of the man." Matthew shook his head, his focus decades distant.

Beatrice focused on the practical. "What did the police say?"

"Not a great deal. They would like statements from us tomorrow but don't see anything to warrant further investigation, pending the coroner's verdict. Let's face it, Vaughan Mason was a hard-drinking, heavy smoker who gambled daily with his health, even aged seventy-one. Looks like his luck ran out." Matthew placed a palm over his eyes and squeezed Beatrice's hand.

She squeezed back. There was nothing else she could do.

Chapter Two

The atmosphere after Vaughan Mason's death affected the whole village. Not a soul referred to him by nickname. People recalled his literary talent and long-distant fame. Everyone was just a little kinder and more appreciative of one another, grateful for the simple fact they were still alive. Guilt crept into the conversation, with many voicing regret they had not called to check on him since he drunkenly left the pub on Friday night. Platitudes and reassurances such as, 'Nothing you could do', 'It wasn't unusual for him to get plastered', and 'How could you have known?' echoed from the bakery to the delicatessen to the post office.

Matthew had become quiet and withdrawn since returning from the police station on Monday morning so Beatrice chose not to press him. He spent hours in his study, out for long walks, or assisting Mungo in trying to find Vaughan's family and making funeral arrangements. She knew he would talk when he was ready.

As it turned out, circumstances came knocking, whether he was ready or not.

On Wednesday morning the sun came out, melting the frost and casting a delicate light over the overgrown mess which would one day be their garden. Matthew and Beatrice finished breakfasting on bagels with salmon and cream cheese, while reading their respective papers. It had been three days since Matthew had mentioned the obituaries. He stacked the dishwasher and Beatrice pegged a basket of laundry onto the garden washing-line, to make the most of the weather. So the first thing she knew of their visitors was when a tall uniformed police officer came out of the kitchen door and across the lawn.

"Excuse me, Ms Stubbs? My name is DS Perowne. Sorry to bother you. Could we have a word?"

Beatrice stared at the young sergeant who had appeared from her own house.

He nodded at the clothes fluttering on the line. "They forecast rain for later so keep an eye on the sky," he said with a wonderfully gentle accent, and gestured for her to go first.

Indoors, a young woman in plain-clothes sat at the kitchen table with Matthew. She rose to shake Beatrice's hand and show her ID. Close up, her face led Beatrice to revise her estimate. Late forties but rather well preserved.

"Good morning, Ms Stubbs, and apologies for turning up out of the blue like this. My name is Detective Inspector Axe and you've met DS Perowne."

The young man pulled out a chair for her. She sat, checking Matthew's expression and finding a worried frown.

Beatrice recovered her voice. "DI Axe?"

The woman shrugged with an easy grin. "Believe me, I've heard every joke going. When I was a DS, I had a colleague called Stabb. We could never work on the same case because people wouldn't stop laughing."

Beatrice examined the open face with wispy trails of hair escaping her ponytail and instinctively warmed to DI Axe. A soft exterior with a core of steel.

"I can imagine. Would you like a coffee or anything?"

"No thanks. My guess is you'd like us to state our business and leave you in peace. So we will. We're here about the death of Vaughan Mason. I know you were both friends of his and Professor Bailey was one of the two men to discover his body. The coroner had some concerns about the way he died and requested an autopsy. It looks very much as if Mr Mason ingested a poisonous substance. There was a pot of meat stew on the hob in his kitchen which we had tested. It contained significant amounts of a lethal toxin from a local strain of fungi. Now, this could easily be accidental if Mr Mason made a mistake collecting wild mushrooms. In a far less likely scenario, it could have been deliberate."

Matthew recoiled in his chair. "You surely don't mean he killed himself?"

"We don't believe it was intentional. Poisoning is a very unpleasant way to go. No, by deliberate, I mean another party introduced the element without his knowledge. What we need to do is ascertain how much Mr Mason knew about local vegetation, whether he was a mushroom collector and anybody who might have wished him harm. We'd also like to know who visited him the last few days before he died. We were hoping you could help."

Beatrice looked at Matthew. "I don't have a clue. What would you say?"

Matthew massaged his chin, still frowning. "Good God, I have no idea. I mean, I've known the man for over thirty years, but as for his knowledge on woodland flora, I am clueless. Look, he had a routine. We played golf on Sunday mornings, me, Mungo and Midge. Tuesdays he often had a few people round to play cards. I never attended as I don't play and certainly don't gamble. Friday night, he was nearly always to be found propping up the bar at The Angel. Other than that, there might be a dinner party, faculty event or cultural gathering where we crossed paths. He was a reasonable cook when sober, but also an awful snob. No offence, DI Axe, but describing his *Cassoulet Toulousain* as a meat stew would have wounded him to the quick. He often boasted about it. He'd make it on a Friday and eat it all over the weekend. One of his favourite quotes was 'a good cassoulet always tastes better the day after'. Midge always ordered his food online and hand-selected his meat from the butcher in Crediton. I have never in my life seen him in a supermarket, nor can I imagine him digging up truffles in the forest."

DS Perowne leant against the worktop, scribbling in his notebook. "I understand Midge was a nickname, sir?"

"Yes, a silly thing. Years ago, there used to be a children's programme called *Mary, Mungo and Midge*. I can't even remember who started calling us Matthew, Mungo and Midge, but it stuck. Probably because it irritated the hell out of Vaughan. Such a towering ego to be known as Midge? He hated it but slightly less than *The Last of the Summer Wine*, which was what people occasionally said about us three old farts pottering around together. He still saw himself as *l'enfant terrible*."

"What do you know of his family, Professor?" asked DI Axe.

"Precious little. He was married once and I believe there was a child, but I don't think he is in contact with either. Mungo and I have had no luck in tracking them down."

"Oh that's all right. We have contacted his daughter, officially next of kin, and his ex-wife. They'll be at the funeral on Monday. I just wanted an insight into how he felt about them, that's all."

Matthew ran his hands though his hair. "He must have mentioned them, or I wouldn't have known they existed, but all I know is that he hadn't spoken to his ex-wife for years. As for the daughter, all I recall is his ranting that she never thanked him for Christmas and birthday gifts."

"The funeral is still going ahead for Monday?" Beatrice asked. "Despite an open investigation?"

"Yes, it is. Thanks to the Professor and Mr Mungo Digby, all arrangements have been made and there is no need to delay interment. The investigation will proceed independently. Well, unless there's anything else you'd like to add, we'll leave you to get on with your day."

The DI pushed back her chair just as a spatter of raindrops hit the kitchen window.

Beatrice hadn't even noticed the encroaching thunderous clouds. "Oh hell!"

DS Perowne took two strides and was out of the kitchen door. "I'll get the laundry. You stay in the dry."

Matthew pulled on his wellingtons and followed the officer out to the washing-line. The two women watched from the kitchen window as they tugged at garments and pegs, throwing them into the wicker basket.

"I hear you used to be in the same line of work as me," said DI Axe.

"Yes. I retired three months ago as Acting DCI of the Met."

Axe turned to her with a wide smile. "I know. Your reputation precedes you. It's a pleasure to make your acquaintance. Do you miss it?"

"Every day." Raindrops slithered down the glass, rendering activity in the garden a blur. "So if you think I can be of any assistance..." Beatrice tried to sound casual and not at all needy.

DI Axe turned to face her. "I wish I could call on your expertise. But protocol, you know how it is. Anyway, this one we can handle."

Two wet men burst through the door, wiping their hands over their faces and dropping the basket on the mat.

DI Axe applauded. "Hey, DS Perowne, you just got your Boy Scout Laundry Rescue Badge! Thanks for your time, Professor, Ms Stubbs, and we'll see you at the funeral."

Beatrice kept to her routine of domestic duties in the mornings and knuckling down to write in the afternoons. Domestic duties had become a great deal more onerous now she had a wedding to organise. In just under a fortnight's time, she would see her former neighbour, friend and all-round favourite person marry the love of his life. Adrian and Will had chosen the Sunday before Christmas and a small Devonshire village of all the locations in the world to commit to each other, and Beatrice could not be more delighted.

The theme was Narnia, so everything would be white, silver and sparkling. She met with the hotel catering staff, local florists, a pastry chef and even a candle-maker. Instructions came daily from Adrian and the assistant in his wine shop, Catinca. And on Saturday, all three would arrive for a week of preparations. Hopefully, that would distract Matthew's attention from the loss of his friend. At least for a few days. Her new dress and crystal bejewelled jacket were tucked away in the wardrobe, so she could devote her attention to creating the perfect day for Adrian and Will.

She was happy and totally fine and not at all disappointed by the Devon and Cornwall Police Force refusing her help. Why on earth would they need a retired old lady who happened to have an impressive track record, collaborative kudos and until recently a high ranking position in the London Metropolitan Police? Had she been in DI Axe's position, she would have done the same. All correct and proper. There was no place for her in such an investigation and she should be relieved.

Except she wasn't.

Chapter Three

The drive from London to Devon in showery conditions meant the roof of the Audi stayed on. Catinca grumbled sporadically from the back seat, stressing her whole travelling outfit had been assembled to show off her Jackie O shades and powder blue headscarf to envious passing motorists. Will tried to reason with her about temperatures and wind chill and motorway spray from lorries in their faces, but she was not convinced. Eventually Adrian told her what happened to Isadora Duncan and her scarf in an open-top vehicle. That shut her up for a good ten minutes.

The car was packed to the gills. Four suitcases – one each for the following week and wedding, with a separate one for Adrian and Will's honeymoon in the Caribbean – filled the boot while beside Catinca were boxes and bags containing various elements of 'magic' she had collected for the wedding reception. Every available nook and cranny was stuffed with a bottle of wine or champagne.

Adrian's mind looped back, as it did at least once an hour, to his shop. His pride and passion. Harvey's Wine Emporium, the jewel of the East End, now left in the hands of his two part-time employees for the busiest fortnight of the year. He closed his eyes and breathed. Jed and Ezra might be so hip it was painful, but they were both conscientious, and another good sign, nervous.

"I need a wee," stated Catinca, her chin poking through the gap between the front seats. "Can we have a piss stop soon?"

"It's called a pit stop. You're as bad as Beatrice," Adrian replied.

"Yeah, but I got an excuse. I'm a foreigner."

Will glanced at the rear-view mirror with a half grin. "If you can hang on for twenty minutes, there's a lovely old pub just before Stonehenge. We could stop for lunch then stretch our legs with a walk to see the standing stones. If you want to?"

"I want to! I never seen Stonehenge. Yeah, I can wait. After lunch, can I have a go at driving? Give you a break?"

"No, you can't."

"You don't trust me," she pouted.

"With no insurance, no experience and a car that handles like a racehorse? No, I don't. How about we have some music on?"

"Yes!"

Will hit the stereo and Adrian sighed. He had no hope of choosing something sophisticated with these two in the car.

Their excitement built to a crescendo as they arrived at Beatrice and Matthew's cottage. When the sun had finally come out with conviction, Will put the roof down and all three of them belted out the chorus to Foo Fighters' 'My Hero' as they cruised along the country lanes to their destination. Wind rushed through Adrian's hair and colour flooded his cheeks. Will gave a cheerful toot of the horn as they pulled into the drive and Catinca got to her feet, clutching their headrests for support, yelling, "Hello, Devon!" at the top of her lungs.

Their exhilaration was short-lived as they got out of the car. The welcoming party was not at all what Adrian had expected. The door remained closed for a minute, then Beatrice slipped out, acknowledging them with a brief wave, before locking the door behind her.

Adrian sensed Will's glance at him but kept his focus on Beatrice. She trotted down the steps and across the drive to embrace each of them with a warm hug.

"So good to see you all!" Her voice was subdued and under-enthusiastic. "Listen, Matthew's feeling a little under the weather, so what say we head straight to the pub? You can check in and freshen up, then join us in the bar for drinks."

No one spoke for a moment, disconcerted.

Will took charge. "How is he coping, Beatrice?"

She shook her head with a quick frown. "Let's chat at the pub. I'll take our car and lead the way."

The three of them piled back into the Audi and Will closed the roof. The little blue VW drove down the drive and waited for them to catch up before leading them back the way they came.

Catinca was the first to speak. "What's up with Matthew?"

Adrian looked over his shoulder. "A friend of his died last week. I told you, remember? Matthew found the body."

"Oh shit, yeah. Poor old geezer. Something you never forget, innit?"

"Losing a friend?" asked Will.

Adrian closed his eyes in anticipation bordering on dread. He'd heard far too many of Catinca's experiences to expect a simple articulation of empathy.

"Nah, finding a body. Back in Romania, I found three. Two was accidents. Drowned kid in a river and old woman. Horse kicked her in head. Bloody sad. But other one killed hisself. Mate, never seen a worse mess in my life."

Adrian stared straight ahead, failing once again to imagine Catinca's world.

"Were any of them your friends?" asked Will.

"The kid and old lady not really. Neighbours is all." Catinca took out her phone and snapped a photo of thatched cottages as they entered the village. "Suicide was my uncle. Shot hisself in the mouth. Me and my cousins had to clean his brains off the ceiling."

So much for the party atmosphere.

The Angel won Best-Looking Village Inn by a country mile, with each window shutter wrapped like a Christmas present and fairy lights around the door twinkling across the green. After heaving all their boxes and luggage upstairs, Adrian sat for a moment on the window seat, absorbing the rustic Devonshire view and trying to realign his thoughts.

Yes, the wedding would be the biggest day of his and Will's lives. No, he could not expect everyone else to live and breathe the million little details which add up to perfection with the same intensity that they (or more truthfully, he) did. The timing of Matthew's friend's demise was unfortunate, true, but unlikely to wreck their day. He had to keep a positive mind-set and provide a joyous celebration to lift everyone's spirits.

He inhaled and gazed out at the vivid colours of Upton St Nicholas in crisp wintry light, releasing his breath and egomania in one long exhalation. Will was clattering around behind him, unpacking bags and grumbling about the amount of stuff Catinca had packed.

"What are you looking for? Will, just stop messing everything about and tell me what you want. I understand her system," Adrian asked his husband-to-be.

"The presents! We're going downstairs to meet Beatrice and Tanya, who have both put in an enormous effort for us. Not to mention Luke."

"Look in that Riedel box by the wardrobe. We packed all the presents for friends and family in there." Adrian looked up at the heavy oak beams and whitewashed ceiling. "This is such a lovely room. Do you suppose they gave us a bigger one because we're about to be the bridal couple?"

Will ripped off the parcel tape and opened the box. "Dunno. Maybe. But we're not spending our wedding night here, are we?"

"Of course not!" Adrian tutted. "We are guaranteed the bridal suite at Moor Hall for our actual honeymoon night. I've told you that."

"Oh yeah. For the amount it cost, we'd better get all kinds of extras as the newlyweds. Here they are! Luke's, Tanya's, Beatrice's, Matthew's and Marianne's."

"You may as well leave Matthew's and Marianne's there. He's poorly and we won't see her till the day of the wedding. If she even turns up."

Will didn't answer and closed the lid. He took great care to place each gift in his backpack, his expression innocent.

Adrian smelt a rat. "You invited Marianne. Here. Tonight." It wasn't a question.

"Yeah, I did. My thinking was we should clear the air now and not have any tension on the big day." Will slid behind him and placed a chin on his shoulder. "I asked her to come as a personal favour. We should bury any hard feelings after the summer. She's split up with that tosser who abducted Luke and now realises her so-called boyfriend was a narcissistic piece of shit. She made a mistake, Adrian, but if her father and sister can forgive her, I think we should do the same."

Adrian stared out at the window, where a man was throwing a stick for an eager retriever. He sighed again.

"Fine. She's Matthew's daughter. Of course we need to be forgiving and polite. I just wish you'd mentioned the fact she'd be here this evening. Does Beatrice know?"

"Everyone knows. Let's go, we'll be late."

"Any more surprises, DS Quinn?"

"Maybe. But I guarantee you'll like them." He kissed Adrian. "Come on, they'll be waiting."

Chapter Four

Gordon Hancock, the landlord of The Angel, went out of his way to be friendly every time Beatrice and Matthew popped into the public bar. But today Beatrice was not in the mood. She would need all her energy to cope with the wedding party and their understandable enthusiasm, so she ordered a tonic water, exchanged pleasantries and took her drink into the empty snug at the back. The rendezvous was scheduled for six o'clock giving everyone time to finish their busy days and get ready for a reunion.

Adrian, Will and Catinca needed to settle into their respective rooms, unpack and freshen up.

Tanya would fetch Luke from school, give him some food and change his clothes, before driving him out here to say hello.

And Marianne, if she turned up, would join them after she left work in Crediton. Beatrice practised a conciliatory grin. Since the family holiday in Portugal that summer, which had gone so horribly wrong, Beatrice and Marianne had not yet come face to face. Beatrice squeezed her eyes shut, blocking out the memory of Luke's kidnap and the agonising hours of uncertainty. The real courage had come from Will, not only rescuing the child but standing witness for the prosecution. Now that Marianne's ex-boyfriend had been tried and imprisoned, she had finally stopped defending him. That whole episode was over for everyone. Or at least for those who could forget.

Outside, dusk threw shards of pink and grey across the sky and in the last glow of sunset, a breeze whirled a pile of leaves into a cartwheel of colour, reflecting the open fire in the hearth. The beauty of the moment left Beatrice frozen. She grimaced and faced the truth. She needed an appointment with James. After leaving London she had navigated relocation, a new house, and an unexpected death, plus planned a wedding and what with Christmas looming, it was no wonder she was discombobulated. Her counselling session could wait no longer. She checked no one was around and reached for her phone.

To her surprise, the receptionist at James's practice knew who she was, required no explanation and found her a slot on Tuesday. Tuesday! After the funeral and before the wedding. She rang off, elated and guilty in equal parts, and mildly puzzled as to why James's schedule was not overbooked as normal. Perhaps she just got lucky. She raised her face to the window and allowed herself a deep sigh. Tuesday. She would just have to manage until then. Now to continue with the domestic goddess routine.

"Susie?"

The landlady twisted to look over her shoulder while pouring a pint in the public bar.

"Hello, Beatrice, didn't see you in there. You all right? Where's Matthew?"

"He'll be here in a bit. We've got a half a dozen people joining us tonight. Could I order a couple of bottles of Prosecco?"

"Course. I'll bring them round with an ice bucket and glasses. Give me half a tick."

Beatrice was practising imaginary responses to James when Susie bunted the door open with her hip and carried a silver bucket into the room, with champagne flutes between each finger.

"Two bottles of the standard dry and six glasses. Shout if you need more. How's Matthew doing? Must have been a terrible shock for him."

"Thank you, Susie, you're very kind. Well, he's struggling, to be honest. Like many people, he blames himself, but in his case, he actually found the body. Most unpleasant."

Susie held up a hand. "No details, please. I'm even avoiding the newspapers this week. I tell you, I've had enough. It's the only topic of conversation in the bar."

Beatrice rubbed her eyes. "Of course it is. That's one of the reasons Matthew has stayed home. He despises idle speculation. And just when I thought he was coming out of the tunnel, the police turned up."

"The police! What did they want?"

"To ask some questions. The coroner..." Beatrice remembered she was not at work and in a village this small, information was currency.

Too late. Susie had caught a whiff of a rumour. "They got the coroner involved? Why on earth would they do that? From what I heard, Vaughan drank himself to death. Something the whole village has been predicting for years."

"Not sure. They only spoke to Matthew," Beatrice lied. "Probably just turning stones. It's just police procedure."

Susie set the glasses on beer mats and went over to poke the fire. With her back to Beatrice, she said, "You of all people should know how it works. You reckon they'll want to talk to us? Last place he was seen that Friday night was here, before he staggered off across the green."

"Susie, as I've told everyone I've met this week, this is not your fault. It's possible the police will want to talk to you to establish a pattern of Vaughan's behaviour, but there is no reason whatsoever you should be a suspect. All of us feel guilty, but how much responsibility can any of his neighbours be expected to take?"

A log popped in the fire and Susie replaced the fireguard. She heaved herself up from her knees with a groan. "You're right. I said the same to Gordon. We're publicans, not nannies, I said. Are you coming to the funeral?"

"Of course. I have to support Matthew. If I'm honest, Vaughan was not one of my favourite people, but he was definitely one of Matthew's. I imagine there'll be quite a turnout, what with locals and the literati."

"Yeah." Susie's intonation fell flat. "So I'll be making sandwiches all morning and cleaning up all afternoon while they get maudlin and sentimental. Here, you wouldn't fancy giving me a hand with waitressing, would you? The week before Christmas is always chock-a-block and with a funeral on top I could use an extra pair of hands."

"All right. At least it will give me something to do. Is Francesca not coming?"

Susie turned back to the fire, picked up the poker and rearranged the logs. "I appreciate that, thank you. No, we've not seen her for months. The gallery is doing great business at this time of year, so it makes sense for her to stay put and sell as much as she can. She'll be here over Christmas, of course. By the way, she calls herself Frankie now." She looked back at Beatrice and rolled her eyes.

The door burst open. A small person rushed into the room, red of nose and cheek and wearing a duffle-coat. He spotted Beatrice and like a heat-seeking missile, cannoned into her midriff, wrapping his arms around her and squeezing hard.

"Oof! Have a care for my old bones," she said, squeezing him back. "Where's your mum?"

Luke looked behind him. "Talking to that lady from the garden centre. Guess what I got in my spelling test today?"

"Rhinoceros."

"Not what words, what marks?"

"Was it marks out of ten? Then I'd say you got seven and a half."

"Nope. Ten! Me and Samantha Lake got full marks and Mr Howard says we should both enter the spelling bee at the end of term."

"I think that's a very good idea. Who's Mr Howard? I thought Ms Shaw was your teacher. Would you like a glass of juice?"

"Yes, please."

Susie ducked behind the bar and lifted up two bottles. "We've got orange or pineapple. Which would you like?"

"Orange, please." Luke unbuttoned his coat and rolled it into a ball. "He's our substitute teacher. Ms Shaw's off sick. Where's Grandpa?"

The door opened again and Matthew's daughters walked in. Tanya broke into a big smile on seeing Beatrice, but her sister looked far less enthusiastic. Beatrice assessed Marianne as she came forward to greet them. She'd put on a good deal of weight since the summer, but it actually suited her. Beatrice opened her arms for a hug.

"Hello, stranger. I've missed you."

Marianne's expression was relieved and she embraced Beatrice warmly. "I missed you too. Is Dad not joining us?"

"He'll be along in a bit. He just needed a little more time. This whole Vaughan Mason business has knocked him for sticks, you know."

Marianne opened her mouth to respond but shut it again as the landlady approached with Luke's juice. She placed it in front of Beatrice and dropped her voice, even though Luke was in animated discussion with Tanya over the nutritional value of a packet of Frazzles.

"He's not the only one. Heather Shaw has taken compassionate leave. She and Vaughan, you know..."

Beatrice frowned. "I thought that was all over after that row at Halloween?"

"Bonfire Night, you mean. They were always on and off..."

"Shall I open the fizz?" Tanya interrupted, reaching for a bottle. "Luke, I said no. You've had a snack already and we'll be having dinner soon." The landlady took the hint and retreated behind the bar.

"Can't stand gossips," Marianne muttered.

"Course you can't," said Tanya. "Because most of the time they're talking about you. Pass me those glasses in case this spills."

"At least I give people something to talk about. Here."

Tanya shot her sister a mock-fierce glare but the banter was teasing and good-natured. Relief suffused Beatrice as she handed over Luke's juice.

The cork popped and Tanya hurried to get the bubbles into one of the flutes, then looked up with a huge beam.

"The happy couple! Talk about timing!" She thrust the bottle at Marianne and rushed over for a three-way hug with Adrian and Will. "You look right gorgeous, both of you! This is going to be wedding of the year, I reckon. Come on, I just opened the Prosecco."

The first contact between Marianne and Will was likely to be awkward. How would he break the ice when it was he who had pursued the incarceration of the man she loved?

Beatrice decided to give them some space. "Luke, you didn't answer my question. Can you, in fact, spell the word rhinoceros?"

With wonderful intuition, Tanya picked up her cue. "He's pretty good at big words, but that one is at least ten letters. What do you think, Lukey?" She continued pouring Prosecco as Beatrice observed the Dance of the Buried Hatchet from the corner of her eye.

"R-H-I-N-O-C-E-R-O-S," spelled Luke, with an air of invincibility.

Everyone applauded his success, just as Catinca and Matthew walked into the room. Catinca gave a deep bow, as if the applause were intended for them.

Scanning Matthew's face for signs of his mood occupied Beatrice's attention fully, so it was only after he'd flashed a warm reassuring grin and gone to greet the bridal couple that she noticed what Catinca was wearing. A man's tweed jacket with rolled-up sleeves over a white shirt and Fair-Isle tank-top with a baggy pair of plus-fours and on her feet, as always, a pair of Converse trainers. She looked like an extra from Oliver Twist and at the same time, quite fabulous.

Prosecco and presents distributed, introductions made and

conversation buzzing, their party seemed to fill the small Snug Bar. Those who looked in, searching for a seat, soon withdrew and left the noisy group to themselves. Initially shy, Luke soon found a way to attract Will's attention by challenging him to spell difficult words. Beatrice was pleased to see Marianne join in, making an effort to recognise Will's place in the family group. This left Matthew and Adrian chatting in a corner, which was no bad thing. Catinca and Tanya, as Beatrice had predicted, bonded instantly and were already laughing at some Catinca classic comment.

This was her family now. All she had to do was keep it together.

Chapter Five

Thanks to great maturity and hard-learnt lessons of the past, Beatrice had opted for a cup of herbal tea as a nightcap. She and Matthew rehashed the events of the evening, judging it to be a positive occasion all round and anticipating more of the same in the week ahead. His mood was expansive and optimistic, the best he'd been for days. She chose not to mention her anxiety or her urgent need to see James. This was not all about her.

Matthew reiterated for the fourth time how pleased he was that Will and Marianne were getting along. She agreed, again, and once her yawns got the better of her, retired to bed while he stayed up with a glass of Macallan. Her last thought before sleep was, *three more days*. Three more days until she could talk to James. Three more days until she could get her head cleaned.

As a result of her relative sobriety – a minority in their party, it had to be said – she was awake and alert before six in the morning. She lay in the dark and considered the day ahead. *Choose outfit for funeral. Break news to Matthew about London trip on Tuesday. Organise trains and ask Dawn if I can stay over. Call Tanya to see if she can keep an eye on Matthew. Warn Adrian about weather forecast. Check if florist has sourced sufficient gypsophila for bridesmaids' bouquets. Call bakery about the cake decorations.*

"Beatrice?"

She jumped. "You gave me the frights! I didn't know you were awake."

"You should have realised. For one thing, I wasn't snoring. Anyway, I've been awake for a while, thinking." Matthew's voice had a portentous tone.

"Yes, that's often what wakes me too. Was it about Vaughan?"

He didn't respond for a moment. Beatrice sat up in bed but instinct warned her against turning on the bedside lamp. Some things are easier voiced in the dark.

He shifted his back up against his pillows and reached for her hand. "Look here, I know you were not his greatest fan. I accept that. However, he meant a great deal to me. And even had he been nothing more than a drunk I passed in the pub occasionally, I would not want to see anyone suffer such a fate."

"Nor would I. But accidents do happen, especially to the heedless. It's very sad, but you should not feel a personal accountability."

"Hmm."

Beatrice waited. She could almost hear him marshalling his thoughts.

Finally, he cleared his throat. "Something bothers me about what the police said. Poisoning as an intentional act. Vaughan was not suicidal, that much I can say. He may have had a death wish, insomuch as he indulged his pleasures to an irresponsible degree, but he had no intention of meeting the Grim Reaper halfway. He used to joke with us, when Mungo and I hinted at moderation, that 'the old bastard will have to bring his scythe and drag me off the golf course'. Nor can I see him foraging for mushrooms when he had everything delivered from Waitrose."

"What are you saying?"

He sighed deeply and released her hand. The dry sound of skin on skin told her he was rubbing his face. She waited.

"I am not unaware of the irony in this. For years, I have tried to deflect your attention from solving crimes and looked forward to the time when your investigative days were in the past. But this is different. I should like to ask a personal favour. I wonder if you could poke around a bit, ask a few questions and see if you can discover any evidence that someone deliberately introduced a toxic substance into Vaughan's system? You see, I have the feeling the police are far too likely to write this off as an accident."

Moments passed in silence as they both absorbed the impact of his words.

Beatrice patted blindly around her bedside table until she located her water glass. She took several gulps. "Do you seriously think anyone in this village would want to poison our famous resident?"

"Hand on heart, yes, I do. Famous he might be, but popular he was not. Vaughan made a lot of people very angry, some even bitter. He could be arrogant, aggressive, snobbish and a boor. He hurt a lot of people. It would only take one to shut him up permanently."

"For someone you call a friend, you have an unromantic view of the man."

"That's because I knew the real Vaughan. The rest was showmanship. What do you say, Old Thing? Do you think you could help? I know about the whole 'I have no official jurisdiction' business but that's never stopped you before."

Beatrice leaned against him and rested her head on his shoulder. "To be honest, my love, this might be exactly what I need."

When she entered the kitchen after her shower, Matthew was making pancakes. Her all-time favourite breakfast and a sure sign he wanted to butter her up. She seized the moment to announce her London trip.

"And if James can squeeze me in just when I need to talk to someone, I really have to go. I know it seems selfish, the day after your friend's funeral, but this has been building for some time and..."

"If you need to see him, you must go. In point of fact, the timing is perfect. Mungo and I intend to spend Tuesday morning at the golf course and lunch at The Boat as our own private farewell. After that, we plan to offer our house-clearing services to Midge's family. I'll be busy all afternoon, I imagine. Ideal day for you to take a day trip to London." Matthew placed a pile of fat little pancakes in front of her. "Here. Ricotta and buttermilk."

"Ooh, these are fluffy. Thank you. Rather than a day trip, I think I will stay overnight, even if Adrian and Will aren't there. It's a chance to catch up with Dawn and..."

"...get your London fix. I understand. So long as you're applying your mind to this Vaughan situation, I feel I've done right by him. I owe the man that."

Beatrice decorated her pancake with a Jackson Pollock splatter of maple syrup and inhaled the scent of freshly brewed coffee. "I've already started. While I was in the shower, I compiled a list of anyone who might see Vaughan as an enemy."

Matthew sat opposite and scattered sugar and lemon juice onto his plate, his expression preoccupied.

"You might want to add a pancake to that," Beatrice suggested. "What do you know about his relationship with Heather Shaw?"

He looked at his empty plate, shook his head and forked two of his concoctions from the pile. "Not much more than you. They were an item for a while, big row a few months ago and it was all off. You recall that screaming match on Bonfire Night. Very embarrassing for all who were present."

They ate in silence for several moments, listening to the piano concerto from the CD player and the clatter of magpies in the garden. A small shape passed the kitchen door and settled on the mat. Beatrice watched it for a minute, tucking into her second pancake, her mind elsewhere.

"So Vaughan had a casual relationship with the local schoolteacher for a couple of years then ended it rather brutally in public. Or am I misremembering?"

Matthew laid down his cutlery and rubbed his face. "No, you remember right. Midge, I mean Vaughan, was a total swine that night. Heather would have had every reason to wish him harm. As would her son, Gabriel. If I'd been in his shoes, I'd have knocked the old bugger's block off for talking to Heather like that."

Beatrice opened the fridge and poured herself a glass of orange juice. She raised it to Matthew but he shook his head, patting his stomach in explanation.

"Tell me about Gabriel," she said.

"Nice lad. Polite, well-mannered, respectful and truly committed to his work. Forestry Commission. Never heard anyone wax so lyrical about trees. He had quite a passion for Tanya at one stage. He's very handsome so I thought she'd be thrilled, but as usual, Tanya wanted nothing to do with a nice single man. And he's also a hunter. Deer, foxes, rabbits and badgers, to keep the population under control. You can see why that partnership would never work."

"Oh dear. That's a pity. Was his animosity to Vaughan in general or only after the acrimonious spilt?"

"They didn't like each other at all. You see, that Bonfire Night wasn't the first time Vaughan and Heather had fallen out. One might call theirs a volatile relationship and much of it played out in public. Vaughan could be verbally ... crude."

"Yes, I remember," Beatrice replied, with a flare of irritation at Matthew's diffident defence of a vulgar, unreconstructed bully.

They ate without speaking for several seconds and Beatrice acknowledged her judgemental tone. She had asked for information. Her job was to listen and filter witness facts from witness emotion. The picture would only get muddier if she dragged her own prejudices into the mix. The only way in which she was relevant was as a non-suspect. She had certainly not poisoned Vaughan Mason, even though she had wished the man gone from the face of the earth on more than one occasion.

Matthew stirred his coffee, his gaze over her shoulder at the garden. "As I say, all part of the persona. He couldn't stop acting his role, especially after he'd had a drink. Just to set the record straight, I am not excusing his rampant chauvinism. I took him to task over several instances. He'd been thrown out of The Lazy Toad twice, was permanently barred from The Star and I believe he was only tolerated at The Angel because of his friendship with the landlord. Gordon is part of the card-playing contingent. Is that a cat on the doorstep?"

"I think so. Probably belongs to one of the neighbours so don't go feeding it. I know what you're like. So Heather, the dismissed lover, would have a motive. Her son, a forestry worker, would have both motive and means. The card games – were they playing for money?"

"Oh yes. They took it awfully seriously, and one chap got into such debt he declared himself bankrupt. I recall the police became involved, suspecting a gambling den and all that. Vaughan smoothed it over as a gentlemen's gathering with a civilised game of cards."

"Hmm. I'd like to talk to Gordon and some of the other attendees. Thank you for the pancakes and the intelligence. Now I need to hit the beat. Just one last question. If I asked you, from sheer gut feeling, who you think might have wanted to kill Vaughan, which one single name would you give me?"

Matthew's brow creased horizontally, vertically and relaxed. "I couldn't give you a single name."

"Really?" Beatrice's tone was incredulous. "Not one single name?"

"No. But I could make you a shortlist of half a dozen."

Chapter Six

As predicted, the crematorium was packed. Vaughan Mason's funeral was the event of the year and the village showed up en masse. Absentees were conspicuous, one of whom was Gabriel Shaw, the schoolteacher's son. Heather herself was present, in velvet layers of black and red, with a dramatic veil over her face.

Matthew and Mungo took on the role of hosts as none of the relatives had offered, and stood in the porch, shaking hands and conversing with each mourner quietly. Beatrice seated herself near the back with Tanya, both feigning expressions of sorrow while gossiping in whispers.

"See that one with the red feather in her hat?" hissed Tanya. "Vaughan's neighbour, Demelza Price. She's on the parish council and she hated his guts. He deliberately annoyed her by sunbathing nude when she was gardening or playing Eminem out of his bedroom window on her book club evenings."

Beatrice sighed. "He really went out of his way to upset people. I'd say a good half of this congregation is secretly celebrating."

"Probably more than half. Look at all these publishing luminaries. There's Whatsisname. You know, the bloke with the teeth. Vaughan trashed his comeback novel in a review for *The Guardian* and called his agent 'an undiscerning vampire'. And those two beside him are the presenters of *ArtScene* on Channel Four, which Vaughan always referred to as *Asinine*. Tell you what, the pub is going to shift some champagne today."

Beatrice watched the room fill and her eye was caught by a pair of older ladies, whom Matthew escorted to the front pew, directly below the pulpit. Their white heads looked familiar, but without seeing their faces, she had no idea where she'd seen them before. They crossed themselves as they faced Vaughan's floral-clad coffin and settled themselves to the left.

Whispers rustled like sea grass through the crowd as a woman strode down the aisle. Short and plump, she wore huge sunglasses, and black glossy ringlets framed her face. Her shimmery black dress seemed more appropriate for an awards ceremony than a family funeral. Draped over her arm was a large handbag with chains instead of seams. Each hand twinkled with rings, bracelets and slick dark nail polish and her feet were clad in black high-heeled ankle boots. She acknowledged no one as she sat on the first pew on the right, opposite the old ladies.

Beatrice, like everyone else in the crowded church, was staring.

Out of the corner of her mouth, Tanya whispered, "Bet you that's his daughter. She just flew over from New York, where she works for a lifestyle magazine. Doesn't she just ooze glamour?"

"She reminds me of a Vietnamese pot-bellied pig," said Beatrice, with total honesty. "Well groomed, certainly, but with little trotters and a snout."

"Ssh!" Tanya snorted as the organ struck up and the vicar ascended to the pulpit.

As funerals go, it was on the brief side. The eulogy touched on Vaughan's youthful fame, the undeniable contribution he had made to literature and the number of friends he had made in the second phase of his life, in his adopted village. He regretted the loss borne by the family, gesturing to the front pews. Rose was Vaughan's ex-wife, and Grace their only daughter. The fact that the white-haired lady and glamour puss sat on opposite sides of the aisle seemed to confuse him as much as everyone else. Nevertheless, he assured the assembly that Vaughan Mason had been dearly loved and would be greatly missed.

Beatrice thought it a good thing that people were not given the opportunity, as they were at weddings, to stand up and object. *Speak now or forever hold your peace.* No, in church people would hold their tongues and go along with the vicar's airbrushed version of Vaughan. Only once the first wine glasses had been emptied in the function room at The Angel would vengeful knives come out. And Beatrice intended to be all ears.

No one cried as the curtain hid the coffin from view, not even Heather, who was infamous for her theatrics. Beatrice kept her gaze on Matthew, who sat on the second pew behind the family. He sat still and stoic beside Mungo, his gaze resting on the space where the coffin had been, saying his goodbyes. Her heart ached for him. She'd never understand their friendship but his loss was real and genuine. As was his pain.

The widow and daughter gave no indication of their feelings, facing front and ignoring each other. On an impulse, Beatrice reached over and gave Tanya's arm a squeeze.

An hour later, the upstairs function room at The Angel was heaving with black-clad mourners. Beatrice flittered about with sandwich trays and canapés, ostensibly giving Susie and her staff a hand. Her intention of eavesdropping was easily disguised in the role of waitress. It took a while to hear anything juicy and she began to get bored. As usual at these kinds of events, one had to wade through all the conventional bullshit to get to the truth of the matter.

"Ground-breaker, forerunner, rebel, game-changer, nonconformist, old school, unapologetic, icon, trailblazer..."

Beatrice sniffed. *Blah, blah. Are you people devoid of original thought?*

She put down her tray and snatched a glass of white wine. It was warm and overly sweet, but it was wine. And even if she was caught drinking on duty, she didn't give a...

"Beatrice Stubbs?"

The white-haired widow stood in front of her, with a disbelieving smile. "It IS you. I thought my eyes were playing tricks.

Do you remember me? We met in Greece, on The Empress Louise. Rose Mason."

Beatrice set down her glass in astonishment. "Rose? I don't believe it! I thought you looked familiar, but ... oh my God, Rose *Mason*? You were Vaughan's ex-wife?"

"Small world, eh? C'mere!" She opened her arms and Beatrice embraced her thin frame with heartfelt warmth.

"It is so lovely to see you again. I'm just totally thrown by the circumstances. How, what, who, why?" Beatrice gazed into the bright blue eyes before her.

"You're not the only one with questions. Come over and sit with us. Maggie's over here, complaining about the food as usual."

Maggie looked exactly as Beatrice remembered. The three of them met on a cruise ship where Beatrice was investigating suspicious deaths. Both had proved to be useful allies and loyal friends. But realising the compartments of her life were not as discrete as she'd imagined made Beatrice feel exposed and vulnerable.

"You're here too!" She hugged Maggie with a respectful gentleness. "I'm so delighted to see you both again, but completely confused. I may need another glass of wine."

Rose hailed a waitress with the air of a Roman empress and accepted three glasses of Chardonnay. "Cheers, Beatrice! A pleasure to see you."

They toasted and looked from one to another as they drank.

Rose spoke first. "Kindly explain why a detective from Scotland Yard is attending the funeral of my ex-husband, if you wouldn't mind."

"No detectives at this funeral, apart from the official one over there." She indicated DI Axe, who stood near the door with a cup of tea. "I'm retired. The only reason I'm here is because of Matthew, my partner and long-suffering companion. Vaughan Mason was one of his best friends. But when I met you, as Rose Mason, I had no idea of the connection."

Maggie and Rose exchanged a glance.

"Not something I used to shout about," said Rose.

"Nor something to shout about in the future," said Maggie, her eyes hard. "We just keep our heads down, quiet little old ladies, and go about our business."

Her words struck a chord with Beatrice and a strategy unfurled itself as if someone had unrolled a map. "It is *such* a pleasure to see you both again. How long are you staying?"

Maggie shrugged and jerked her head towards Rose. "Ask her."

"The reading of the will is tomorrow and we have been invited to attend. I also want to try to have a conversation with..." Rose looked across the room at the black-clad woman with the piggy eyes, laughing with a cluster of publishing folk.

"Your daughter?" offered Beatrice.

"We've not spoken for years. This might be a chance to repair some damage." Rose's voice was faint but raw. "So I thought we might stay on a few days."

Beatrice grabbed her chance. "Listen, now is not the time, but what do you say we have drinks before dinner this evening and catch up? I think we have a lot to discuss and if you're interested, I could use your help."

Rose and Maggie's faces wreathed into smiles.

Take that, DI Axe. This old dog can still follow a scent.

Chapter Seven

The Moor Hall viewing had been scheduled for weeks. Adrian and Catinca, giddy with excitement, waited in the pub foyer for Will, anticipating and second-guessing every aspect of how the venue's reality would meet their expectations. Having pored over the webcam on its site and studied all the images available online, they were as familiar with the layout as they were with Harvey's Wine Emporium.

At last, Adrian had the project back on track. The funeral was over and now was the time for everyone to focus on the big event. Six more days till the most important day of his life. Catinca's enthusiasm buoyed him. Her obsession for detail matched his. Together, they would make it work. All he needed from Will was the bare minimum, such as showing up. Which he still hadn't done, after ten minutes of waiting.

"Where the hell is he? We have an appointment for six o'clock and it's a good half an hour's drive. I'm going to call him. I am getting sick and tired of trying to get him interested. It's like he couldn't actually give a shit." Adrian exhaled his frustration.

He hit speed dial and heard Will's ringtone come from the bar. He opened the door to see him sitting with Beatrice and two old ladies at a table in the corner. Will winced, held up an apologetic palm and said his goodbyes before hurrying towards his fiancé.

Adrian folded his arms, jaw set. "I understand why Beatrice

and Matthew lost interest for a few days. Bereavement does that to you. But you, the person who proposed to me, are showing less enthusiasm for our wedding than I could muster for an episode of *Top Gear*. If you have better things to do than marry me, William Quinn, maybe we should save ourselves the effort and expense."

Will sighed and closed his eyes for a second, then opened them to direct an imploring gaze at Catinca.

She shook her head. "Nah, don't get me involved. He's right. Pull the finger out, mate. Can we get in bloody car already?"

Will put on his coat. "Yes, let's get in the bloody car. Come on, I'm sorry, and from now on I will devote all my attention to this stuff. Promise."

Adrian opened the front door and faced the cold. "This stuff?" His tone was as icy as the wind.

"This lovely, weddingy, marriage stuff. I am on it. Quick, it's freezing out here!"

The approach to Moor Hall, even in the dark, took Adrian's breath away. The building itself looked like a wedding cake, spotlights illuminating the fabulous façade. Catinca grabbed Adrian's shoulder and he returned her excited grin. Even Will seemed impressed.

"Wow. That building is the perfect backdrop for photographs. Good choice."

"That's one of the main reasons Catinca and I chose it. Plus the bridal suite is to die for. I hope we can get to look at it this evening. But if we can't, it will be an extra surprise for you on our wedding night. The most important thing today is to confirm the menu, discuss decorations and finalise the timing. At least we're not late for our appointment. God, I'm so nervous, my pulse is racing."

Will parked the car and squeezed Adrian's leg. "Stop worrying! After all the time and effort you two have put into this, it will run like a military operation."

They entered the main door with expressions of wonder and delight. Moor Hall was opulent, dramatic and the most photogenic building Adrian could imagine. Catinca was almost breathless at their surroundings. "Mate! Look!" she whispered, pointing to the grand staircase leading up from the foyer.

Two blonde women looked up from computer screens as they approached, and Adrian smiled warmly. Always important to get staff onside from the get go.

"Good evening. My name is Adrian Harvey. This is my fiancé Will Quinn and my assistant Catinca Radu. We have an appointment with Mr Roper to view the ballroom and discuss the wedding arrangements for Sunday."

The women exchanged a glance Adrian could not decipher. Surely theirs was not the first gay wedding the hotel had hosted?

"Just one minute, sir, I'll give him a call," said the blonder of the two.

It took all of thirty seconds before a man appeared from a door beside the reception desk, with a folder under his arm. His handshake was weak and his expression apologetic.

"Mr Harvey, a pleasure to meet you and Ms Radu in person. And this must be Mr Quinn. I'm the general manager of Moor Hall, Gerald Roper. Delighted. Please come this way." He led them to an L-shaped sofa in the foyer and seated himself on the shortest arm.

"Before we begin, I want to say that I fully understand the importance of your wedding day. It should be filled with memories you will treasure for the rest of your life. Nothing should spoil your celebrations. Which is why I am so very distressed at what has happened and will put every effort into finding a solution. The fact of the matter is that our drains became blocked yesterday evening, leading to the flooding of our ballroom. This is not simply a matter of mopping up as it is a sprung floor, designed for professional dancers. The plumbing company came out first thing this morning and their estimate is that a full repair will take four to six weeks. Quite apart from the disruption to your wedding celebration and our schedule of Christmas events, the smell has forced us to close our main dining room, which requires our current guests' meals to be accommodated in either our bistro café or the bar."

Adrian could not speak. He couldn't trust his voice. Will appeared equally dumbfounded. So the silence stretched until Catinca cleared her throat.

"That's shitty for you, mate."

To everyone's surprise, the manager snorted with laughter. "You hit the nail on the head there, young lady. The cause of the blockage and subsequent flooding was nappies. Rather than dispose of them properly, someone simply flushed their child's soiled nappies down the toilet."

Catinca wrinkled her nose. "Nappies? Some people are disgusting. But sympathy an' all that not gonna solve our problem. Sixty people coming to Devon on Saturday to celebrate a marriage and we got nowhere to go."

Roper shook his head. "We will not let you down. I meant what I said. We will make your day special." He opened his folder. "The way I see it, we have three options. The ballroom is unusable, so we can offer you a marquee in the grounds. Obviously it is December so we would provide outdoor heaters and the catering would remain more or less the same. Option two would be to relocate the entire event to our sister facility, Silverwood Manor. It is some distance from here, closer to Crediton, but a five-star location which can meet all your needs. They are willing to host you and your party for the same price we quoted. Thirdly, we can refund you in full and offer you first choice of a rescheduled date next year at a twenty percent discount. I am genuinely sorry this happened and will do anything I can to make this work."

Will and Catinca accepted the brochures showing example marquees and the Whatever Manor, discussing pros and cons with the manager. Adrian sat still and mute, all his elation draining away. This wedding was doomed to failure. It was not meant to be. He'd never call himself superstitious, but when portents throw themselves in your path like potholes, it's time to take note. The death of Matthew's friend, Beatrice preferring to play Miss Marple than matron of honour, Will's lack of enthusiasm and now his dream venue wrecked by a dirty nappy. Oh, the irony. He wanted to a) cry and b) call the whole thing off.

The manager shot Adrian a furtive glance. "What say I leave you to discuss preferences? Can I get you any drinks at all?"

Catinca ordered a Coke and Will asked for a still water. Adrian looked up at the man's watery grey eyes and said, "I'll have a Bloody Mary, please."

He nodded and headed towards the bar. Rage bubbled in Adrian like lava and he refused to look at either of his companions. They continued to flick through advertising material but both had the good sense to keep quiet and not attempt a positive spin on the greatest let-down of Adrian's life.

A waitress deposited the drinks on little paper coasters and Will muttered his thanks as the girl walked away, Adrian picked up his glass, wishing he'd chosen a whisky or something more suited to a dramatic down-in-one gesture, removed the curly celery and drank a good third in three gulps. His eyes watered and heat rose in his cheeks like a blush.

"Right." Catinca scooted past Will to sit beside Adrian. "You pissed off, mate, I know. But listen for a minute is all. When you and me was looking at wedding venues, we liked that place with the fountains, 'member? Big posh gardens like a BBC drama, closer to Matthew's village and bedrooms real old school. All that wooden shit in the ceilings. You loved it. But we couldn't have it. They said minimum guests gotta be hundred people." She rapped her nail on the glossy brochure. "This is it, mate! Silverwood Manor. Bloody gorgeous. Was our first choice. Adrian, look!"

She caught hold of his chin and forced him to look at the beautifully shot images of a country house. He brushed her hand off his face but kept looking. He remembered the fantasy of snowflakes settling on their heads as they posed in front of that fountain. He recalled the imaginary thrill of chasing Will through the maze. He recognised the classic William Morris decor of the dining room. Flipping the brochure to the back, he checked the map. Catinca was right. This was the venue closest to Beatrice and Matthew's cottage and a classic Jane Austen country manor, perfect for a family wedding.

Will leant across Catinca and reached for Adrian's hand. "I don't want to wait till next year to marry you. Nor do I want to get married in a tent and spend our first night as a married couple in a place that stinks of sewage. Let's be adaptable, switch venues and have the wedding we want. Over the top, glamorous, beautiful and every bit as stylish as you are."

Adrian knew he was being manipulated. He looked at the pictures again. White tablecloths, gilt-edged glasses, sparkles and all the magic of Narnia.

"Go and ask him how soon we can see it."

Will released his hand to high-five Catinca, and Adrian drank the rest of his Bloody Mary.

Chapter Eight

After Beatrice left her two co-conspirators at the pub, she took a brief detour before heading home. Rose and Maggie had been thoroughly briefed to make the gentlest and most innocent enquiries to the staff and management at The Angel. Who could suspect two white-haired old ladies of snooping? That left Beatrice to pursue Heather Shaw and her son, then to try and coax some opinions from Mungo. Tonight offered the perfect opportunity, as Matthew had invited his old friend round to dinner. Mungo's brilliant but impatient wife had already returned to Oxford to continue her research, so the poor chap would be glad of the company. And as chilly as Beatrice's feelings had been towards Vaughan, she adored Mungo, his clever spouse and exceptionally intelligent offspring.

She drove out of the village, wipers on to clear the windscreen of sleet, and followed the country lane another mile until she saw the sign to Sweetham. Heather Shaw's bungalow, lit from within, had an enticing air. The warm glow, smoke curling from the chimney and twinkling fairy lights in the windows made her quite convinced she could smell gingerbread. As soon as she rang the doorbell, a barrage of barks echoed down the hallway and she could hear the scrabble of claws on parquet flooring. The door opened and out poured a cascade of canines, in all shapes and sizes, circling, sniffing and wagging their tails.

"Hello, Beatrice. What are you doing here? Get down, Peanut, for goodness sake."

"Just popped by to check you're OK," Beatrice said, not quite truthfully. "Today can't have been easy for you."

"Oh you are thoughtful. Come in, come in, it's bitterly cold out there. Your timing is perfect. I just took a batch of mince pies out of the oven. Tea?"

"I'd love a cup, thank you." Beatrice waded through the dogs, who escorted her back into the house. The scent of spices and baking filled her nostrils as she hung her coat on the over-crowded rack by the door. "Is your son here?"

Heather glanced up at the enormous kitchen clock. "No, Gabe won't have finished work yet. And he usually goes home to change before coming round here for his tea. Did you want him for anything in particular? Because I can give him a ring if you like?"

Beatrice sat at the kitchen table while Heather put the kettle on the stove and unhooked a couple of mugs from the dresser. "Not at all. I only asked because I didn't want to disturb your dinner."

"We don't usually eat till sevenish. I often have a snack when I get home from school, otherwise I'd be ravenous by five. But I've been off this week. The head gave me compassionate leave for a fortnight."

"That's kind of him. It occurred to me today that despite recent circumstances, you were probably the closest person to Vaughan."

"Yes." Heather wiped her hands on a tea towel. "We had our ups and downs but we'd been together for seven years, give or take. Sugar?"

"One, please. That long? I asked Matthew and he couldn't recall."

"Matthew's probably seen so many women come and go from Vaughan's life, he's lost count. Let's face it, the man was never short of admirers."

To avoid replying, Beatrice reached down to pet one of the dogs, a Border Terrier with a pronounced underbite. Most of the other mutts had retired to their beds scattered around the cosy kitchen, satisfied the new arrival posed no threat.

Heather sat opposite and poured the tea from a battered enamel pot. "Have a mince pie. They're vegan. No animal products whatsoever."

Beatrice wasn't sure she liked the sound of that. How did one make mince pies without butter? But she bit into one anyway, and found it just as sweet and crumbly as those in Ashton's of Crediton. "Mmm, these are absolutely delicious. I didn't know you were vegan."

"I'm not. I don't eat red meat but I'm perfectly happy with fish or dairy or the odd organic chicken. But Gabe has very strong views on the damage done by industrial farming. That's why most of the meals I cook are purely plant-based."

Beatrice wanted to pursue this line of conversation, recalling Matthew's mention of the man as a hunter, but remembered her stated mission. "So how are you feeling? I hope today gave you some sense of closure."

Heather drank her tea, absently stroking the large hairy wolfhound at her feet. "It did and it didn't. You were there on the fifth of November. Even if you didn't hear what he said, you must have got the gist from local gossip. I swore I would never forgive him for that night. Even so, I still wanted him to apologise or show some contrition. That was the usual pattern. Big fight, weeks of silence, then he'd worm his way back in."

"When you say 'fight', do you mean physical violence?" asked Beatrice.

"No, no, he never used his fists. Let's face it, he was eighteen years my senior so if it had come to that, I could have flattened the old sod. His form of cruelty was mental. He could be vicious and nasty, particularly to those he really cared for."

Alarms went off in Beatrice's head. That mantra of he-does-it-because-he-loves-me chained so many women to abusive relationships. How come Vaughan had male friends of thirty years he had never abused verbally, with whom he had never had a big 'fight' and made up? Why was it only a series of women who suffered his arrogance and public humiliation? Her temper rose and she drank more tea, reminding herself of her situation.

"Heather, do you mind if I ask you a personal question? Did you love Vaughan?"

"Love him?" Heather started, as if the notion had never crossed her mind. "No, I couldn't say that. I love my son, my animals and I'd even say love my job most of the time, but I didn't love Vaughan. Not really. I was fond of him and he was very good company most of the time. I liked the sex and the attention, and I won't deny I enjoyed reflecting in his celebrity status, but I couldn't say I loved him. At our age, it's more about the companionship, don't you think?"

"I'd say that depends. What time do you usually get home from school?"

"About four, if there's no after-school activity."

"Do you remember what time you got back the Friday before Vaughan died?"

"Yes, I do. It was late because we had rehearsals for the St Nicholas Day choir. I didn't get home till gone seven. Why do you ask?"

Beatrice looked down at the little brown terrier whose teeth stuck out as if he were grinning. He wagged his tail and flattened his ears. "Just wondering. What's this dog's name?"

"She's called Huggy Bear. Gabe rescued her from a puppy farm." She looked around the room. "Almost all these dogs and cats are rescues. I admit I impress upon the whole school the importance of responsibility when it comes to pets, and try to persuade their parents into adopting. I don't suppose you'd be willing to take on an elderly cat?" She reached over to an open drawer at the bottom of a dresser and ran her hand over some grey fur. "Dumpling here lived with a pensioner till a month ago when he passed away. Poor old fella finds all these dogs and cats and people quite stressful. He hides in the drawer most of the day."

Beatrice looked into a pair of weary yellow-green eyes while still stroking the terrier's ears. Having a creature to care for might make Matthew focus on the here and now as opposed to mourning his friend. New house, new garden, new furry companions ... a spark of energy made her impulsive.

"Why not? We have a big garden and peaceful environment. I'd be delighted to take Dumpling. Is there any chance we could adopt Huggy Bear too?"

In many ways, it was a relief to see Mungo's car in the driveway. Firstly, the two men would have already discussed the idea of Vaughan's accidental death being anything but accidental while preparing dinner. Secondly, Matthew would accept their new adopted housemates with far greater equanimity in front of his friend. Thirdly, the spare room was already made up, so Beatrice would insist Mungo enjoy a second glass of wine and stay the night, ensuring he was not alone.

When she opened the hall door, weighed down by cat carrier and bags of pet equipment, she was dragged forward regardless by the determined Border Terrier on the end of the lead. Huggy Bear's tail whipped a frantic rhythm, straining to get to the kitchen and the scent of roasting chicken. Beatrice unclipped the lead, released the dog and deposited her baggage on the floor. First things first; butter.

In the kitchen, Mungo sat at the table, a glass of red in his hand, distracted by the small brown hairball bouncing between himself and Matthew with delirious joy.

"Hello there, where did you come from? You're a friendly little chap, aren't you?" Mungo offered the back of his hand to Huggy Bear, who sniffed and wagged then rushed to sit at Matthew's feet, nostrils twitching.

"Good evening, gents. Sorry I'm a bit late. I went to visit Heather Shaw and came away with more than I bargained for. This little lady is a rescue dog called Huggy Bear and in the hallway, we have an ancient Persian Blue called Dumpling. They needed a home and I thought we could give them one," she said, meeting Matthew's alarmed eyes.

He blinked, shook his head and sighed. "As I've always said, there's never a dull moment when you're around." He turned to the stove and reduced the heat. "A Persian Blue called Dumpling? I assume that is a cat? In which case, we shall need some butter. Mungo, would you hold onto Huggy Bear while we offer a formal welcome to Dumpling? Feel free to give her a bit of chicken skin."

In the hallway, Matthew gazed into the cat carrier with a benevolent smile. "Let's take him into the laundry room. It's warm and quiet and he won't be disturbed. Shall I butter his paws or should you?"

"I think that would be best coming from you. I'll fill his litter tray and get food and water. Matthew, are you sure you don't mind?"

He creaked up from his crouching position and looked into her eyes. "I don't mind. In fact, I rather missed having a cat. Huggy Bear might be more of a challenge, but one I think I could meet. I'll get Dumpling settled in. You go and chat to Mungo."

At nine o'clock, the atmosphere in the kitchen was relaxed and comfortable. The chicken had been despatched, followed by several slices of custard tart and in front of the wood-burner, curled up in a nest of old bedsheets, a small brown hairy ball slept off her chicken scraps, occasionally twitching along with her dreams.

They had dissected the funeral and passed judgement on most of the guests. Beatrice and Mungo had their inevitable debate about whether Mungo should stay the night and Beatrice won, with greater ease than usual. Before heading to the cellar for a second bottle of Burgundy, Matthew confessed to a certain amount of chagrin. His offer of assistance in clearing Vaughan's house had been met with a polite but firm refusal from his daughter.

"She actually said that Mungo and I would receive a memento in good time but before making any bequests, she first needed to assess her father's estate. As if our motivation were to scavenge through Midge's belongings!" He snorted like a bull and left the kitchen. Beatrice noted he took a carton of milk with him.

Beatrice turned back to Mungo. "I've already asked Matthew, but who do you think would have wanted Midge dead?"

"Not the right question, my dear. Half the village are feigning regret in public whilst rejoicing behind closed doors. Who wanted him dead *and* had the cunning to carry it through? That's what we need to ask ourselves."

"And who might that be, in your opinion?"

"My money's on the Shaw boy. As I told the police, his dirty great vehicle was parked outside Midge's house when I drove past on Friday afternoon. No love lost between the two of them, so even at the time I thought it odd."

"What were you doing over that side of the village on a Friday afternoon?"

Mungo's wine-stained lips stretched into a smile. "They do say a police officer never retires. Well, ma'am, my lovely wife instructed me to return a book to Demelza Price. They're in the same *book* club, you know." His fingers made inverted commas around the word 'book'.

Beatrice raised her eyebrows, inviting him to expand.

He took another sip of Côte de Nuits. "Better described as a drinking club with a reading habit, if they're honest. Anyway, I went over on Friday afternoon because I knew Demelza had a parish council meeting. Don't get me wrong, she's a good sort but can't stop talking. So I put the book in a carrier bag and hung it on her front door handle. I can even tell you the title. *A God in Venice* by Kate Atkinson."

"*A God in Ruins*. Your wife has excellent taste. Now tell me what you thought of Grace Mason?"

Mungo shuddered and clutched his arms as if cold. "Same way I feel about black ice. Chilly, nasty, dangerous and to be avoided. I'm jolly well relieved she refused our offer of help, tell the truth. Do you know, she offered not one word of thanks for organising her father's funeral? She said that as long as we could provide receipts, her solicitor would reimburse all expenses once the will has been read. She seems very confident Midge left her everything."

"She may well be right." Beatrice dabbed up a few crumbs of shortcrust pastry with her finger and popped them into her mouth. "Who else should inherit what's left of his fortune? If it includes his intellectual property, she stands to gain a great deal in the next few months. His books will almost certainly be reissued and his work will have a last gasp of fashionability."

"Oh God," Mungo groaned. "I'm almost glad the old devil's not here to see that. He'd be insufferable. My only hope is that she doesn't publish his current work-in-progress, if indeed there is such a thing. Midge always had an elastic relationship with the truth."

"You think he was writing again?" Beatrice asked.

"So he said. But Matthew and I are of the same mind. We believe it was more of a threat than a promise. He told us he was writing Exeter's version of *Lucky Jim*. Of course, any kind of university-set satire would put Matthew and me in the firing line. He never stopped claiming I stole his tenure, despite the reasons behind his dismissal being an open secret. If he has written his own exaggerated version of the university in the 1980s, inevitably celebrating his own conquests, it will leave a very sour taste today."

Beatrice wrinkled her nose. "When women are calling out power abuse and sexual harassment in every industry? No publisher would touch it with a bargepole."

"I do hope you're right." Mungo's jowls drooped and he gazed into his wine glass. "Anyway, dish the dirt on the ex-wife. Matthew says you're old pals so you'll have the insider info. Doesn't she have any claim on his wealth?"

"Not old pals exactly. I met her in the course of a case. Despite her surname, I never suspected a connection. I just liked her and Maggie very much. As for claims, Rose has been deranged from both Vaughan and Grace for years."

"You mean estranged."

"Whatever. They're divorced, he brought Grace up himself, so I can't see any reason he'd leave Rose something as part of his legacy. I was actually surprised to hear she'd been invited to the reading of the will."

Mungo's eyes flicked to hers with a glance of concern. "You don't think he'd do something ... unpleasant?"

Beatrice shook her head. "Sticking the knife into your ex after forty years? No, Vaughan had his faults, but I don't think even he'd be that vindictive."

Even as the words floated into the warm kitchen air, Beatrice knew neither she nor Mungo believed them. They lapsed into a thoughtful silence.

Matthew returned to the table and topped up each glass.

"How's Dumpling?" asked Beatrice, with a pointed glance at the milk carton.

"Purring. He seems quite content so I might let him out to explore the house tomorrow. Then if all goes well, he can roam the garden in a few days. I think he and I might rub along quite nicely. Two old gents enjoying a peaceful retirement."

Mungo leaned to look at the snoring Border Terrier, appraised Beatrice and raised his glass to Matthew with a smile. "With your womenfolk around? Good luck with that."

Chapter Nine

Will was trying hard, but it didn't come naturally. Adrian could see that by the constant expression of confusion on his fiancé's face. While happy enough to send emails to all their guests explaining the switch in location, Will seemed bemused by the rest of the arrangements, as if everyone was speaking a language he didn't understand. He drove them to Crediton and accompanied Adrian and Catinca to the florist's. While the gypsophila emergency was under discussion, he glazed over while looking out of the window. At the bakery, he made several positive cake-related comments even though he had never encountered the concept of wedding favours. His questions to the candlemaker were distracting and unnecessary. All things considered, Catinca and Adrian would have worked more efficiently without him.

After they'd finished briefing the coach company on alterations to pick-up and drop-off locations, Adrian had every intention of releasing Will from his duties until the venue viewing tomorrow morning. They emerged from the travel agent's onto the high street and Adrian opened his mouth to speak.

"Oi!"

Almost everyone in the town turned to the source of such a foghorn bellow. Adrian, Will and Catinca stopped short at the sight of Tanya running awkwardly towards them in her work skirt and high heels. Her hair blew around her head like a jellyfish's tentacles and her face glowed red with exertion and cold. She caught up with them, breathless, and clutched hold of Adrian's arms.

"Tanya, what's the matter?" he asked, horrible scenarios flashing through his mind. Matthew, cold and blue as his pyjamas, alone in his bed. Beatrice falling down an escalator in a London Tube station. A crumpled boy's bicycle, one wheel still spinning. The wedding that was not meant to be.

"Guys... we have a problem," she gasped, her eyes wide. "I've been looking for you since... I got the email. You cannot... cannot get married at Silverwood Manor!"

"What?" Adrian snapped.

Tanya shook her head with real vehemence and bent over to regain her breath.

Adrian took advantage of the momentary silence. "That is ridiculous! Didn't you read Will's message? Moor Hall has a burst drain and the wedding must be moved. Silverwood can take us..."

"Was first choice!" added Catinca.

"...for the same price and number of guests..." Adrian continued.

Will interrupted, "And we've spent all morning making the rearrangements."

"...so there is no alternative. We either get married at Silverwood on Saturday or we don't get married at all!" Adrian finished with a theatrical hand gesture as if sweeping a table setting to the floor.

Tanya heaved herself upright, her complexion blotchy and suggesting tears, still shaking her head.

Will placed a hand on her shoulder, his voice gentle. "Tanya, we've put a lot into rescuing this after the disappointment of that other venue. What possible reason can you have against us relocating to Silverwood?"

Tanya turned to Adrian, eyes flooded. "Because... the Head of Event Management at Silverwood Manor... is my mum."

Adrian covered his eyes with his palms. "Oh dear God."

When he took his hands away, Will and Catinca were wearing the exact same expression of total bewilderment.

Tanya clutched his arm. "Listen, I called an emergency meeting. Dad and Marianne ... they're going to be at The Angel in Upton. I faked a migraine to get off work ... Beatrice won't be back till tomorrow ... we have a couple of hours to fix this."

"I don't understand," said Will.

"Where's your car? Come on, let's go. I can explain on the way."

No one had spoken for the last two miles. The sound of brains racing for solutions or processing information was almost audible. Will braked sharply to allow a pheasant to scuttle across the road, a sprinter breasting the finish line. The jolt seemed to wake everyone from their internal worlds.

Will was the first to speak. "Let me see if I understand correctly, in tabloid speak. Nearly thirty years ago, Matthew Bailey ran off with Beatrice Stubbs, who happened to be his wife's best friend. In the process, she wrecked a marriage, initiated a bitter divorce and two young girls became the product of a broken home. Pamela, Matthew's ex-wife and mother to Marianne and Tanya, has never spoken to Beatrice since. The family take care to ensure their paths never cross. Until Saturday, when it becomes unavoidable."

Tanya leant forward from the back seat. "Tabloid speak? Will, I'm surprised at you. If I can damn well come to terms with what happened, I don't expect judgement from someone who wasn't even there. The reality is that Dad has never been happier since he and Beatrice fell in love. Mum was very angry and hurt for years, understandably. Marianne and I have learnt never to mention Beatrice in her presence because it only upsets her. Now she has a career and a husband who worships the ground she walks on. She's fulfilled and successful but still has a blind spot when it comes to Dad and Beatrice."

"And if the wedding goes ahead as planned, they will come face to face for the first time since it happened," Adrian added.

Catinca sighed. "Shit gonna hit the fan."

"I'm sorry, Tanya." Will met her eyes in the mirror. "I really was trying to look at it from the worst-case perspective to be prepared for what Catinca calls shit-hitting-fan. No disrespect intended."

"Yeah, OK, I get a bit defensive about the whole parents thing. And just a word of warning, Marianne is even worse. She's Mum's first-born and Beatrice's god-daughter, so even the most innocent comment can send her into a tailspin. Tread softly."

Adrian was about to quote another poet, but in his case Philip Larkin, when Will elbowed him. "How come you never mentioned this before?"

"It's not my place. I only found out myself by accident. Matthew let slip a comment about his divorce and I realised he and Beatrice must have already been together. I pressed him and he explained, but even then he played it down. As for Beatrice, I've never spoken to her on the subject. Too scared."

Catinca spoke, her face directed to the window and voice wistful. "Families. What a mess. Should be grateful for each other, innit? I got three sisters and two brothers. Only in contact with one sister and my dad. Shame."

"What about your mum?" asked Tanya, her voice solicitous and kind.

The car pulled onto the green. Adrian saw the pub and breathed a sigh of relief. Time to focus on the wedding, not old family feuds. This was a new start, a new family, a new life for him and Will.

But Catinca hadn't finished. "When I was little, Mum got new boyfriend. Left Dad, took us all kids and moved in with him. Bad guy. Tried messing with me and younger sisters. One year, after he killed pig for Christmas, Mum found him and older sister in bed doing same kind of squealing as pig. Massive fight and older brother got stabbed in leg. Stupid cow sister married that arsehole and Mum don't talk to none of us no more."

"Oh my God, that's awful. What about..."

Adrian cut in. "Parking space at ten o'clock, Detective Sergeant Quinn. Ladies, focus please. We have a wedding to rescue."

Only Matthew sat in the snug, doodling in the margins of *The Times*, the crossword not even begun. His forehead, with well-worn wrinkles, was more creased with worry than usual as he looked up to greet them.

"Well, this is a bugger's muddle and no mistake. What are our options, do you think?" He looked from one face to the other, finally fixing his gaze on Will.

"Look," Will began, throwing himself heavily into an armchair, "I've only just heard the back story to all this, so I might be out of line. But is it at all possible that this is not quite the disaster you think? It all happened nearly three decades ago. Perhaps Beatrice and Pamela are prepared to forgive and forget, or at least behave in a civilised manner when they meet?"

Tanya shook her head. "We have tried to get Mum to bury the hatchet. She won't even enter into a conversation on the subject. I honestly think we need to find another venue. Dad? Is there anyone at the golf club you could ask?"

Matthew's frown deepened. "It's awfully short notice."

"Tanya, this is ridiculous!" Adrian said, his jaw tight. "I am not changing venue again. Sorry, Will, but I would rather cancel the wedding than have nasty sandwiches in a draughty golf club to celebrate marrying the love of my life. We found our dream venue and by a stroke of luck, it fell into our laps. There must be a way to have our perfect wedding with *all* my favourite people present."

Silence followed his speech, as the implications of the last line hit home. No one had dared suggest it but Adrian had cut off the thought before it could even be voiced. Beatrice would not be excluded, regardless of ancient history. The door opened and Marianne came in, her face pale but eyes bright.

"Hi, all. Sorry I'm late, couldn't get away from the office. Listen, I called Mum from the car on the way over. Just for a casual chat. And I think we might just get away with this."

"How?" demanded Tanya.

"She is Head of Event Management, which means she works Monday to Friday. When they do weddings, she organises all the staff, decor and catering to run like clockwork, so she doesn't need to be there on the day. As long as we leave the arrangements to Adrian, Will and Catinca, there's no reason she would even know Beatrice and Dad are involved."

Catinca drew down her arm in a fist pump. "Yes!"

"Are you sure about that?" asked Matthew, his forehead slightly smoother.

"Yep. I didn't ask outright, but checked on her plans for the weekend in case she fancied some last-minute shopping. She said an emergency wedding relocation was taking all her time this week, but she is off work from Saturday till Wednesday. So we're going into Exeter together on Sunday morning. I'll be back for the wedding, don't worry."

Tanya released a huge sigh. "Why didn't I think of that? This is why having a sister can occasionally come in handy. So, are there any flaws in this plan? Will, why don't you apply your detective's brain to this one?"

Will reached out to shake Marianne's hand. "You've saved our day. Thank you. I couldn't have gone through all the rearrangements again. All right, let's think this through. Nameplates and seating plan will need aliases for Matthew and Beatrice. Maybe we should take our own photos of this family group, to keep them out of the official shots. Erm, are we going to tell Beatrice about all this?"

Everyone turned to Matthew. His brow concertinaed for a moment and then he shook his head.

"One more thing she doesn't need to worry about. Let's simply suggest she takes a back seat to allow the happy couple and their wedding planner to take over. She's usually in an excellent mood when she comes back from London so I am sure she'll understand."

The whole party expressed agreement, and relief bubbled

up in Adrian. "Right, let's order some lunch and then Tanya, Catinca and I need to make plans. The viewing is at ten in the morning. Will, just leave the talking to me. You may be a professional detective but I am an experienced actor, well versed in the art of charming an audience."

Will gave him a sideways glance and picked up the menu.

Chapter Ten

Islington High Street bustled with last-minute shoppers, a sound system played George Michael's 'Last Christmas' through the air, and frosty sunshine lit rosy cheeks and glowing eyes. Beatrice inhaled the spicy scent of the café's Christmas cookies and for an instant she was overcome with a rush of affection for London. Sentimentality, of course. Had she still been a resident, she would have cursed the man with the awkwardly pointy John Lewis bag on the Tube and rolled her eyes at the giggling office workers with tinsel in their hair tumbling out of Zizzi's.

She sipped her coffee and wondered why on earth she had felt such urgency last week. Everything was fine. She was fine. When James asked the reason for her hastily arranged appointment, she would feel a fraud. Even worse, if he asked about her mood-stabilisers, she would have to tell a small untruth. Overall, she did take them regularly. She'd just had a lot on her mind and forgotten a few times. She checked her handbag, knowing as she did so the packet was still in the drawer in her bedside table. No matter. She'd be home tomorrow and would definitely take one then.

The clock read three-fifteen and the festive decorations adorning the street glowed a little brighter as daylight began to fade. She finished her drink, picked up her gloves and bag, left a tip for the waitress and crossed the street to James's practice. After her session, she would have half an hour to get to Westminster to meet Dawn after work. She smiled to herself, picturing the pair of them in The Speaker with a bottle of wine, sifting through the latest internal police politics. Maybe that was all she needed. Just a little trip to London and she was back on an even keel.

James did not tut or sigh deeply when she announced the complete absence of any reason to be there. Instead he asked her to describe her feelings when she had made the emergency appointment.

"Oh, the usual panicky stuff like nerves before a big event you're dreading. As if it would only take one more thing to push me over the edge." She explained about the death of Vaughan Mason, preparations for Adrian's wedding and her own buoyant mood since arriving in the capital.

James lifted his gaze from his notes. He looked directly at Beatrice and then his focus changed, to a picture on the opposite wall. She knew it well, a print of *Beach at Low Tide* by Degas.

"Would you say that since you moved to Devon you associate being in London with satisfying a need? Not only your counselling sessions here but personal therapy on more than one level?"

"I suppose I do," Beatrice considered. "It's Me-Time, when I get to be my old self again."

"I see." He made a note on his pad. "How would you describe your progress in these sessions since your move?"

"Well, it's not really a question of progress, is it? The way I see these appointments is more like a check-up. Just making sure I'm still balanced and not going wobbly again."

"More a question of standing still than moving forward?" James gave her a gentle smile, his pen resting on his chin.

"Yes, standing on my own two feet, with the support of my stabilisers. That would be you, my medication and Matthew."

He wrote rapidly, far more than her latest statement seemed to deserve. Finally, he looked up, his focus on the ivory gauze curtains veiling the window. "That concept of stabilisers is an interesting one. Some would say you don't need stabilisers to achieve stasis. It's only in motion extra support is required."

The word 'stasis' stung Beatrice. "There's been plenty of movement, James. I have coped remarkably well with all the recent changes in my life. You make it sound like I have been slacking!"

"My job, as we chose to define it, is to guide you. I lead you to examine and understand your own behaviour and patterns of thinking. It is reassuring to hear that you are not in reverse gear due to your retirement, move, wedding planner status and the emotional support you're providing to your partner in a bereavement situation. That said, I would be 'slacking' as you put it, if I lost sight of the aim of our meetings. We need to move forward, Beatrice. Just coping is not enough. As a matter of fact, I wanted to raise the matter with you in our next scheduled session."

Beatrice frowned, a sense of foreboding darkening the mellow room. "What do you mean?"

James placed his notes on the desk and leaned forward, clasping his forearms and holding her gaze. "My feeling is that in order to make the necessary progress, you need to step outside what has become a comfort zone. The association between your therapy and where you used to live conflates two very different emotions. This will be counter-productive in the medium to long term. Managing your mental health is daily diligence, homework, a commitment to doing the hygiene. Regarding that as part of a weekend jolly tells me you are simply treading water and not learning to swim. I think it might be time to find you a new therapist, someone local to Devon. I did some research and would like you to try a person who comes highly recommended."

Over the years in James's office, Beatrice had cried, yelled, sulked and apologised more times than she could remember. He'd seen her naked. Not physically, but mentally, and that was by far her ugliest aspect. Whenever he probed her tender spots and slammed the gates on her escape routes, she'd told herself she should change therapists. What did this pretty blond thirty-something know about what it was like to be her? Yet she had stayed, returning week after week, month after month, coming to see this man as sanctuary, this process as healing. He'd seen her at her worst and refused judgement. His and hers. Now, after all these years, *he* was rejecting *her*. She couldn't find her voice.

"I don't want to attempt to influence your decision, because it must be you who decides. All I ask of you is to attend a couple of trial sessions with Gaia with an open mind and see how you get on. This folder has all her details and all email conversations I've had with her about your case. I want this transfer to be totally transparent. It's a big step, which I understand is unsettling after all your recent changes, but I am convinced this could realign your commitment to constant vigilance and modification of behaviours that make you unhappy. Perhaps you'd like to think this over. Or if you have questions right here and now, I am ready to explain my rationale."

Beatrice shook her head, her gaze on the floor, her throat tight. "No, I ... no. This requires some thinking time. I'd better get on. I'll be in touch, probably in the New Year."

"Beatrice, hold on a minute..."

"Merry Christmas, James, and thanks for everything."

She grabbed the file and fled out into the sleety evening. Tears blurred her vision as she made for the Tube, her chest tight and one phrase echoing through her mind.

He doesn't want me anymore.

By the time Dawn had shoved her way through the throng of smokers huddled outside The Speaker, Beatrice was on her second glass of white. She raised a hand and despite her grim frame of mind, managed a smile at the sight of her friend. She stood up for the greeting hug, Dawn's cheek cold against her own wine-warmed face.

"New hairdo?" she asked, reaching for the wine bottle and filling the spare glass.

"Yeah, thought I'd have some highlights done in a pathetic attempt to stave off old age." Dawn shrugged off her coat and glanced at the half empty Sauvignon Blanc. "You been waiting long? I thought you were seeing James this afternoon?"

In lieu of a reply, Beatrice lifted a glass. "Cheers! Here's to girls' night!"

"Cheers!" Dawn chinked her glass and took a sip, her steady grey eyes on Beatrice.

"So fill me in on all the gossip. What's the latest at Scotland Yard? Who's doing what with whom?"

Dawn shook her head with a vague frown. "In a minute. When we spoke at the weekend, you couldn't wait to see James. So how did it go today?"

"The counsellor-client relationship is confidential, you know that. It's not something I can talk about."

Dawn placed her glass on the table and sat back with her arms folded. "Beatrice Stubbs, you are an unbelievable hypocrite. When it suits you, you'll talk about your therapy sessions till my ears fall off. And in any case, I'm not asking for a blow-by-blow account. I just wondered why you got here so early. Did you or did you not see James?"

"Yes," Beatrice muttered. "But I won't be seeing him again. He's dumped me."

Dawn gazed at her in silence and waited for her to continue. Beatrice should have known her calm and sensible friend would not rise to the bait of melodrama.

"He thinks we're not making any more progress and I'm using him as a crutch. He wants me to see another counsellor, in Devon. After all these years, he wants to pass me on to some tie-dyed flake from Totnes who makes dream-catchers, wears crystals and will want to interact with my inner child. It must be against some kind of medical ethics to chuck out clients whose mental health depends on their counsellors."

"It probably would be, if that is what he's doing. But it sounds to me like he's got your best interests at heart. It would be more convenient to see someone local, and a change could be exactly what you need."

Beatrice tutted in exasperation. "And now *you're* siding with him. Is there no loyalty left in this world? It was incredibly difficult for me to see a counsellor in the first place. Many people never find someone they can talk to openly and honestly. I got lucky with James and he has proved a lifesaver. And I say that literally, without fear of exaggeration. How can he just end it all, after everything we've been through?"

"Talking of exaggeration, how do you know the new counsellor is... what did you call her? A tie-dyed hippie? Have you already met her?"

"No," Beatrice admitted. "But he told me her name."

"Which is...?"

"Gaia."

"Gaia?" Dawn repeated.

Beatrice took a large slug of wine. "Exactly. I think that tells me all I need to know."

"Good gracious, you're absolutely right. I don't blame you in the slightest for building a wall of prejudice and judgement based on the simple fact of her name. Giving her a chance by actually meeting the woman would be foolhardy in the extreme. Far better to fume and rage at James for randomly picking some name out of the ether with no consideration for whether you would be a good match. Typically cavalier and unprofessional of him."

Beatrice glowered at her from under her eyebrows. "You're not making yourself any friends here, you know. He gave me a file of their correspondence and some background information on her to read and consider."

"Let me guess. You took the file, stomped out of his office and spent the last hour winding yourself up into a state of self-righteous pity rather than reading it in order to make an informed decision. Top-up?" She poured them both another glass with a knowing smile.

"I'll read it tomorrow. Tonight I want to drink wine and feel sorry for myself."

"In that case, that is exactly what we should do. Then when we've raged against the injustices of the world and condemned everyone in it, can we get a curry?"

With some reluctance, Beatrice gave in to a smile. "Sounds like a plan."

Chapter Eleven

The following day, on the 12.20 from Paddington to Exeter St David's, Beatrice made several decisions.

Firstly, she bought two bottles of water from the buffet car to assuage her hangover. Then she read the file James had given her, forcing her ego into the background in order to appreciate the care and consideration these two professionals had shown in her development. Gaia Dee was from Marazion in Cornwall, a qualified counsellor and Registered Member of the British Association for Counselling and Psychotherapy. Her emails in response to James's query appeared professional, if there were a few too many questions about her potential client's dietary habits for Beatrice's liking. *Why on earth would she need to know what I eat for breakfast?* she wondered, and immediately had a fancy for a bacon sandwich. All things considered, she decided to give the woman a try.

She dragged out her phone and sent a polite email enquiry.

'Dear Ms Dee, Re: Change of Counsellor. Would there be any chance of a brief chat sometime in the New Year? Best wishes, Beatrice Stubbs.'

She hesitated over James's name in her contacts, an apology in mind, but chose to delay any conversation until she'd met Gaia.

Remembering her manners, she sent a flurry of text messages. One to Dawn with thanks for the emotional support and guest bedroom. One for Matthew to let him know she was en route and needed collecting from the station. One to Adrian asking if

Moor Hall had met all his requirements. After a quick trip back to the buffet car for a bacon sandwich and a cappuccino, she withdrew her 'case file' and settled down to work.

Suspects in the case of Vaughan Mason's unexpected death (by poisoning?)

Heather Shaw (ex-lover, familiar with his habits)

Gabriel Shaw (Heather's son, detested Vaughan, at property on Friday)

Gordon Hancock (gambling landlord, monetary debts?)

Bankrupted card-players?

Neighbour he aggravated – Demelza Something?

Rose Mason (ex-wife, estranged)

Grace Mason (Vaughan's daughter, lives in NY, likely heiress)

Mungo Digby (friend, key to house, worried about potential book)

Matthew Bailey (friend, key to house)

To Dos

Debrief Rose and Maggie for news on Gordon

Ask Matthew to grill Gabriel, interview Grace myself

Probe Rose and Mungo on relationships with deceased

Check each suspect's alibis from Friday to Sunday

Ask each if they know anyone who would wish Vaughan harm

Contact DI Axe for any forensic clues (off-the-record?)

Research toxic local fungus

Find out what happened at reading of the will

Pick Heather's brains – Vaughan's passwords?

The next concern was where to take Maggie and Rose for a debrief. The likelihood of their having found something significant was slim but the truth often lay in the most mundane detail. Discussing the hosts of The Angel on the premises was evidently a bad idea. Yet it seemed equally inappropriate to invite them to the cottage with Matthew in situ. A coffee shop? A walk in the woods?

An envelope flashed up on her laptop.

'Hello, Beatrice. I'd love to have an informal chat. This is a quiet time of year for me, so I could offer you a slot this afternoon, if that suits you? I'm available from 3pm-5pm. Let me know if you can spare half an hour and I'll send you a map. My house isn't easy to find. Otherwise, of course we can find a time to meet in the New Year. I look forward to meeting you. Best wishes, Gaia.'

Hmm. Nothing hokey at first glance, but these people were good at maintaining a normal façade whilst being off-the-scale weird when you met them. Still, an optimistic start and her address was not that far from their own cottage. Beatrice decided to give it a try, already composing a smug message to Dawn in her head.

'Dear Gaia

That is very kind of you. I could manage half an hour today – can we say four thirty? I look forward to meeting you too. Best wishes, Beatrice.'

There. An adult, professional and mature response. James would be proud of her. As if she cared what he thought. She finished her water and wondered if it was too early to have lunch.

She was still puzzling over how and where to do her interviews as the train pulled into Exeter. Her concerns soon turned out to be unnecessary. Matthew took her case in his left hand and embraced her with his right.

"Good trip, Old Thing?"

"Yes and no. But more of that later. How are our houseguests?"

"This way, the car's over here. Well, Huggy Bear won't let me out of her sight. I gave in to her whining last night and took her bed into our room. She settled down instantly and we both got a good eight hours. Dumpling emerged from the cellar and has chosen the conservatory as his personal sun spot. Both eating well and apparently content. Although I do have to go out this afternoon, so I'm glad you're back. It feels a touch too early to leave them alone."

"That's fine with me. I want to proceed with my investigations and will invite witnesses to my interrogation room, also known as the kitchen. Where are you going and who with?"

Matthew placed the case into the boot and opened Beatrice's door for her. "Been summoned, don't you know. Vaughan's daughter wishes to speak to me and Mungo. We have arranged to go round at two. I've left lunch for you and all the other creatures in the fridge."

Beatrice looked at her watch. "Best crack on then. There are one or two things I'd like to do myself, starting with a decent meal."

Matthew started the car and smiled. "Wine and doubtless Indian food with Dawn last night, egg muffin at the station or possibly on the train, several coffees, a bottle of water and a light snack around Westbury but she's still hungry."

"Travel broadens the mind and expands the appetite. What's the latest on the wedding? Is Adrian calm?"

Matthew glanced in the rear-view mirror before pulling into the stream of traffic. "All going like clockwork. Catinca has it all under control. That girl is incredibly attentive to detail, I must say. Speaking of which, I was presumptuous enough to ask Adrian and Will if they could handle the arrangements from here. You've done the grunt work, so I thought you'd prefer to hand over the baton and focus on your core competence. Good Lord, I just said 'Core Competence', didn't I? Please don't leave me. I promise I can change."

Beatrice laughed to cover her discomfort. She hated hiding

things from Matthew. She hated it even more when he hid things from her, but somehow she wasn't ready to talk about the whole change of counsellor issue. She would make up her own mind and then tell him her decision. Snowflakes spattered the windscreen and muddied the view of the road ahead.

When she called them to arrange a debrief meeting, Maggie and Rose surprised her by refusing the offer of a lift. They had their own transport, Rose assured her, complete with Satnav and would arrive at the cottage no later than three pm. Beatrice was laying the kitchen table with tea things and trying not to trip over a skipping Huggy Bear when she heard a vehicle crunching over the gravel. She opened the door to see a huge battered beast of an old Land Rover parked on the drive. The driver's door opened and rather than a shotgun-wielding farmer in gaiters emerging, a slight figure in shades of powder blue hopped out with a wave.

"Hello, Beatrice! How's that for timekeeping?" Rose called, turning to reach something from the cab. Maggie slammed the passenger door and came across to greet her.

"What a lovely cottage! You are so lucky to have so much green space. And who's this wee creature?"

"That's Huggy Bear. We've only had her for a couple of days so please excuse her manners. Whose vehicle is that?"

"Ours! Rose bought Black Betty for a song at an auction years ago and fixed her up. All-terrain, four-wheel drive, bags of room for everything we need in the back. We've taken her all over Europe and she's still going strong. A wee bit worse for wear after a few scrapes but when you drive one of these, no one gives you any bother."

"No, the main reason people leave us alone is because I stuck a picture in the back window of Maggie's face after she ate a vegetarian haggis. Beatrice, we brought you these. Going local," said Rose, handing over a bag from the bakery.

Beatrice ushered them in from the cold and set the scones on a plate. Once they were settled around the kitchen table with a fresh pot of tea, Maggie got straight down to business.

"Right, we did as you asked and got chatting to staff, customers and management at the pub. Based on what we learned and our own observations, we have identified a prime suspect. Have we not, Rose?"

Rose nodded once. "That's our conclusion, right enough, but Beatrice needs the whole story. She's the professional here. We took notes on all the conversations we had, although the last one gave the most away."

"Didn't he just!" Maggie's expression was bright and knowing. "Ply them with drink and they'll give you their life story."

Beatrice took a sip of tea. Scotland Yard this was not.

"First things first," said Rose, clasping her hands together. "Breakfast was a bit chaotic at the pub this morning. Only one waitress and no chef. Poor girl was trying to handle the whole thing on her own, so Maggie and I rolled up our sleeves and pitched in to help. We fried and toasted and grilled while Amanda served. When things calmed down, the three of us sat down and ate the leftovers. Apparently it's not the first time this has happened. Amanda arrives to find no prep done and Gordon and Susie either still in bed or too hungover to cook. That's usually at the weekend, but after the funeral..."

"Drink was taken and they had a row," said Maggie, her expression full of significance. "Apparently. We heard nothing. It was a late night for us because we had a nightcap with your lovely friends. They are just charming! I've a real soft spot for gay men, always have, and those two are so..."

"Maggie, Beatrice needs the facts. As she says, we had a drink with the lads and turned in before last orders. So we can't honestly say we heard a thing."

"Not personally, no. But other guests reported a fierce commotion in the wee small hours."

Beatrice looked from one to the other. She could remember faster, more pertinent reports from her detective sergeants. "Is there anything else to this than a couple having a drunken argument? I can't see how this leads anyone to a prime suspect."

"Nor could we," Rose acknowledged. "Only when we started discussing the disturbance with other guests did we start to form a theory. Mr Anderson is a regular and stays in Room 8. He heard them blaming each other for all the money Vaughan had taken."

Maggie spread jam on a scone. "Two of the customers backed him up. One friendly old dear with a dog like yours told me Susie hated Tuesday evenings. She was left at home to pull pints while Gordon went out to play cards. He wasnae good at it. That weekly poker game pulled in some big spenders. Most people were losers, but Vaughan Mason made a lot of cash."

"Then after dinner last night, we met Lionel," said Rose, with the tone of someone with the Royal Flush. "He used to drive the school bus until the council let him go. A Londoner originally, he used to work in a casino. When he heard about Vaughan's card nights, he wangled an invitation. He knew the tricks and thought he could earn a bit from these wealthy amateurs."

Beatrice narrowed her eyes. "I think I know Lionel. Bit of a morose sort, drinks rum and coke and often gets miserable of an evening. Always sits in the corner?"

"That's your man. Last night, he and Maggie fell into conversation and she bought him a rum and coke. She made it a double."

The two women smiled at each other with impish glee and Beatrice set aside her impatience for facts. She sat back and listened between the lines.

"Oh aye, the rum loosened his tongue, "said Maggie. "Everything he had, he said, Vaughan Mason took from him. He's a very bitter man, after gambling away his pension and losing the love of his life to a man who treated her like dirt."

"But that's not all," Rose interjected. "He told us Vaughan was a blackmailer. He seduced wealthy women and threatened to tell their husbands unless they paid him hush-money. According to Lionel, Vaughan was dropping some very heavy hints about how much money Gordon had lost and how awful it would be if Susie were to find out."

"That convinced us. Gordon Hancock had two very good reasons to want Vaughan Mason dead."

Rose nodded her agreement. "Frankly, Beatrice, all the above tallies with the man I married. He was then, and clearly remained until his death, an absolute shit."

Beatrice poured more tea, trying to sort gossip and personal enmity from useful detail. Snowfall and darkening skies made the kitchen gloomy so she switched on the lights. Huggy Bear sat up in her bed by the Aga, only relaxing when Beatrice returned to her seat.

"Before we go any further, I have some questions about what you've told me."

Rose and Maggie exchanged a glance. "You might like to hear the most important part first. Yesterday morning, we went to the reading of the will."

She glanced at the clock. Twenty to four. If she intended to make her meeting, she would have to leave in the next fifteen minutes. Maggie and Rose waited, alert and engaged, willing to share an insider's perspective. This was business. She had far too much to do to go traipsing around Devon meeting total strangers who knew all kinds of details about her personal life. In fact, all things considered, she wasn't even sure if she wanted a new counsellor. She came to a decision.

"Give me two minutes to cancel an appointment and let's get to work. Rose, would you boil the kettle? We're going to need more tea."

When Matthew arrived home, Beatrice was still hunched over the kitchen table amid the tea things an hour after her guests had left. She had filled half a dozen sheets of paper with questions and theories and a mind map of connections, with Vaughan Mason at the centre. Huggy Bear heard the door open and rushed to greet Matthew with bounces and wags. Several guilty sensations slithered around Beatrice's insides.

She hadn't walked the dog. She'd prepared nothing for dinner. She hadn't checked in with Adrian all day. She had cancelled her new counsellor. And she was still sitting at a dirty table in the half dark, obsessing over Vaughan Mason's attitude to women, when she should have been wrapping Christmas presents or baking a plum pudding.

"Hard at it, Old Thing?" Matthew stuck his head around the door.

"Got carried away. Sorry. Why don't you take the dog for a stroll while I clear up and start dinner? Then you can tell me all about his daughter and I can fill you in on the latest developments."

"Sounds just the thing. If I'm allowed to make a request, comfort food would fit the bill tonight. The journey back was touch and go in this weather. We won't be long."

Beatrice heard the clatter of claws on tiles as Huggy Bear skittered about at the sight of her lead. What had they done without that bundle of energy before now? She turned her attention to dinner but her mind ran on parallel lines.

Fish stew. With fresh crusty bread. She cleared the table and rummaged in the fridge for the ingredients. While she set the oven to heat, a name popped into her mind.

Gabriel Shaw. She'd not spoken to him on the subject of Vaughan Mason's death and nor had anyone else, at least as far as she knew. At her surprise visit after the funeral, she had intended to catch him and his mother together. Just a friendly chat with them both, to reassure them of her neighbourly concern. But Gabriel had not materialised.

She chopped onions, garlic, celery and leeks, and ran through her options. Matthew knew and liked Gabriel. He might be able to initiate a conversation. Whether he could steer a dialogue as well as a seasoned detective, who could say? She herself would be a far more reliable interrogator, if he chose to talk. But she'd never spoken to the man in her life, so she would be coming in cold, with no emotional leverage.

A thought occurred as she threw chunks of potatoes into boiling water. If Matthew was to be believed, a romance with Tanya had once been on the cards. Smart, emotional, empathetic, strong and principled Tanya. Who could resist her engaging manner, enthusiasm for life and persistent questions?

Beatrice grinned to herself as she filleted the fish. It might even enable a deeper understanding between the two and reignite the flames of passion. And it wasn't beyond the realms of possibility that this time next year, they might be celebrating all over again. A shadow slunk into the kitchen and rubbed around Beatrice's ankles.

"Hello, Dumpling! Fancy a bit of fish skin? It'll do wonders for your hair and nails." She offered a piece to the grey fluffball, who sniffed Beatrice's offering and opened his mouth. "Mmm, that barely touched the sides. Here's a bit more. You've got quite an appetite! When Matthew gets back, he'll give you some kibble and tomorrow, if the weather's not too hideous, you can go out in the garden."

The chartreuse eyes blinked and Beatrice returned her attention to the stew, adding the fish stock cubes and stirring. Dumpling padded off, licking his lips. When Beatrice looked up from adding stock and aioli, he had curled up on the battered old armchair beside the Aga, better known as Matthew's chair. She smiled again and tore some parsley from the plant on the kitchen window.

Matthew's chair!

Her head snapped around, staring at the cat. Matthew's chair. Lionel's corner. Vaughan's tankard. Being a creature of habit could be deadly.

Chapter Twelve

"I think we should go to the police with all this," said Matthew, emerging from the bathroom in his pyjamas, smelling of toothpaste and talcum powder.

Beatrice glared at him from the bed. "With a half-baked set of suspicions founded on rumour and hearsay? Don't be ridiculous. I need to conduct several more interviews before I can offer any kind of theory."

"What interviews? We already have three likely suspects. The police can pursue these leads with all their resources and arrest suspicious sorts without us getting involved. You did what I asked and I'm grateful. Now we should turn our findings over to the police and our attention to the future. Adrian's wedding for one thing."

"We don't have three likely suspects at all. A suspect must have motive, means and opportunity. Look, Maggie and Rose are completely sure it must have been Gordon. He lost money at those card games, he had access to Vaughan's personal tankard and ample occasions upon which he might have added a toxin to a pint of Badger's Backside or whatever they call that foul swill he drinks. Used to drink."

"That's what I mean. We have credible evidence which needs investigating by the professionals. Shall I switch the big light off?" Matthew asked.

"Yes, go ahead. But when I presented you with 'credible

evidence' against Lionel Ruddock, you dismissed it out of hand. In your own words, Lionel is a miserable man who had a brief affair with... what was her name again?"

"Josephine. Very pretty girl who worked at The Star."

"Yes, exactly. Lionel tells it as if Vaughan stole his soul mate. Whereas you describe it as a summer liaison which finished long before Josephine ended up in Vaughan's bed."

Matthew got under the duvet, folded his arms behind his head and exhaled. "When I said three suspects, I certainly didn't include Lionel Ruddock. He's a moaner and full of resentment, but he thrives on that. He wouldn't ever do anything about it. In fact, he's probably even more bitter that Vaughan is dead because he has no one else to blame. Hate can be just as energising as love, you know."

"True, but love is much healthier." Beatrice leaned over him to look at Huggy Bear, fast asleep in her bed. "So the other two suspects you mention would be?"

"Is this an exercise to prove how dim I am? The second suspect would be his daughter. Grace Mason is his sole heir. She's a very unpleasant, grasping person whose grief took the form of evaluating his possessions and chucking anything she saw as 'tat' towards Mungo and me. We weren't beneficiaries, we were house cleaners. She wanted nothing more than financial gain. To tell you the truth, her demeanour made me feel physically sick."

"She's not his sole heir, though, is she? Vaughan left her everything except the rights to *An Empty Vessel*. Those he left to Rose. Why would he do that?"

"I don't know why. But I do know it upset Grace Mason dreadfully. She was in a terrific temper, muttering on and on about it. Called her father some appalling names and I won't repeat what she said about Rose. I told you she intends to contest the will?"

Beatrice nodded then shook her head slowly. "Some people are just... vile. But while Grace does indeed have financial gain as a motive, I don't see means. How do you poison someone from the other side of the Atlantic?"

They lay in silence for several moments.

"Regarding the intellectual property rights, I tend to agree with what Rose said. It was a reciprocal gesture," Matthew offered. "While they were married, Rose was the breadwinner. She supported him while he wrote that novel, which propelled him into the upper echelons of the literary world and made him a fortune, not to mention reputation. But by then, they were already divorced, so..."

"Yes, yes, I know," Beatrice interrupted. "But that makes no sense either. If he felt beholden to her, why not give her some money back then? He's never written anything equal to *An Empty Vessel* since, so it has to be his main source of income. If you leave all your worldly goods to your daughter, why deprive her of its greatest jewel? He must have known it would widen the rift between mother and daughter."

"As I say, a debt of gratitude. They split up months before its publication, so I doubt Rose reaped the benefits of her sacrifice. I'm surprised she holds no bitterness."

"Hmm. She described him this afternoon as 'an absolute shit', but I got the impression she was stating an objective truth rather than a subjective opinion."

Matthew did not reply so she opted to steer the conversation into safer waters.

"Suspect Three?" she asked.

"To me, it seems obvious to suspect Heather Shaw. The jilted lover. Crime of passion, cold vengeance sort of thing is her motive. Plus intimate knowledge of the man and his habits give her means and opportunity. She cannot be dismissed."

"Crime of passion and cold vengeance are quite different means of operation. But yes, she does have opportunity. She was rehearsing in Upton till seven. She could have easily made a detour via Vaughan's house, knowing full well he'd be in the pub. Does she have a key too?"

"No. He was adamant none of lady friends had access to his house. The only spare keys are with me and Mungo and his cleaning lady."

"Right then, tomorrow I need to find a way of getting into Gabriel Shaw's head."

Matthew yawned, rubbed his eyes and leaned over for a goodnight kiss. "Sleep well, my love. And this may be an old romantic speaking, but the best way into Gabriel's head is through his heart. If I were you, I'd call Tanya."

"What a marvellous idea! I'll do that first thing in the morning. Goodnight, Matthew, you are quite brilliant, you know."

He grunted as he switched off the bedside lamp. "You had every intention of calling her anyway. I just gave you permission."

She squeezed his arm with a smile. He did know her awfully well.

When she awoke on Thursday morning, something had changed. The world was brilliant and quiet, in a Sundayish sort of way. She sat up and realised why. The garden was under a thick white cover of snow. Shrubs, furniture, plant pots had been transformed into unrecognisable lumps and the weak winter sun sparkled off the crystals, turning an unkempt wilderness into a wonderland perfectly in keeping with the wedding theme. She beamed at the beauty of the scene in front of her, willing it to remain until the wedding on Sunday. Would that not be the perfect present for Adrian?

By the time she descended, Matthew and Huggy Bear were returning from their walk. Through the frosted glass door to the porch, she could see him stamping his boots, drying the dog and removing his outdoor things. She went into the kitchen and prepared the coffee machine. Dumpling, curled up like a dustball on Matthew's chair, looked up at her and mimed a miaow.

"Good morning to you too. Would you like some milk?"

A rattle of claws announced an excitable terrier who jumped

up to leave wet paw-prints on Beatrice's trousers until Matthew broke off his rendition of 'Good King Wenceslas' and whistled her back into the hall for some food. Beatrice poured some milk into a bowl for Dumpling and the rest into a pan for their coffee, her attention drawn repeatedly to the white-shrouded foliage outdoors.

"Looks like Adrian may well get his wish," said Matthew, closing the kitchen door as he came in. "Forecast is for more of the same."

"I do hope so. I know it's disruptive and dangerous and going to get on my wick in a matter of days, but this morning, it's beautiful."

"It certainly is. You know I'd swear Huggy Bear has never seen snow before. She went quite daft this morning, rolling and diving and trying to eat it. Have you spoken to Tanya yet?"

"No, I decided to leave it till she got to work. Weekday mornings trying to prepare oneself and a small child before leaving the house must be very stressful. I'll call her when she gets to her office. Best catch her when she's bored out of her mind."

"But she's not at the office today. Oh, is that coffee?"

"The black liquid bubbling away in the Moka pot? Could be. Do a taste test to be sure. Why isn't she in the office today?"

Matthew made quite a performance of tasting the coffee, by which time Dumpling had returned to his seat and Huggy Bear was scratching outside the kitchen door.

"Nothing like a punchy Brazilian brew after a walk in the snow. So, what had you in mind for breakfast?"

Beatrice sniffed. "I asked you a question. Why is Tanya not at work today?"

"Oh she *is* at work, as far as I know. She simply mentioned she was doing site visits this morning. I was worried about her, trying to negotiate country lanes after all this." He waved an arm at the window and let the dog in.

Beatrice dismissed his dissembling as vagueness and focused on her tasks ahead. She handed Matthew a jar of oats. "Crack on and make us some porridge. I'll call Adrian first and then get hold of Tanya. Don't forget, add salt after ten minutes. Once it's cooking, you might want to feed the cat."

Adrian did not answer his phone. Odd. It was always on his person like some kind of life support. Why would he ignore her? She left a message offering any help or assistance required. Next she called Tanya on her mobile. The ring tone buzzed for an age before a familiar voice came on the line.

"Beatrice! You all right? How did London go?"

"Fine. Completely fine. Now I'm home and keen to progress with my enquiries. Tanya, how well do you know Gabriel Shaw on a scale of one to ten? One being you'd not recognise him in the street and ten being a knowledge of his whereabouts at any given time."

Tanya laughed. "Six, I suppose. We're the same age and went to school together. He's local and we stop for a chat now and then. Why?"

Beatrice launched into her request with a great deal of specific detail. Tanya listened, clarified and agreed to ask Gabriel out for lunch in a few hours' time. They said their goodbyes and Beatrice ended the call with a satisfied smile. That was when suspicion set in.

Tanya, contrary to expectations, had been the opposite of defensive. She was engaged, curious, knowledgeable and very well informed. Beatrice realised the ground had been prepared. Someone had got there before her and she had a good idea who. She glared at the kitchen door, listening to the sounds of the *Today* programme and Matthew's muffled but cheerful voice talking to the animals.

She got up and strode to the kitchen, determined to call him out on such interfering deviousness on a case he had asked her to take. Her purpose was delayed by the ringing of the doorbell. She opened the door intending to get rid of the postman as rapidly as manners would allow. But standing in the snow, a good deal smaller than the postie, was a pale-faced Rose Mason.

"Sorry, Beatrice. It's early, I know. I'm sorry to disturb you. It's just I could do with some support. I need to talk to my daughter. This might be the last chance I ever have to build a bridge between us. I can't ask Maggie as she takes the concept of partisan to a new level. Could you spare me half an hour? I really must talk to Grace and I..." Her voice broke. "I don't want to do it alone."

Beatrice reached out to grasp Rose's shoulders. "Of course I'll come with you. Hold on one second while I get my coat."

The Land Rover proved a real asset in the country lanes and Rose's driving skills left Beatrice in awe. Seventy-something years old, the woman used the vehicle more as an attacking weapon than a means of transport. No wonder it was covered with scars and dents. Within fifteen minutes, they pulled up outside Vaughan Mason's semi-detached, Beatrice reflecting on how some of the best drivers she'd ever met were women.

They rang the bell and waited, small talk out of the question. Sounds within indicated someone had attached the chain. The door opened a crack to reveal a sliver of Grace Mason. One eye, abundant curls and dark red fingernails.

"You shouldn't be here. We have nothing to discuss. I made my feelings clear on Tuesday. Further communication should be via our respective legal teams. I'm gonna have to ask you to leave."

Her voice had a strangled quality, as if she'd inhaled the opposite of helium, and her American accent sounded affected.

"Grace," said Rose, her tone sincere, "I come here with open hands and if you'll forgive me, an open heart. I only want to talk. This is my friend Beatrice. She knew your father. Can we just sit down and have a chat?"

"We're going to be in court in a few months. I think any contact is unwise. How do I know who this woman is and why you brought her? Why would I be dumb enough to let you into this house, putting myself and my father's legacy at risk?"

She spoke as if she were being recorded. Perhaps she was.

Beatrice snorted and turned away from the door. She followed the passageway between the house and its neighbour, opened the kitchen door and walked up behind Grace as she continued to spout soap opera dramatic phrases at Rose across a chain.

"Open the door and talk to your mother like an adult. To see a grown woman behaving like a petulant child is embarrassing for all of us, not to mention the fact it's downright rude to leave an elderly lady out in the snow. Open the door. Now!"

Her temper surprised her. The heat in her voice obviously touched Grace, who closed the door, released the chain and allowed Rose to enter. She walked away from them, into the kitchen and made a point of locking the back door.

Beatrice shot an apologetic glance at Rose. "Perhaps I should wait in the living room, give you both some space."

Rose gave an emphatic shake of her head before Grace turned from the window with an imperious glare. "I don't think so. The living room is full of my father's personal papers. I won't allow a total stranger to go snooping through his things." She gave Rose an insolent once over. "I'm extremely busy so would you ever just say your piece and get out?"

"Very well." Rose looked at the chairs around the kitchen table as if she would like to sit down, but Grace folded her arms, demonstrably unwilling to show even the most basic hospitality.

"I came here to tell you that I would very much like to get to know you. We've missed out on many years of a relationship and now we have a chance to change things. I appreciate you may not feel you need a mother figure in your life, but it would mean a great deal to me if we could be friends."

"Friends? Ha!" Grace's face twisted into a wholly unattractive sneer. Beatrice had the urge to slap her.

"Please, let me finish. Yes, I have been foolish enough to imagine we might be friends. I know it is more realistic for us to continue as we have done for the last forty years, with no contact whatsoever. The one thing I cannot abide is that we should become enemies. Grace, you are my only child and I will do anything I can to avoid a legal battle with you over your father's estate."

"In that case, we can settle this right now."

"Yes, I think we can." A tone of infinite calm entered Rose's voice, as if she'd arrived at the terminus after a very long journey.

Grace hesitated, but only for a beat. "All you need do is legally transfer the intellectual property rights to *An Empty Vessel* to me and our problem is solved." Her eyes narrowed to slits. "No courtrooms, no lawyers' fees, no publicity. I could certainly see that as a basis for a civilised future relationship."

Beatrice ground her teeth. This manipulative piece of work was using a possible future connection with her own mother as a bargaining chip to get the rights to Vaughan's most famous work. If Rose had any sense, she'd keep as far away from the noxious female as possible. *Don't give in*, she willed Rose. *Don't fall for it!*

To her surprise and relief, Rose shook her head. "I can't do that, Grace. I'm sorry."

"The hell you are! You get the biggest slice of pie and you're sorry? Why are you here? Just to gloat? Yeah, sure, I got his house, his estate and the rest of his trash but Vaughan Mason left his most valuable possession to you. Someone who walked out on him over forty years ago and has made no effort to create a relationship since."

Rose gasped, her eyes wide. "No effort? Grace..."

"Save it, Rose, I'm not interested. I'm his only child and should inherit everything. After all these years, why the fuck would he give that book to you?"

"Because it's mine."

Something about Rose's quiet conviction stilled the room. In the silence, the sound of melting snow dripping from the roof counted the seconds like a metronome.

"What do you mean, yours? You seriously think you have

any claim to that work because you spent a couple of years of your miserable marriage grubbing a wage while he created something people still want to read today? Give me a break! You know what I think? I think his drinking took its toll and he lost his mind. There's no other reason he would leave it you." Grace's face scrunched in contempt.

"He didn't leave it to me. He returned it. Sad to say, your father made few honourable gestures in his life, but in death, he finally did the decent thing. He gave me back my book."

Grace's expression darkened as if under a thunderhead. Her voice was low and menacing. "For the final time, it is not your book."

"Beatrice, I'm afraid I've brought you here under false pretences. It wasn't simply emotional support I needed, although I am grateful you gave your time so freely. The truth is I needed a witness to this conversation. Someone neutral, discreet and with a working knowledge of the law. Who better than a police detective inspector?"

Beatrice stared, at a loss for something to say.

Rose turned to Grace, words tumbling from her mouth in a rush. "I started writing *An Empty Vessel* in 1964, two years before I met your father. In those days, I shared a tiny flat in Putney with two friends and couldn't afford to go out. So I stayed home and I wrote. When I met Vaughan, I never breathed a word. He was The Writer, the would-be *wunderkind* poised to take the world by storm. Except all his ideas for books and plays were derivative and only lasted until he realised Kerouac, Orton and Tynan could do Kerouac, Orton and Tynan better than he could. His ego suffered and he sought the company of easily impressed young women while I lay pregnant with you. Bed rest was such a bore, I taught myself to touch type on his machine. My manuscript was perfect practice, even if I did wear out a few ribbons in the process. Once we had you, money became a problem. His occasional article didn't bring in enough for the gas meter, so I became a temp, working whenever and wherever they paid me. Your father took on the role of house husband which did not suit him. When you were not yet two, I came home one afternoon to find you locked in the bathroom, crying. He was in bed, otherwise engaged with one of our neighbours. After a furious row, I packed a few things for both of us and tried to take you with me. He wouldn't let you go. He threw me out but insisted you had to stay."

"Stop it! I don't need to hear this. You are trying to mess with my head. My father always put me first."

Rose's expression was sympathetic as she shook her head. "I spent eighteen months fighting to get you back because I knew Vaughan would never put anyone's needs above his own. I lost the case, of course I did. He had been your primary care-giver. I'd left our family home; I was sleeping on my friends' floor and couldn't provide for you. They granted him custody and he made damn sure you didn't want to see me. The first few times I visited, you screamed the place down. I couldn't win. So I left London and moved as far away as I could get."

Grace said nothing, her expression blank.

"It took me a while to realise what he'd done," Rose continued. "Newspapers in the north of Scotland don't tend to focus on the antics of the London literary crowd. By the time news of Vaughan Mason's *An Empty Vessel* reached my ears, I'd made myself a new life. In any case, I had no desire to see another courtroom for the rest of my days. Sometimes, I was even proud the book did so well and found myself mildly entertained by the interviews. 'How did you get into the female mind, Mr Mason? How long did the book take you to write? What are you working on next?' And always, 'Mr Mason, where did you get the idea?' Strangely enough, he never gave the correct answer: 'Well, Michael, I found it in a shoebox under the bed'. Your father stole my book, Grace, and now he's finally given it back."

The three women stood immobile after Rose finished her speech, Grace's eyes locked with her mother's. Beatrice recalled monochrome footage of atomic bombs, a mushroom cloud of destruction exploding in silence.

"NO!" Grace pointed her index finger at Rose's face. "Get out of here this minute! You dare defile my father's reputation IN HIS OWN HOUSE? Get out! I am ashamed that we're related. You are not fit to shine his goddamned shoes. As if you could have written that book. You are a joke! See you in court. Now get out and take your witness with you!"

Grace's fury was ugly and violent, her voice hoarse. Beatrice moved to stand beside Rose, who placed a reassuring hand on her arm, still calm and dignified.

"If you insist on contesting your father's final wishes, I will demonstrate that the book was and always has been mine. All my notebooks, interviews and research were still in a hatbox in Putney, which I took with me when I moved north. There's no doubt they are genuine and will prove incontrovertibly that I wrote *An Empty Vessel*. So not only will you lose the case, but you will destroy your father's reputation and any value attached to the rest of his work. Your call, Grace."

Rose sailed down the passageway to the front door, head held high. It was all Beatrice could do not to applaud.

Chapter Thirteen

Pamela Harding hit it off with Catinca from the second they met. The Head of Events Management did not even raise an eyebrow at the small dark dynamo in trapper's hat, faux fur jacket, silver leggings and moonboots taking control of the meeting. Catinca, for her part, pulled from her tomato-red satchel all the numbers, dimensions, timings and precise table dressings required and targeted her questions with pinpoint accuracy. Mrs Harding evidently appreciated her professional approach to wedding planning and stated that Catinca was one of the best prepared organisers she'd met.

The two women beamed at one another and Adrian caught Will's look of awed respect at the diminutive Romanian. But Adrian would not be rendered superfluous. After all, it was his day.

"I wonder, Mrs Harding, would it be possible to have a look at the honeymoon suite? If it's not occupied, of course."

Pamela Harding gave them an indulgent smile. "Of course you can. It's rarely occupied during the week. Let me buzz Jason, our porter, and he can show you the way. I already know you are going to love it. Did you see the one at Moor Hall? Let me tell you, ours knocks that into a cocked cat. It has an outdoor hot tub so you can sit in steamy water and drink champagne while catching snowflakes on your tongue."

Adrian let out a little moan of bliss and Catinca clapped her hands like a child.

"You read his mind, Mrs Harding," said Will, placing an arm around Adrian's shoulders. "All I have to do is persuade him not to record the moment on video."

A young man appeared in the doorway, sporting an eager smile with startlingly white teeth. "Honeymooners? This way."

Will and Adrian left Catinca to handle the arrangements and followed the porter upstairs to gush and fawn all over their accommodation. Their first night as a married couple would be spent in an Emperor-size bed under Egyptian linen, with a private balcony, hot tub and gasp-worthy views of snow-capped Dartmoor hills.

"It's perfect," said Will, after Jason had beaten a discreet retreat. "Just perfect. The whole organisation and military planning is important, I know that, but honestly? I cannot wait till it's all over and it's just you and me, here, wearing our wedding bands. When all the fuss and celebrations are over, this is what it's all about. Us two, together."

"True. This is where I should say I don't care where and how it happens, because what matters is you and me. But isn't this the most blissful place to start our life as a married couple? That bed! That tub! Will, listen to me. You're under-excited by all the detail, I get that. Catinca and I have it under control and in three days' time, we say our vows with all our friends and family. Then we get to look back on it for years to come as we grow old and wear cardigans."

Will kissed him and shot a glance at the bed. Adrian pulled back and shook his head with some emphasis. "No way. The room, if not the groom, stays a virgin till our wedding night. Come on now, let's go and make sure Catinca hasn't given the game away."

After two more hours of discussion and poring over alternative menus, Adrian had ticked every item off his list.

"We'll go with your suggestion of chestnut and sage soup for the starter, Mrs Harding. It sounds divine and as you say, it's seasonal. Catinca, is there anything else we need to discuss?"

"Nope. We done the menu, canapés, timing and decorations already so all we need is fix rehearsal tomorrow. What's that bloke called, one doing ceremony?"

"You mean the registrar?" Pamela Harding checked her notes. "That's Mr Kirkpatrick. In his email, he said he would be available between five and seven tomorrow evening. I generally leave at five-thirty, so can I suggest five o'clock for any final questions and then I'll leave you to it?"

"Fine with me," said Adrian, with a prod at Will who was playing with his phone. "Five o'clock for wedding rehearsal tomorrow afternoon, OK?"

Will attempted to look engaged. "OK, yes, yup, that sounds perfect." He gave Mrs Harding a winning smile. "All this talk of food has given me quite an appetite. Is your restaurant open for lunch today?"

"Unfortunately we have a private function booked in, a Christmas party. Those sorts of affairs can get rather boisterous, if you know what I mean. But there are lots of nice pubs nearby. Which direction are you going?"

"Upton St Nicholas," said Adrian, without thinking. Will tensed beside him and Catinca shot a furious glare in his direction.

"Oh, so close? I'd assumed you were staying in Exeter. Well, on the way there's The Red Hart, and Upton St Nicholas itself has The Angel and The Star, all of which do good food. To be honest, you don't want to be eating here today. Don't look before you peep, save it for a special occasion. Like Sunday." Her kind face crinkled into a smile and she patted Will's arm. "Now I've got a lot to do to prepare for your big day. You take this poor boy away and feed him. I'll see you all tomorrow at five."

They took their leave and crunched their way across the gravel towards the car, snowflakes falling onto their coats.

Catinca released a huge sigh. "This is how I imagine England before I got here. Country house romantic, horses, flowers, snow and Mr Darcy. London was nasty shock. Good to know it is real after all."

Will unlocked the car. "It's not real. We just keep a few places for the tourists."

"I am tourist! And so are you, mate. Beautiful building, innit? And that lady is proper lovely. Wish we could tell her we know her family. But better play safe. If Adrian don't put foot in it again, this wedding gonna be perfect."

Adrian fastened his seatbelt, ignoring the jibe. "Lunch at the pub or shall we stop on the way?"

"Let's try somewhere different," said Will. "Beautiful as the village might be, I kind of miss the range of choices we have at home. I don't think I'm cut out for country life. What do you say to The Red Hart?"

Adrian looked back at Catinca, who shrugged. He turned to Will. "Why not? Let's give it a go. Matthew's ex-wife is very nice, I agree. Did either of you notice anything funny about the way she speaks?"

Will switched on the wipers and shook his head. "Apart from the West Country accent, no."

Catinca said nothing, busy taking pictures on her phone.

"She has that Beatrice tic, mixing up her expressions. You know how we talk about her Bea-lines? Well, Pamela Harding does exactly the same thing."

"Whatcha talking about?" Catinca scooted forward to stick her head between the seats.

"When she was describing the honeymoon suite, she said it knocked the one at Moor Hall into a 'cocked cat'. Not hat. There was another one later but I can't remember it now. I'm just used to saving these because of Beatrice, so it jumped out at me. You didn't hear it?"

Catinca leant back, evidently bored. "Nah. Wouldn't notice anyway. Not my mother tongue."

Adrian looked to Will. "Do you know what I mean?"

"Not really. I was concentrating on the honeymoon suite. There's the pub. Thank God, I'm starving."

The Red Hart was a low-ceilinged classic country inn with

enticing warm lights and a real fire. Will strode to the bar, ordered drinks and asked for menus while Catinca went off to the ladies. Adrian took in his surroundings and spotted a familiar face at a corner table, in earnest conversation with a man. Tanya. She glanced up and saw him. With an almost imperceptible shake of her head, she turned her attention back to her companion.

Adrian got the message. Do Not Disturb. He guided Will and Catinca to the other end of the bar and settled them at a table to choose their food.

He'd already decided. "Monkfish goujons for me, with salad not chips. Listen, Tanya's over there, talking to a man. She gave me a very clear sign I should not interrupt. So let's eat our lunch and leave her in peace."

"Where?" asked Catinca, her eyes wide. With her trapper's hat still on, she looked like a bushbaby.

"To the right of the fire. Don't stare. Have you decided what you want to eat?"

"Fish and chips." She got to her feet. "I'll get this, it's my turn. Will, shut up already. Least I can do is pay for pub lunch after all you two done for me. Anyway, I wanna see Tanya's boyfriend."

She went to the bar, gave their order and paid. Then with classic Catinca chutzpah, walked past Tanya without a glance, up to the fire and warmed her silver-clad behind, allowing her a clear view of Tanya's companion. Her fashion sense and evident 'otherness' drew plenty of stares from the clientele, but Catinca was unfazed. She strolled back, smiling vaguely and picked up her glass of cider. She took a swig and indicated the couple by the fire with her glass.

"She got good taste. He's hot."

Will laughed. "And you are completely unsubtle. If the guy missed you checking him out, he's either short-sighted or fixated on Tanya."

"My guess is the latter," said Adrian. "Look, he's not even eating, just talking to her while his food goes cold."

"Stop staring!" Will whispered. "Poor woman can't even have

lunch without people gawping and gossiping. This is another reason I couldn't cope with life in a village. No privacy."

Catinca faced Will, her eyebrows drawn into a severe frown. "Village life is all some people got. You always go on about London, your choices, nobody knows your name. Good for you. Not everybody can afford it. Some people depend on neighbours. Yes, means they know more of our business. Also means they care. Don't judge the way other people live." She pointed a finger at Will, then at Adrian. "You two spend way too much time judging other people. Make your own choices and let them make theirs."

Stunned, Adrian stared at a particularly twee watercolour on the wall and assessed his own behaviour. Whatever had they done to give Catinca such an impression?

Will seemed equally dumbstruck and an awkward silence hung over the table until the barman approached with their food.

"Two fish and chips, one monkfish. Can I get you anything else?"

"Yes please," said Catinca, her eyes not leaving Adrian and Will, her jaw set in defiance. "I would like some ketchup."

"Sure." He fetched a bottle from behind the bar.

Adrian raised his glass. "I'd like to propose a toast. To choices. May they always be right for us."

Catinca cracked a smile. "To choices." She looked at his plate, back at her own and grinned at him. "Bet you wish you choosed fish and chips now, innit? Cheers!"

On the drive back to the village, Adrian's mobile rang. Guilt crept over him. He hadn't even acknowledged Beatrice's message. But the name on the screen was Jared, Adrian's ex-boyfriend and their wedding photographer.

"Hello, Jared! How's it going?"

"Adrian, hi. Not great, in fact pretty shitty. Listen, I'm so sorry about this but we aren't going to make it on Sunday. Alejandro is in hospital with suspected meningitis."

"Oh my God! When did this happen?"

"Last night. He was crying but didn't want us to pick him up. He already had a rash and I thought it was that. But Peter was convinced something was wrong. Then Alejandro started puking and his temperature shot up. Peter called the children's hospital and described the symptoms and we took him in at four in the morning. They are doing tests but he's very, very sick. I'm so sorry to let you down, my friend, but I have to stay by his side."

"Jared, don't even think of apologising. Of course you must stay with your son. I just hope it's not what they think it is. You must be worried out of your mind. Listen, don't give us a second thought but please keep me in the loop. Give Peter a hug from me and I'll be crossing my fingers for Alejandro. Take care of yourselves."

"Thanks, Adrian. I hope the wedding is wonderful and send my love to Will. I'll call you when I have news. Bye."

"Bye bye." He hit the End Call button. "This is the final straw. My godson is in hospital with suspected meningitis, Jared and Peter can't come, we have no photographer and I seriously believe this wedding is cursed. I think we should call it off."

Will kept his eyes on the road. "Don't be such a drama queen. How is Alejandro?"

"Very poorly. I mean it, Will, we should call this whole thing off. I wanted it to be the best day of our lives. Instead, it's been stress and hassle from the beginning. How can we enjoy our day knowing that tiny baby is in intensive care, fighting for his life? How can you have a wedding without any pictures? It's a disaster."

"Call it off now? I don't want that, I'm sure Jared and Peter don't want that, no one who's worked all these months on the arrangements wants that either. It seems it's only you. What is it, Adrian? Are you having second thoughts?" He pulled into a parking space in front of The Angel, switched off the car and faced Adrian. "Every single hiccup results in you deciding to cancel our wedding. At first I put this down to your natural tendency to histrionics, but now I'm beginning to wonder if you're just looking for any excuse to escape. Do you still want to marry me?"

Adrian couldn't reply. His throat constricted and he stared out at the snowy village green. He heard Catinca slide out of the back seat. He expected her to close the door quietly, leaving them to talk in peace but instead she threw a powerful punch at his headrest. He jolted forwards and bounced back as the door slammed shut.

The shock to his senses startled him out of his unhappy introspection. He caught hold of Will's hand. "I do want to marry you. I really do. It's just all these problems with the venue, deceptions with Beatrice, a suspicious death, a sick child and now we don't even have a photographer."

Will put his arm around him and drew him close. "I am going to fix this. You are going to stop panicking. We are going to get married on Sunday. There's still a lot to do and if I were you, I'd start by apologising to your wedding planner. You were lucky that seat was in the way or she'd have given you a cauliflower ear. Go inside and appease Catinca. I'll call Beatrice and between us, we'll locate a photographer. Leave it with me but please, Adrian, no more high drama and threats of calling it off. It's how we solve problems together which makes us such a good couple."

Adrian nodded, feeling Will's stubble graze his cheek. "You're right. Maybe it's just nerves. Come on then, we can do this." He took a deep breath and prepared to face Catinca.

Chapter Fourteen

A promise was a promise. Beatrice had given her word to Rose. She swore to tell no one of the conversation that morning, and the truth of Vaughan Mason's deceit would remain a secret. Unless Grace chose to go public about her father, no one would know the *enfant terrible* of 1960s literature had been much worse than a plagiarist. He was a common thief.

After Rose dropped her back at the cottage, Beatrice stood in the porch, pondering what to do next. The snow continued to fall, muffling all sound. The temptation to tell Matthew what she had learned ate at her like an itch. *Now why would that be, Beatrice? Surely not a nasty urge for vindication by puncturing the Midge bubble? You're better than that. And a promise, after all...*

"Yes, yes, I know," Beatrice snapped. Sometimes her conscience was an insufferable little prig. What she needed now was to talk to someone about the potential poisoning and train her attention on the case. The 'case'. Under normal circumstances she would throw ideas around with her colleagues when all leads resulted in a dead end.

Will? He would leap at the opportunity but Adrian wouldn't thank her for distracting him from the wedding. Although Rose and Maggie were enthusiastic amateur detectives, their idea of crime solving came from Sunday night TV dramas. Tanya was busy grilling Gabriel Shaw, so the only option available was for Beatrice to continue with all the diligence she'd normally have delegated to her sergeants. With a clap of her cold hands, she made a decision to return to the pub for a friendly chat with Gordon. She stamped the snow off her boots and opened the door with a breezy, 'Hellooo?'

Her only reply was a bark and a clatter of claws. Huggy Bear tore out of the kitchen and across the black and white tiles to bounce up at Beatrice with her toothy grin and blur of a wagging tail. A note lay on the kitchen table.

'Gone to golf club with Mungo to arrange memorial. Police called – DI Axe's no. below. Pls call her back. Running errands this afternoon. Could you feed Huggy Bear? My slipper was not to her taste. Mx'

Beatrice dialled the number with anticipation, keen to share her findings with a well-trained police mind. DI Axe answered after three rings.

"Thanks for calling back, Ms Stubbs."

The civilian moniker stung. Shouldn't police, like military officers, retain their titles in perpetuity? After all, they had earned them.

"My pleasure. How can I be of assistance?"

"It's more the other way round, to be honest. We received a complaint this morning, from Grace Mason. She wanted to register an official complaint of unauthorised entry to her property without an official warrant. She seemed to think you were part of the local force?"

Heat rushed into Beatrice's face as she struggled for words. "That is ridiculous! I didn't say I was police, I wasn't trying to..." She began pacing, the dog at her heel. "Look, Rose Mason asked me to accompany her this morning to be present at a conversation with her daughter. I admit to entering via the kitchen without invitation but only because she wouldn't open the front door to her own mother. I can assure you I never tried to present myself in an official capacity."

"I see. Well, I think we've managed to talk her out of it now she knows you're not one of ours. That said, given the circumstances, it might be better if you keep a distance from the whole Mason situation. We're following a few lines of enquiry and trying to keep it subtle. Don't want to ruffle any feathers, do we?" DI Axe's voice was friendly and warm, with the sound of tapping on a keyboard in the background.

Beatrice sniffed. "As a matter of fact, I have made done some surreptitious digging of my own and would be only too pleased to share my findings with the official investigators. Would you like me to come by the station at your convenience?"

There was a pause before Axe softened her tone, as if she were talking to some curtain-twitching old busybody. "Thank you, but that won't be necessary. I appreciate you have a personal interest in this case but even what you perceive as 'surreptitious digging' might have a negative influence our own investigation. I'd say after all you've achieved over your career, you deserve a well-earned rest. Best leave us to get on with the donkey work. Is that OK with you?"

Message received and understood. Butt out.

"Of course," Beatrice said, her voice cold. "You're the investigating officer."

"Thank you, I appreciate that. Oh, and by the way, merry Christmas!"

"Likewise. Goodbye." Beatrice ended the call and flung her mobile at the sofa cushions. Fits of pique were all very well but repairing a smartphone just before Christmas was a headache she could do without. "The arrogance of that bloody woman," she muttered and clenched her fists. Huggy Bear looked up at her, tail wagging and teeth protruding.

Beatrice exhaled and relaxed her frown. "Right, pooch, it's lunchtime for you, me and Dumpling. Then you're coming with me on covert ops. First stop, the pub. Old dogs don't necessarily need new tricks."

Thursday afternoon in the public bar at The Angel was quiet. A couple of locals were finishing a pie and a pint while browsing the paper, but there was no sign of the wedding party or Rose and Maggie. At least a friendly face was behind the bar.

"Afternoon, Susie. All right to bring the dog in?"

Susie glanced up from her magazine. "Hello, Beatrice! I didn't know you had a dog. Yes, of course, bring him in. No way should people leave them outside in this weather. What can I get you?"

"A pot of tea, please, I'm driving. This is a new addition to the family. Heather Shaw persuaded us to adopt. It's done Matthew the world of good."

Susie twitched her lips in a half-hearted smile. "Yes, Heather's very persuasive. How did the viewing at Silverwood Manor go this morning?"

Beatrice settled on a stool, tucking the dog's lead under her leg. Before being told, Huggy Bear sat at her feet. "Good girl. I don't know anything about the viewing because I didn't go with them. Adrian and Catinca have taken over now and that's fine with me. Gives me more time to work on..."

"The dog," said Susie, with a wise nod. "Rescues need a lot of fuss at first."

Beatrice scanned the bar and reminded herself to be professional. *Do not mention the case!* She closed her eyes for a moment, focusing on her aim. She wanted information from, or about, Gordon. Susie was an interviewee, not a sympathetic acquaintance. There must be no gossip, no idle conjecture, but facts. She opened her eyes with a smile.

"You on your own this afternoon?" she asked, as Susie placed a tea tray on the bar.

"As always. He won't usually get out of bed till tea-time, depending on how much he drank the night before. He'll get down here before the girls arrive for the evening shift and then I get a break. If they all turn up, that is. Otherwise, I'm on my feet all day."

"That's a long shift," said Beatrice. "And I suppose it will be busier than ever over Christmas?"

"Yeah. Usual stuff plus your wedding crowd. I could cope if I had reliable staff, you know? Not to mention a reliable husband."

Beatrice poured the tea, leaving a gap for Susie to steer the conversation. Change the subject or continue – up to her.

"It's not easy being business partners as well as husband and wife," said Susie, dropping her voice. "Lots of couples argue about money, I know. But when it's our livelihood at stake, it's not fair. Not fair at all."

"No, it isn't," Beatrice agreed. She reached down to stroke Huggy Bear's ears and cast a glance at the weary woman in front of her. Susie's roots were showing under her harsh blonde dye and her skin was dull. Her expression was one of permanent worry, wrinkles forming an arch between her brows.

"It's a question of trust, really," Susie spoke, half to herself.

Beatrice lowered her voice and spoke gently. "You mean you don't trust him in the financial sense?"

"His heart's in the right place, but his weaknesses get the better of him," Susie sighed, rubbing her lip with a thumbnail.

The gesture touched Beatrice. Susie needed a comfort blanket, or perhaps a willing ear. Beatrice saw her chance to serve both agendas.

"The drinking or losing to Vaughan Mason at cards?"

Susie's expression changed. Two furrows appeared between her eyebrows. "There's no truth in that. Village gossip, no more, no less."

"Maybe. But I should mention that one line of the police investigation is the gambling ring Vaughan ran in order to fleece his neighbours and friends. Have you spoken to the police yet?"

Susie shook her head, her features sagging. "They called in yesterday. Gordon got stroppy and insisted they make an appointment. To be fair, it's such a busy time of year."

Beatrice looked around the sparsely populated bar.

"We had a Christmas lunch party in when they arrived. It wasn't convenient. We've agreed to talk to them in the morning. I really don't know why they need to speak to me. Gordon was Vaughan's buddy but I had nothing to do with the bloke. All I ever did was pour his pints."

Huggy Bear sneezed, pre-empting Beatrice's own snort of disbelief. Something about Susie's evasive behaviour and weak mendacity made Beatrice curious. She knew more than she was letting on. The police may have rejected Beatrice's offer of experience and local knowledge, but Matthew still valued her opinion.

"Susie, you have nothing to worry about. As an ex-detective myself, I'd say all they'll ask you is who his friends were, if he had any enemies, that sort of thing. Obviously they'll ask you where you were the weekend Vaughan died, just to eliminate you from their enquiries." *Use enough police speak and people will not think to question your assumptions.*

"Yeah, we're ready for that one. Both of us were here from Friday morning to Sunday night. It was St Nicholas's Day weekend, so we were rushed off our feet and can provide plenty of witnesses."

"Exactly. All you need do is tell the truth. After all, you'd known the man for years. You and Gordon could give a pretty accurate picture of his drinking habits and romantic liaisons, presuming you can remember that many names."

The light from the beer pumps threw an orange glow onto Susie's face but Beatrice detected a blush even in the low lighting. Susie and Vaughan? This was a complicating factor Beatrice had not considered.

The door banged open and a voice said, "Here you are! I've been looking for you everywhere. Why aren't you answering your phone?" Tanya pushed back her hood, scattering clumps of snow onto the carpet.

Beatrice sat upright and bit her lip, recalling her dramatic gesture after her conversation with the police. "I must have left it at home. Do you want a drink and a debrief or do you have to get back to work?"

"No viewings in this weather so I can file my paperwork from home. But I have someone who wants to talk to you. Come on, leave your tea and let's go. Bye, Susie!"

Beatrice scrambled to her feet. "Bye, Susie. Tell Gordon if he wants a chat before he talks to the police, just give me a call. I'd be only too happy to help."

Two minutes later, Beatrice sat beside Gabriel Shaw in the front seat of his Land Rover with Tanya in the back and Huggy Bear at her feet. The dog gazed up at him with a look of total adoration as he reached down to stroke her chin. Beatrice could understand. He was her rescuer. While the forester eyed humans with great suspicion, he was naturally comfortable with animals and nature. Handsome in an uncompromising way, Gabriel Shaw had a monobrow above dark, thick-lashed eyes. His hands were calloused and his face unshaven but not in a neat-hipster-stubble way; more tumbled out of bed and straight into his moleskin trousers. It was all very dangerous and D. H. Lawrence and if Beatrice was in Tanya's position, she'd cast off her conscience for a roll in the hay.

Good God, woman, get a grip.

"You don't want to come in for a drink, Gabriel?"

He shook his head, attention still on the dog. "Thanks, but I have to work this afternoon. Tanya said you're trying to find out what happened to Mason."

Tanya tapped Beatrice's shoulder. "The police paid Gabriel a visit yesterday. They asked a lot of questions about a particular mushroom, or group of mushrooms. *Anamita...*"

"No, wait a minute." Gabriel held up his hand to stop Tanya. "Why do you want to know, DI Stubbs?"

"My partner wants to know if Vaughan was killed deliberately. I know the man had quite a few enemies, but what I'm trying to work out is how many would have access to the poison that killed him."

Gabriel exhaled with a grunt. "Everyone has access. It grows in the forest."

He looked into Beatrice's eyes for the first time and spoke in a rush. "There are a group of mushrooms which contain amatoxins, including the Death Cap. Most of them can be found in Devon's woodlands, but they're pretty rare. The one they think poisoned Mason is *Amanita virosa*. You can find it on the edges of woodland and it looks innocent enough. No stink, no red or yellow warning signs. Some people, the stupid kind who have no idea what they're doing, make the mistake of thinking it's edible. They usually die within two days. What's really vicious about *Amanita virosa* is that you puke and crap all over the place, as if you have a stomach bug. Just when you're ready to call the doctor, it seems to be over. You think you've recovered. Meanwhile, it attacks your liver and kidneys and by the time it comes back and you call for help, it's too late."

"That's horrible! I assume the police's toxicology report led them to suspect this particular fungus?"

Gabriel shrugged. "I suppose. They didn't tell me much. I just told them what I know. Where it grows, how to spot it and what it does to the body. For someone like Mason who spends Friday in the pub and sometimes sees no one till Sunday morning, it's ideal. He ingests *Amanita virosa* on Friday afternoon and goes to the pub as usual. He gets sick late Friday night, has a few hours feeling bad, recovers on Saturday and when it comes back on Saturday night, his system is so badly compromised, he can't even raise the alarm."

In the silence after Gabriel's speech, a logical conclusion must have occurred to them all. They all spoke at once.

"How many people have..."

"The thing is, Gabe couldn't..."

"DI Stubbs, *I* didn't do it."

Huggy Bear yawned loudly and leaned sideways onto Gabriel's foot, settling her chin on his toe.

Beatrice pressed her fingers to her temples. "First things first, I'm no longer a DI, so please just call me Beatrice. Secondly, I assume you told the police all this and therefore you must be considered a suspect. You have motive, means and very possibly opportunity. But they've not taken you in for questioning. Why is that?"

Gabriel shrugged and shook his head. "No idea. I don't have an alibi for Friday as I work alone in remote locations. No one can vouch for me. I was at the St Nicholas Day parade with my mother on Saturday afternoon and in Brixham the rest of the weekend. The police are checking my 'story' and 'looking into my background'. They don't intimidate me. I'm prepared to be honest with you and give you my view on what happened, DI Stubbs, because you treat me with respect. Just take this at face value. I hated Vaughan Mason's guts. I'm glad he's gone somewhere he can't treat anyone else the way he treated my mother, and many other women before her. He was scum.

"But I don't get to choose who lives and who dies. You said I have motive, means and opportunity. That is true. I could poison the old git with a mushroom, but will that give my mother her dignity back? Or any of the other women he treated as disposable? And..."

Beatrice waited, her nerves alert. "And?" she prompted.

His eyes flicked up to the rear-view mirror. "Part of my job is maintaining the ecological balance of the forests. That means chopping down trees and sometimes killing animals to control the population. If I have to kill something, I do it as fast and humanely as I can. No animal should suffer. Nor should any human. Poisoning is cruel and unnecessary, a method used by cowards who don't stick around to see the agony they have caused. If I was going to kill Vaughan Mason, I'd have told him to his face why he deserved it, then shot the arrogant bastard in the head with my twelve-bore."

Seconds ticked by as Beatrice laced her hands behind her neck, leaned back and stared at the torn fabric of the Land Rover's roof, turning it all over in her mind.

"Mushrooms are a specialist interest. You'd know about them because of your job. Is there anyone else in the area who would know where to find and how to use that kind of toxic fungus you describe?"

Gabriel's eyes unfocused for some seconds. "One or two at

the university for sure. But not many locals, at least not any more. The last woman who knew everything in the forest was Hannah Gwynne but she's been dead for two years."

"Mrs Gwynne?" Tanya's voice had a note of incredulity. "You don't mean Susie's mother? Wasn't she a bit ... off the grid?"

"That's the one." Gabriel's smile came from a distant place. "A formidable woman who could have taught us a lot if anyone was prepared to listen." He looked out the window at the lengthening shadows and encroaching dusk. "DI Stubbs, I need to get on the road. If you have any more questions, give me a call. Tanya, cheers for lunch. See you around, yeah?"

Beatrice scooped up Huggy Bear and held out her hand. "Thank you so much for all you've shared with me. One last thing before you go. Could you tell me again the name of the poisonous mushroom?"

"Sure. *Amanita virosa.* Most people call it The Destroying Angel."

Chapter Fifteen

It took Adrian twenty minutes to get Catinca to open the door and a further fifteen before she would speak to him. He used every means of apology he could think of and finally she hissed at him like a feral cat.

"Shut up! Shithead!"

He closed his mouth and looked at his shoes. His role was to take the tongue-lashing with humility. He didn't have to wait long.

"Is not all about you! Beatrice been weeks working on arrangements, I spent loads of time making atmosphere perfect and Will found dream honeymoon! And all you can do is throw toys out of pram every time we have hiccups. Sick of it, mate! One more time and you can do crappy wedding on your own."

"I know and I am truly sorry. It must be nerves. I don't usually overreact like this."

Catinca's eyebrows shot up and she managed to look down her nose despite being a foot shorter than him.

"OK, OK," he admitted. "I'm not the best at handling stress. I really couldn't cope without your advice and help and Beatrice's practical good sense. I'm lucky to have you on my side."

"Lucky to have Will an' all."

"I am and I wake up every day grateful to have met the only person in the world who could put up with me. I do want to marry him and I will stop seeing omens where they don't exist.

The wedding is happening on Sunday whether we have a photographer or not, even if the snow melts, even if we have to put Beatrice in a burkha to avoid confrontation."

"On Sunday, we don't need no burkha. But what we doing about tomorrow?" Catinca demanded.

"What do you mean?"

"Rehearsal, mate. Five o'clock tomorrow, we meet Missus Harding and registry bloke. Beatrice is matron of honour. She gotta be there."

"Oh my God, you're right. Don't panic, we can sort this out. Pam said she leaves at five-thirty. That's fine. We'll talk to her and the registrar first, and get Beatrice to arrive a bit late, maybe quarter to six. Then a quick walk through and no one will be any the wiser."

Catinca twisted her lips sideways. "Cutting it fine, innit?"

"Yes, but we can pull it off. We just have to work together."

"Yeah, I guess." She sounded unconvinced. "But for photos, I got an idea. We get all guests to take own pictures and share online. We pick the best and make album."

Adrian nodded, deep in thought, recalling all the dreadful drunken images shared on Facebook of friends' weddings. "That *might* work. Perhaps if we ask people to upload to a shared folder and we can choose the ones we want made public."

"You are such a snob. Whatever. I'm going to hairdresser in half an hour. You wanna call Matthew and plan tomorrow? I reckon team meeting tonight at six *without* Beatrice. Maybe not here either – too many gossipers. Know a different pub?"

"No, but I'll find one. Yes, good point to keep Beatrice out. Otherwise someone will say something they shouldn't. Why are you having your hair done this afternoon? The wedding's not for three days."

Catinca whirled around, her hands on her hips. "In case they cock it up! Still got two days to fix, innit?" She snatched up her satchel and with a shake of her head flounced out of the door.

Adrian sat on the bed for several seconds, her words echoing in his head. 'Still got two days to fix, innit?' He reached for his mobile and dialled Matthew.

At ten past six that evening, Adrian and Matthew entered the bar of The Star Inn to find Will, Catinca, Tanya, Marianne, Rose and Maggie settled at a large table in the bay window. Adrian's surprise at seeing the septuagenarians present was nothing compared to his double take when he saw Catinca's hair. Long platinum ringlets cascaded over her shoulders with a thin plait in the same gleaming silver circling her head. She caught his expression and grinned.

"They didn't cock it up, mate. On Sunday, I'm The White Queen."

"You look amazing!" Adrian breathed.

"She always looks amazing," said Will. "Where's Beatrice?"

Matthew heaved himself into a chair next to Tanya. "At home. I told her I needed to run a few errands and would be back for dinner at eight. I told no untruths, but may have alluded to visiting Mungo. I have to say, I find all this skulking around most uncomfortable and would prefer a degree of honesty. I really think if we explain the situation, Beatrice would keep a low profile until Sunday. Thereby upsetting no one but involving no deceit."

"I'd vote for that policy," Will added.

Marianne and Tanya both shook their heads.

"Nope, that's not on." Tanya's tone brooked no argument. "If we're telling lies to keep them apart, we tell them both lies. Otherwise we're being unfair and favouring one over the other."

Marianne chimed in. "It might not make sense to you, but Tan and I have grown up this way, trying to be equally balanced. We never spill secrets or share information with one and not the other. It's a question of fairness."

"Very well," Matthew groaned. "So how do we manage tomorrow night?"

"Before we get to that, I have some good news," Will poured

two glasses of wine for Adrian and Matthew. "We have an official photographer." He indicated one of the little old ladies, Adrian couldn't recall her name.

"Really? That's wonderful, umm..."

"Maggie. Maggie Campbell. I'm an experienced photographer, more of landscapes than weddings to tell the truth, but I will do my best to take a beautiful set of images to record your day. If I could have a wee peek at the venue first, it would be a great help. Could Rose and I come along to tomorrow's rehearsal? Scope out the place and choose some backdrops?"

Her soft face with sharp blue eyes reminded Adrian of a mouse, with its slightly twitchy nose testing the air. He recalled their conversation on Monday, where both women swore a fierce loyalty to Beatrice. It wasn't what he'd planned, but his instinct told him it would be very different to any of his friends' wedding albums.

"That is incredibly kind of you, Maggie. Of course you should come to the rehearsal. We just need to keep quiet in front of..."

"Beatrice. Don't worry yourself, Adrian," said Rose. "We'll keep out of her way. Maggie wants to go shopping in Exeter and now that Grace has returned to New York, Matthew has very kindly given me permission to have a look round Vaughan's cottage. Just in case I want something to remember him by."

Maggie gave a snort of disapproval but Rose ignored her. "Anyway, we won't see Beatrice before we turn up at Silverwood Manor. And then we'll all have far too much on our minds to chat."

Adrian sighed and gave both women a huge, genuine smile.

"Our remaining problem is getting Beatrice to the rehearsal early enough for it to be worthwhile but late enough for her to miss Mum," said Marianne.

"I suppose I shall have to get lost," Matthew said, and took a sip of wine. "She's always telling me I couldn't find my way out of a paper bag, so I'll head off in the wrong direction, take a few wrong turns, park up and study the map until I get a message from one of you saying the coast is clear."

"Yeah, that sounds classic Professor Bailey," Tanya smiled. "You didn't bring the car tonight, did you? You know the police will be extra hot on drink-driving over Christmas."

Matthew leaned over and patted her hand. "Taxi here and I'll be driven back home with a real live policeman behind the wheel. Your old dad's not half as daft as he pretends."

Adrian glanced at Will, pleased to see an affectionate smile on his face. It was all going to work out beautifully.

The White Queen clapped her hands and opened her laptop.

"Good. That's sorted. Right, let's organise schedule from now till wedding. Synchronised watches timing. Who's where, doing what and who needs to know? I got spreadsheet prepared and need few answers. Tanya, what we doing with Luke as ring bearer?"

Chapter Sixteen

Destroying Angel.

Beatrice slipped a shawl over her shoulders and continued scribbling at the kitchen table. If Hannah Gwynne knew poisonous mushrooms, so did her daughter. Susie may have become a respectable landlady, but for many years, she had been an unmarried mother, living on the charity of her surviving parent. Until she met Gordon Hancock.

Gordon Hancock. Like Matthew, he was eleven years older than his partner. Unlike Matthew, he was married and had a stepchild. He and Susie seemed happy enough, even if they argued about money. Their daughter Francesca couldn't wait to get away from the village and ran off to college the minute she finished school. Nothing unusual there; bright lights attract country kids.

Susie had means and opportunity. Gordon had motive. Yet the idea of the pair working together to snuff out Vaughan Mason didn't sit right. She, weary and hopeless; he, drunk and hopelessly optimistic. This was as far from Bonnie and Clyde as one could imagine. But if not a partnership, could either have acted alone?

Gabriel Shaw. Beatrice went through the motions, elbowing aside her gut feeling that anyone Huggy Bear adored could never be a killer. He admitted his hatred of Vaughan. He knew the exact time frame of the poison and the habits of the victim.

His mother had been repeatedly humiliated by the man and his anti-cruelty statement could have been nothing more than an attempt to impress his old crush.

Heather Shaw. She knew Vaughan better than most and had an axe to grind. Motive, means and opportunity were obviously a given but what did she have to gain? If she was to be believed, she had expected him to come back.

Mungo Digby. Innocence claimed by best friends' status. He'd lived in the region for his entire life so might have some knowledge of local flora. The thought of Mungo poisoning Midge for fear of some hypothetical book was ridiculous to Beatrice. But academic reputations were delicate creatures and...

The shrill ring of the telephone woke Huggy Bear, who sat up with a startled bark.

"Hello?"

"Beatrice. Gordon here, from The Angel. Susie suggested you might be up for a chat."

"Hello, Gordon. Yes, happy to oblige. Shall I come to the pub?"

"Not much privacy here. What do you say to a quick snifter at The Star?"

"Suits me. What time?"

"How's half six?"

"See you then. Thanks, Gordon."

"Thank *you*."

The car park of The Star, surprisingly busy for early doors on a Thursday, was riddled with potholes. Easy enough to avoid unless the ground was covered in four inches of snow. Beatrice chose one of the three spaces in the lane, in front of a mud-spattered Land Rover Defender she recognised as belonging to Gabriel Shaw. She sat in the car, wondering if she should call Gordon and relocate their meeting. She'd really rather not encounter anyone they knew, but that was close to impossible round here. Having their conversation in one of their vehicles was inappropriate, going for a walk would be unpleasantly cold, so she would simply have to acknowledge Gabriel and continue with her purpose.

A car pulled up outside the pub and Gordon Hancock emerged from the passenger seat. He leaned back in to speak to the driver, then slammed the door with a laugh and thumped on the roof. The driver gave a pip-pip of the horn and drove off into the night.

Beatrice opened her door to accost Gordon before he made for the pub. "Gordon? I've just this minute arrived. You are punctual."

"Can't keep a lady waiting," he said, with an awkward bow. With a public bar between them, there had never previously been any kind of physical greeting.

She pulled on her gloves and locked the car. "Let's go inside. Just a word of warning, I think that's Gabriel Shaw's Land Rover. Best we say hello to him then retreat to a corner."

Gordon looked over his shoulder at the dirty vehicle, still warm enough to melt the snowflakes landing on its bonnet. "Nah, that's not Gabriel's. Not a local number plate. Hey, Beatrice, you all right to give me a lift home? One of the punters dropped me off, see, and Susie's behind the bar on her own so she can't fetch me. Is that OK?"

They began walking up the path to the pub. "Of course I can give you a lift. It's a detour of no more than five minutes. But if Susie's behind the bar, why didn't you drive?"

"Can't risk the breathalyser." He opened the door. "After you."

They entered the pub, its ambience full of warmth and voices, and made for the bar. Gordon held up a hand. "I'll get the drinks. My way of saying thank you for a bit of inside knowledge. What's your poison?"

She froze for a moment then her thoughts caught up. "A white wine spritzer with soda and ice. Thank you." She looked around the room for a spare table and saw the party in the bay window. Adrian, Will, Matthew, Tanya, Marianne, Maggie and Rose all leaning in to listen to a silver-haired female in fancy dress. Not one of them saw her, so intent was their concentration, so Beatrice melted away to a corner table at the opposite end of the bar. She reached up to the sunken spotlights and twisted one from its socket. Good job she'd kept her gloves on. She sat with her back to the wall in the shadows, watching the group with a cynical eye. Gordon loomed over her, drinks in hand.

"You chose the darkest corner there is! Hope folk don't get suspicious. People might think we're..."

"Thank you for the drink. What other people think is their business. Now, let's talk about Vaughan Mason. I'm going to ask you questions as if I were the investigating officer and you tell me the truth. If I think you're incriminating yourself in any way, I may suggest rephrasing your response."

Gordon took a large pull from his pint and licked his lips. "Ready when you are, Inspector Stubbs."

"You may refer to me as DI Stubbs, just for the duration of this exercise. Mr Hancock, how long had you known Mr Mason?"

"Twenty-five years? Can't recall exactly, but he's been a regular at The Angel since we took over the licence. That was twenty-five years back."

"Would you consider him a friend?" asked Beatrice, with a glance over his shoulder at the group in the bay window.

"Acquaintance, more like. He drank in the bar most weekends, we played cards occasionally, and moved in similar circles. You know the score."

"Gordon, you're not talking to me but a police detective investigating a suspicious death, remember? What are you prepared to say about the card games? And please don't lie, they already know about the gambling. Be as honest as you can."

Gordon drank deeply from his pint glass, his eyes downcast. Across the room, Beatrice saw the silvery goddess rise from the table and make for the toilets. The Converse trainers gave her away. Catinca. So the whole wedding party was present and she had been deliberately excluded.

"This is confidential, right?" Gordon asked, licking his lips.

"Gordon, please. I want to offer my experience as a police officer, not dig about for gossip. Whatever you tell me is in total confidence."

"Yeah, that's what I thought. Right then. We played poker. Table of six, high stakes and Vaughan made a lot of money out of all of us. Everyone thought we could beat him but that sly old git never – not once – ended up on the losing end. Susie thinks I lost over a grand to those games, but she could add a nought and get closer to the truth." He pressed his finger to beer-moistened lips.

Adrian approached the bar and looked around the room as the server prepared his order. Beatrice elbowed her notebook to the floor and ducked to retrieve it. She spent so long digging about, Gordon bent down to offer assistance.

"Got it, thank you." She sat up in time to see Adrian returning to his table. "Now, to return to my questions. When did you last see Mr Mason?"

"The Friday before he died. As usual, he was one of the last to leave, hoping for a lock-in. I kicked him out at half eleven because it was Francesca's birthday and they were waiting for me upstairs. She wouldn't come down to the bar. The old drunks get on her nerves, she says. All I wanted was to go upstairs and have a birthday drink with Frankie. Vaughan must have had four or five pints and at least two whiskies. His speech was just starting to slur, so I told him to go home. Sometimes, Suze will give him a lift if she's in a good mood, but that's not very often these days. Anyway I just wanted him out so I could lock up and spend some time with my girls. I thought a brisk walk in the cold was exactly what he needed."

"Francesca was home that weekend? I thought she was busy with her gallery."

Gordon drained his beer. "She is, but she always comes home for her birthday, even if it is just overnight. I got staff to cover the bar so they could have some mother and daughter time. She misses her little girl more than she lets on. So do I, if I'm honest." His eyes grew soft and misty. "I'm so proud of her, you know."

"So you should be. You raised a lovely young woman. Who do you think..."

Gordon hadn't finished. "Never wanted kids, you know. But when I met Susie, Francesca was part of the package. I fell in love with her mum but that little angel also captured my heart." He sighed.

Beatrice wondered how many the man had already drunk if he was getting sentimental at seven o'clock in the evening.

As if he'd heard her thoughts, Gordon picked up his glass. "Ready for another?"

Beatrice panicked. If Gordon went to the bar, he may well spot the party in the bay window or they see him and the ensuing awkwardness would be unbearable. She couldn't propose leaving just yet as she'd only scratched the surface of his knowledge. Another pint or two would loosen his tongue but how to achieve that when they couldn't risk going to the bar? She sipped at her wine, playing for time. A noisy party entered the pub, baying and shrieking with laughter. They were all gussied up and well-oiled, presumably post-Christmas lunch, judging by the synthetic Santa hats and cardboard reindeer antlers. Time to make their exit.

"Yes, I am ready for another, but not here. Let's find somewhere more conducive to conversation. Come on now, quick!" She grabbed her coat, bag and gloves, left the light bulb on the table and scurried towards the door. Gordon obediently followed at her heels.

Weaving her way through the drunken throng, she excused herself politely at first, until the complete indifference of the people began to inflame her temper. She elbowed and shoved and barged people out of her path, arriving at the doorway to find another group blocking her exit.

Will saw her first. "Beatrice! What are you doing here?"

They all turned to her, every single face a mask of guilt and embarrassment. Matthew reached out a hand.

"Listen, Old Thing, we just..."

"Hello, everyone. Fancy seeing you! Sorry, can't stop. Promised Gordon a lift home. See you all later." She barrelled her way through them and headed out into the snow.

Her enthusiasm for interrogation had faded away entirely. When Gordon opened the passenger door, she gave him a tight smile. "Would you mind if we called it a night? I'll drop you off and if you have any other questions, you can give me a ring in the morning."

He fastened his seatbelt. "Um, yeah, sure. Is everything all right?"

Beatrice started the car and flicked on the wipers to clear the screen of its gauzy white veil. "I'm sure it will be. There must be an innocent explanation of why I've been excluded from the family meeting with the wedding party. No need to take it personally. Maybe I was just surplus to requirements."

They drove in silence back towards the village, snowflakes coming out of the navy-blue night like a cloud of moths, the countryside softening to a festive fairyland.

Gordon cleared his throat. "No one can make you feel inferior without your permission."

"Sorry?"

"I meant that it's up to you. You can choose your own reaction." Gordon inhaled and released a huge beer-scented breath. "I don't really know what I'm talking about, Beatrice. Just one of those phrases that hit me in the right place. Vaughan, Mungo and, sorry, even Matthew make me feel insecure, you know, unsophisticated and a bit of a peasant. Them being such intellectuals and all I do is pull pints. Thing is, Francesca saw a therapist for a while, when she was having a few teenage problems, and that was one of her, what would you call them? Mantras?"

"Yes, mantras or affirmations."

"You know about this stuff?"

"A little. Go on." She drove slowly through the lanes, alert to reflective blue eyes of foxes or cats and the subtext of Gordon's ruminations.

"Inferiority is a state of mind. Depends on your measurement of people's worth. I don't pretend to get all of it, but Francesca came back from every session with live ammo. You know, stuff she could use immediately. I admit to being a bit sceptical at first but anyone could see it made a massive difference. That counsellor made her look at things with a new perspective. She changed Francesca's life. Which in turn had an effect on me and Suze. You know, I've completely revised my opinion on therapy and I've got a lot of time for that woman."

"She sounds quite wonderful. Is she local?" asked Beatrice, indicating left to the village green and the lights of The Angel.

"Hellfire, the pub's packed already. I'd better get in and give Suze a hand. Yeah, Gaia's sort of local. She lives in the back of beyond round Appleford way. Thanks for the pep talk, Beatrice. I'll let you know how it goes. G'night and don't fret too much. It'll all come out in the wash."

Chapter Seventeen

The front door opened. Huggy Bear yipped with excitement and rushed into the hallway to greet Matthew. Beatrice told herself to stand up, to get busy and do something. Yet she remained slumped at the kitchen table, staring at her notes, which seemed to have no more significance than the scuff marks on the floor.

She looked up to see him standing in the kitchen doorway, still with his coat on and snowflakes in his hair. His expression was sombre. "I'm so sorry. That should never have happened."

Beatrice shrugged. "Doesn't matter. Have you eaten?"

"No. As I said, I'd be back for dinner. But before I start cooking, I need to explain."

"Don't bother. I had a sandwich earlier and I honestly couldn't care less about your secret meeting. Adrian's made it quite clear he has no further need of my help, which is his prerogative. It's fine. In a way, it's a relief. I'm going to run myself a bath and get an early night."

"Please just wait a minute. The reason for all this skulking about is quite simple, but in my opinion, also quite unnecessary."

"Whatever it is, I'm not interested." She gathered up her papers in an untidy pile. "I have other things on my mind. By the way, I've fed the animals."

He blocked her path. "Just one moment. The problem is Pam. She's Head of Event Management at Silverwood Manor and thus in charge of these last-minute wedding arrangements. Will and I take the view that you are both adults and can comport yourselves with enough dignity not to ruin Adrian's big day. However, the girls are quite convinced you two must be kept apart."

She said nothing. The idea of meeting Pam again after all these years left her at a total loss. No idea what to think, how to feel or whether it was actually something she wanted or not.

"So the reason we met this evening was to work out a military-style operation to ensure we arrive at the rehearsal after she's gone home for the night, guarantee she will be Christmas shopping on Sunday while the celebrations occur and keep both of you in the dark about each other's proximity."

Beatrice swallowed. "She ... Pam doesn't know either?"

"No. The girls are scrupulous in equal treatment. If they tell white lies to one of you to spare feelings, they do the same to the other. Part of me respects that strategy but it backfired this evening. Now you feel excluded and side-lined which is absolutely not the case. Adrian is distraught. And I..."

"You what?" Beatrice noticed the lines on his face and the pallor to his skin tone. As if he needed any further stress.

"I think it's time we all grew up. This is not about us, it's about Adrian and Will. We've wasted a stupid amount of time chasing our tails and I've had enough. On top of all that, I'm hungry. Did you really have a sandwich earlier?"

"No," she confessed.

"Shall I heat some French onion soup?"

"Good idea. I'll make the cheesy croutons."

Friday morning dawned grey and cold, an echo of Beatrice's mood. She lay in bed running through all the things she had to do, with the deflating conviction they were all pointless. Matthew's gentle snores made her envious. If she could only sleep for the next 72 hours and let them all get on with it. She didn't want to go to the rehearsal later that day. She didn't want to run around hiding and ducking behind curtains as if this were some kind of Brian Rix farce. On the other hand, neither did she want to meet Pam after all these years. What on earth could she say?

If she were honest, she no longer had much interest in going to the wedding. It all seemed far too much effort. And as for pursuing 'Who Killed Vaughan Mason?', what was the point? The police would have far greater access to all the evidence so all she was doing was wasting her own and other people's time. What she really wanted to do was grab her passport, pack a case, drive to the airport, get on the first flight somewhere sunny and disappear for a week.

She slid out of bed and scooped up Huggy Bear, so the yips and barks of delight at waking up to another morning didn't wake Matthew. In the kitchen, she made coffee and stared out at the blank whiteness. There was so much to do! Christmas presents to be wrapped, cards to be delivered, the food shopping, her hair appointment, Matthew's suit to be pressed, Adrian and Will's wedding gift, the pudding to be made ... a jittery electricity ran through her veins and her chest seemed to contract. It was too much. Whose stupid idea was it to have a wedding the day before Christmas Eve? She was exhausted even thinking about it. The idea of going back to bed and curling up with Matthew crossed her mind but Huggy Bear's tufty eyebrows suggested an alternative.

She dressed in her gardening clothes and laced up her walking boots, her limbs heavy and fingers slow. As she reached for the lead, she saw the blinking light on the answer machine she'd ignored when she got home last night.

Three new messages. One from James, asking her to call him. *He wants to tell me off for missing the Gaia appointment.* She resolved not to call until the New Year, when she may or may not have met the woman. The second was Adrian, apologising for last night and entreating her to call. He hoped Matthew had explained they'd only been trying to protect her. The third was a voice she didn't recognise.

"*Hello, Beatrice. Sorry you couldn't make it yesterday but thanks for letting me know. I'm not sure you got my reply? I emailed you back saying I'd be happy to meet you either today or Friday. I know it's a busy time of year, so if it makes things easier, I can come to you or we could meet in a local coffee shop? Have a good evening."*

Gaia. So she and James were both bullying her into a meeting. She shook her head and retreated from the phone. When people ganged up to force her into something she didn't want to do, she turned mulish. The sound of the cistern flushing upstairs galvanised her into motion. She clipped the lead onto the dog's collar, grabbed a coat and opened the front door. A long walk was exactly what she needed.

An hour later, two weary females trudged up the drive. Huggy Bear's delight at the weather had lasted for about half an hour, until they turned onto the lane. The salt and grit got into her paws and she began to limp. Beatrice picked her up and rubbed her feet, but carrying her for more than a few minutes made her arms ache. Cold wind and snow flurries battered them both and every time Beatrice stopped and put her down to rest, Huggy Bear shivered, her tail tucked under her legs, snowflakes sticking to her eyebrows. Beatrice added *buy a dog coat* to her list of things to do and wretched helpless tears increased her discomfort by chilling on her cheeks. Her mind wandered to a beach in northern Germany and a huge hairy man carrying a fully grown Husky as if she were a cuddly toy. That was back when she was DI Stubbs, an international expert in solving crime, in demand all over Europe.

Now she was plain Ms Stubbs and surplus to requirements. At least the dog needed her. She wiped at her face with a damp and dirty glove.

The house came into view and Beatrice continued her reassuring tone. Who she was reassuring was not clear. "Not long now, pooch, we're nearly home. Nice warm house, see, there it is! Cosy blanket by the Aga for you and maybe some milk. Cup of coffee for me and dry trousers. Oof, you weigh a ton."

Once on the drive, she released the dog and caught a strange smell of burnt caramel. Huggy Bear hared away to the door and stood scratching till Beatrice caught up. Caramel or coffee? Whatever it was, it was burnt. She fumbled for her key and let them both in. The stench of smoke hit her instantly. The house was only a degree or two warmer than outside as all the windows were open and the carpet soaking wet.

Matthew, still in his bathrobe, was mopping the kitchen floor.

"What on earth?" she asked, already knowing the answer. Absorbed in her own thoughts, she'd put the Moka pot on to boil and completely forgotten about it. Matthew indicated the hob, a charred wreck, and the blackened mess of once-white splashback tiles. Using an oven glove, he fished out the pot from the sink. No longer silver and elegant, it was covered in crusted brown stains. The pot let out an angry hiss which Beatrice took personally.

"The coffee. I forgot."

"Yes, I gathered that. The spillage caught fire and set off the sprinklers. We have a clean-up operation to deal with but my primary concern is Dumpling. When I heard the fire alarm, I rushed down here to open the door and he shot out like ... well, like a scalded cat. I have no idea where he went. No amount of shaking a box of GoCat has persuaded him to emerge from his hiding place. I'll keep clearing up in here and Huggy Bear can stay with me while you look for the old boy."

Beatrice's throat contracted. She wanted dry clothes, a warm house, a cup of coffee and a massive, uncontrolled crying jag. Instead she muttered, "I'm sorry. It was an accident." She returned to the hallway to remove her wet coat, gloves and boots.

Her mobile rang. Adrian again. She declined the call, shoved it back in her pocket and went in search of the cat.

There were no sprinklers in the cellar, so that was a logical place to start. In the laundry room, the cat carrier was empty. The doors to the pantry and wine cellar were both shut but between them sat empty several cardboard boxes left over from the Christmas delivery.

Beatrice took up her reassuring tone again. "Puss, puss? Come on, Dumpling, it's all over now. Come on out. You must be hungry. Puss?"

Even if he was responding, she wouldn't be able to hear him. His miaows were visible but never audible. She went into the pantry and rummaged around until she found some cans of sardines. She peeled back the lid of one and took it to the boxes.

"Fishies. Sniff that, Dumpling! You like fish, remember?" She smacked her lips. "Mmm, delicious." She placed it on the floor and waited. From above, the doorbell rang and the smothered feeling enveloped her like a damp duvet. *I can't deal with it, whatever it is, not today. Please go away and leave us alone.* She sniffed and swallowed the lump in her throat.

Male voices drifted down the stairs and she guessed it was Adrian and Will. Part of her wanted to escape, to crawl into some hole and hide, far away from weddings and enquiries and relatives and obligations. Perhaps she and Dumpling could find a cosy cardboard box, curl up together and live on sardines till it all blew over.

A soft sound came from the empty carton of Cava nearest to the laundry room. Beatrice sat very still. The light was poor and Dumpling's grey form could have been a shadow or a ghost. Yet the glint of his eyes was corporeal.

"Hello, Dumpling," she whispered. "Come and have some food. Sorry about all the fuss and drama. My fault. Tell the truth, I think I may be losing it. Come out of there, pusscat." She pushed the tin a little closer to his cat cave. "Sardines for you, all the way from Portugal."

He took a cautious step forward, nose twitching. With pea-green eyes on her face, he opened his mouth for one of his silent miaows and approached the tin. His fur seemed dry so perhaps he had escaped before the sprinklers. She backed away at the speed of a sloth and settled herself on the bottom step. Footsteps approached from the floor above.

"Don't come down here!" she said, her tone low but firm. "I'm trying to coax the cat out of his hidey-hole."

No reply came, but neither did any indications someone was descending the stairs.

"Beatrice?" Will's voice was muted. "Can we talk?"

She shook her head, although he couldn't see her. She composed herself. "Not now, Will. As you can see, I've made a mess of things again. I'll talk to you later, at the rehearsal. I will be there, don't worry."

"I'm not worried. Adrian, on the other hand, is climbing the walls. I keep telling him you wouldn't let him down but he won't take my word for it."

Beatrice watched Dumpling nibble at the open can, licking his lips and looking up to blink at her. "I just told you. I'll be there."

"I know you will. The reason I came over was to clear the air and explain. And there's something else. I have new intel on your case."

The chill of the cellar crept into her bones, her hunger made her irritable, the stink of smoke and the towering To-Do list hollowed her out and there was nowhere to hide. The poor old moggy left his sardines and retreated into his empty box. He didn't trust her. She didn't blame him.

Her voice was flat. "There is no case. I've decided to leave this investigation to the professionals. At this moment, I want to persuade this cat out of his hole and you're not making it any easier. Please go and reassure Adrian I will be there tonight as promised."

There was a pause in which she could almost sense meaningful looks being exchanged. "Fair enough, I'll leave you in peace. Could you please call me when the cat situation is resolved? I really do need to talk to you."

Beatrice grunted and pressed her knuckles to her eyes to stem the flow. Spontaneous weeping was a very bad sign. Indistinct murmurs from above ended when the front door closed.

She continued sitting on the step, her arms wrapped around herself, staring at the square of darkness into which Dumpling had retreated.

The sound of the postman's crunchy tread up the path echoed into the basement. Later the phone rang again and Matthew answered. She could hear no detail of either conversation but had no curiosity. The ping of the microwave in the kitchen attracted Dumpling's attention and a little grey-whiskered face moved towards the light.

The slap of slippered feet came down the stairs and she moved over to let Matthew sit beside her. He held a tray in his hands. To Beatrice's surprise, Dumpling gave another soundless mew and padded across to greet him, bunting his head against Matthew's bare legs. On the tray was a mug of hot chocolate, a bagel slathered with butter and honey and a packet of pills. Her mood stabilisers, neglected for ... she'd lost count of the days.

She popped one of the blisters and swallowed one with a sip of hot chocolate.

Matthew handed her the tray. "Take this upstairs and retire to bed for a couple of hours, please. It's still dry as only the downstairs sprinklers went off. The girls and Mungo are coming over to help clear up, I have everything under control and you must not worry."

Her eyes welled up and she shook her head but could find no way of articulating her overwhelming sense of panic.

He took her hand. "Please. Eat, rest and relax. Thank you for finding Dumpling and I'll take it from here. That is not a suggestion but an order."

She pressed his fingers to her lips and did as she was told.

Chapter Eighteen

When Adrian was training for the London Marathon, which he never actually entered after he discovered the nightmare of Jogger's Nipple, he installed an app on his phone with a voice telling him every few minutes how far he'd run, how many calories he'd burned, his average speed and what time it was. What a nightmare. He'd deleted it months ago but still recalled that sense of intrusive internal pressure. A ticking clock, every second implying failure.

That same sense of running but standing still was amplified to stadium levels by five-thirty on Friday night.

Pam Harding and the registrar were still making small talk with Catinca, whose platinum hair gleamed under the ballroom lights, but the flicker of her eyes to the double doors betrayed her concern. Rose and Maggie were yet to make an appearance and there was still no news from Beatrice. Will was making no effort to hide his nerves, pacing the room and checking his phone every thirty seconds.

Adrian shot Catinca a boggled-eyed glare. She knew perfectly well they had to get Pam out of there before Beatrice and Matthew turned up, so why was she still chatting away as if they had all the time in the world? The poor Harding woman was completely unprepared to see her ex-husband and new partner after so long and it was all horribly unfair.

Will's mobile rang and he stepped out of the ballroom to take it. The registrar slid back his cuff to look at his watch. A scream of rage built in Adrian's core and he clenched every muscle he had to keep it within. WHERE WERE THEY? In response, Will came back through the double doors with a smooth smile.

"Our friends got a little lost, but they'll be here in around twenty minutes. Mrs Harding, we've delayed you long enough and I thank you for your patience. I'm sure you have a hundred and one things to do before Christmas. We'll get on with the walk-through and on behalf of my future husband and me, we're grateful for all you've done for us. Merry Christmas and thanks again."

The double doors opened again and Adrian's body tensed. Two white heads popped around the door.

"Sorry we're late, it's all her fault," said Maggie Campbell, jerking her head at her companion. "She had to go poking about in his house one last time. But we're here now. Where are..."

"So pleased to see you!" gushed Adrian, jerking his head at Catinca. "We worried about you in this weather. We're just saying goodbye to Mrs Harding and then we really must do this rehearsal."

Catinca bounced over to introduce the women to the registrar. He and Will gently escorted Pamela Harding from the room, with enthusiastic expressions of gratitude, out to the foyer and into the sparkling snow-encrusted car park. Waving and smiling, they watched her car trundle up the drive, passing another coming in the opposite direction.

Thirty seconds later, Matthew's tatty old Volkswagen cruised to a halt right in front of them. Beatrice got out first, and without a word, gave Adrian a tight squeeze. He squeezed back. Matthew's voice echoed off the façade as he greeted Will.

"Damnedest thing! After scheming to get lost on purpose, I only went and did it by accident! Missed the turning and thought I knew a shortcut, but in this weather one lane looks much like another. Sincere apologies for delaying proceedings. I say, I'm assuming the coast is clear?"

Adrian smiled down at Beatrice. "You just passed her. The registrar is impatient to get started so let's get this show on the road!" He took her hand, but she was looking back at the main road, where a little car was indicating right.

"That was Pam?" she asked, her face turned up to his.

"Yes. Your timing was perfect, if a touch tighter than I'd like. Wedding rehearsal, people, let's go!" Sweat slithered down his spine as he crunched back across the snow.

Nothing more than a walk-through. Just learning the steps. No need for emotion. But when he stood at the table and imagined saying his vows as he looked into Will's eyes, a wave of joy threatened to overcome him. He focused on the registrar's peculiar accent instead. Luke and Tanya turned up just after six and they ran through it all again. He kept his emotions in check that time. As ring bearer, Luke was coached by Catinca to carry his cushion as if it held glass eggs. He took his instructions seriously and paced up the aisle with immense solemnity and care. As he offered the empty cushion to Will and Adrian, Catinca pulled down her arm in a fist pump.

"Yes!"

Luke beamed at her show of approval.

As soon as they'd finished, the registrar rushed off to prepare another couple's big day and the trainee bridal party repaired to The Angel for decompression in the snug.

Beatrice appeared subdued but friendly and Adrian noted Matthew's protective arm around her as they joined the party. He waited till the arrival of Tanya and Luke distracted Matthew and sidled up to see for himself.

"How's the cat?"

She gave a rueful smile. "He's not yet forgiven me for scaring him out of his wits, but I'm sure he'll come round with the aid of some fish. Matthew's the same. Whenever he gets himself into a bate, I can usually win him over with a New England seafood chowder."

"I know exactly what you mean. With Will, my sure-fire winner is paella. Is there some connection between fish and forgiveness?"

A sudden shriek made him jump. Tanya and a barmaid Adrian didn't recognise had spotted each other and squealed in delight. The young woman dashed out from behind the bar to give Tanya an enthusiastic hug. Everyone apart from Matthew and Luke broke off their conversations to listen.

"Frankie! When did you get back?"

"Today. To give Mum and Dad a hand at Christmas."

"I've not seen you for ages!"

"I know. The gallery has really taken off so I've not been home since the summer. Where's Luke?"

"Over there, badgering his grandfather for crisps." Tanya pointed at the back of a small individual still reasoning with Matthew.

"Oh wow, he's ... I was just about to say 'He's grown!' I am a walking cliché. How are you, Tan?"

"Mad busy. Not just Christmas but we've got a wedding on Sunday. Come say hello to Adrian and Will, the groom and groom. Everyone, this is Frankie!"

"FRANKIE!" yelled Luke, hurtling across the snug with his arms outstretched.

The woman's face broke into a huge smile as she yelled back, "Luke Skywalker!" and caught the small body in her arms.

Tanya laughed and turned to Adrian. "Frankie used to babysit Luke for me when she lived here. They used to have so much fun together I think he resented my coming home."

Still carrying Luke, Frankie moved around the room to congratulate Will and Adrian and to say her hellos to Matthew and Beatrice.

Beatrice perked up considerably and actually laughed at one of Frankie's comments. The woman brought an air of excitement into the room. Her looks alone were enough to arouse curiosity. Black hair in a shiny bob, Southeast Asian features, fine bones and skin that actually glowed, she was dressed in an off-the-shoulder Bardot top and black jeans. Striking merely to look at, but her personality illuminated the whole room.

Adrian glanced through to the public bar and watched her unremarkable parents serving customers. There was a story to Frankie, he just knew it.

When Tanya introduced her to Catinca, Adrian held his breath. Usually the person who turned most heads at any gathering, Catinca might not appreciate her fashion icon status being usurped.

Frankie put Luke down and stared at Catinca. "You look incredible! I cannot take my eyes off your hair. Did you get that done in London?"

"Cheers, mate. Found great colourist online, right up road in Crediton."

"Crediton?" Frankie's voice rose an octave over three syllables.

"I know!" exclaimed Tanya. "As soon as I saw Catinca's do, I made an emergency appointment for midday on Saturday. Not for the same look. I couldn't carry it off, just some highlights for the wedding."

"I need that salon's number," said Frankie.

Catinca gave her an appraising look. "You don't wanna mess with yours. Natural look suits you perfect. Where those earrings come from? That green is gorgeous."

Luke looked from one to the other. "What about my crisps?"

After three glasses of Prosecco and much giggling, Tanya reluctantly decided she should take herself and Luke home. Matthew volunteered as chauffeur. Frankie and Beatrice saw them off and returned to the snug. With a deep sigh, Frankie went behind the bar and served a waiting customer. Beatrice parked herself between Will and Maggie. She looked content and engaged.

If Ms Stubbs was returning to her usual equilibrium, Adrian's next key concern would be the photographs.

"Maggie, did you have a chance to look round the venue?

I know it was dark by the time you arrived, which is a shame. There are some stunning gardens which might be perfect backgrounds for your shots."

"Aye, we did. We had lunch there today and if what we ate is anything to go by, Sunday is going to be a triumph. Me and Rose had a wee mosey about and we made a list of good spots for traditional staging and a few more experimental ideas. You see they have a maze? What do you say I go all the way up to the penthouse, if they'll allow me, and take an aerial shot of the pair of ye in the middle of the labyrinth. You found each other!"

"That's a wonderful idea! The penthouse is the honeymoon suite, so you definitely have permission. What other ideas did you have?"

"Plenty. Lookee here, swap places with Rose and I can show you my list."

Rose obliged by shunting over to sit next to Beatrice, while Adrian and Maggie bent over her notepad and browsed the examples on her camera. Catinca came back from the ladies and joined them, oohing and aahing as Maggie displayed her suggestions.

"Love these! And if snow sticks around till Sunday, it's gonna be exactly as we wanted it! Dream wedding!" Catinca clapped her hands in excitement.

Emotion rose in Adrian once again and he could not help but hug the little Scottish lady beside him. "Maggie, you are a treasure!"

"Aw go on wi' ye. All I can do is my best. Just hope my assistant keeps her eye on the ball." With hooded eyes, she looked over at Rose, whose head was bent in conversation with Beatrice and Will.

"They're pursuing their case again, aren't they?" asked Adrian.

"I believe so."

They watched as Rose pushed a manila envelope across the table towards Beatrice.

Adrian whispered, "Do you know what that is?"

Maggie sipped at her Aperol and shook her head. "She found something today, in her ex-husband's house. Must be one of the few items her scavenger daughter missed. That's what made us so late. I don't know what it is; Rose told me nothing. That means it's dangerous. She's handing it over to the right people and I want to hear no more of it. Now tell me, how do you feel about airbrushing?"

The noise levels in the pub on a Friday night made it difficult for Beatrice to hear Will and Rose, but it had the advantage of ensuring their conversation could not be overheard.

"The police questioned Gabriel Shaw again today," said Will, evidently impatient to draw Beatrice's attention to the case.

"How do you know that?" asked Beatrice. "I thought they were writing it off as an accident. Are they going to bring charges?"

He shook his head. "No, I don't think they've got anything but circumstantials." He looked over his shoulder at Adrian, Catinca and Maggie poring over Maggie's camera and dropped his voice. "I found out because Tanya mentioned she'd spoken to him this morning. Everyone knows each other's business round here. You can see why they're putting pressure on Shaw. He has no alibi for Friday, works in the forest with access to poisonous mushrooms and has good reason to detest the victim. But if they didn't charge him, that's all they've got."

Beatrice thought about Gabriel's assertion in the Land Rover. She had believed him then and still did. Something else was niggling at her but she had no time to pinpoint what it was as Rose leant in to whisper.

"I have some news too." She tapped the handbag on her lap. "Your lovely man let me look around Vaughan's cottage this afternoon, in case I wanted some kind of memento. I wasn't sure I did, but curiosity got the better of me. There's nothing of value left after Grace grabbed all she wanted and even if there had been, that's not what I was about."

"So what did you find?" asked Will.

Rose's eyes sparkled. "His diary. A most illuminating read. Along with a stack of pornographic magazines, defaced copies of *The London Review of Books* and what I assume were his trophies."

"Trophies?" asked Beatrice.

"Women's underwear, jewellery, intimate photographs, letters from his conquests, that sort of thing." She scrunched up her nose. "All very tacky."

Will rubbed his brow. "Why didn't Grace take any of that? Not because they're worth anything, just to save him from embarrassment. Although his diary would be worth a mint."

"Because she didn't find it. She's not the kind of person who'd want to get her hands dirty." Rose took a sip of her Lucozade-coloured drink and smiled with feline serenity, her expression mischievous. "When I was married to Vaughan, he used to spend a long time in the bathroom. All men do, that much I know, but he would stay in there for hours. I soon worked out he'd got some kind of ... entertainment hidden away. Sure enough, while I was cleaning the toilet I spotted one of the panels around the bathtub was loose. That was where he hid all the evidence of his affairs. Too vain to throw it away, the man was hoisted by his own petard. Or suspender belt. Except he never got hoisted or exposed or even challenged. Back then, fearful of what might happen to me and my little girl, I never used that knowledge." Her eyes glittered with what might have been grief or rage.

Beatrice glanced at the wedding planners once more and reassured herself they were still occupied. "So you checked if he was still using the same hiding place."

"I did and he was. Vaughan lacked imagination, as I think I mentioned before. He stashed his trove of treasures, including his current diary, in the cavity under the bath. Don't mind telling you I read it, and spent far too long proving to myself what I already knew." She pulled a manila envelope out of her handbag and slid it over the table. "Beatrice, I'm giving this to you because I am quite sure it will help in your investigation. Otherwise I'd set fire to the rotten thing."

Beatrice took the envelope and hesitated with a guilty glance at Will. "We really should take this to the police."

"I trust you to do what's best. Keep it, give it to the police, use it as evidence, whatever you want. Just one word of caution. Don't let Matthew read it. He wouldn't like the real Vaughan Mason."

Chapter Nineteen

Once Matthew's breathing had slowed into his familiar snore-puff, snore-puff rhythm, Beatrice slid from the bed, tiptoed past Huggy Bear's basket and made her way downstairs. It was impossible to forget the package Rose had given her. She had an obsessive need to read the contents and try to focus on the moth-like thought she had not quite captured. In the living room, she wrapped a chunky-knit cardigan around herself and threw another log on the embers of their earlier fire. Curled into the armchair, she slid a finger under the envelope to retrieve a cheap lined exercise book, around two-thirds full.

His handwriting was appalling and some entries impossible to decipher. Only occasionally had he added dates and the only way of telling one entry from the next was ink colour or level of scrawl. Those that were legible made for unpleasant reading. Beatrice flicked through pages at random at first.

15 May: Still nothing from Carson Chambers. Three months without a single royalty cheque. Called Simple Simon to read him the riot act and threatened to take the new book elsewhere. Chinless wonder said unless it was ready by the end of the year, I would have to. Need to up the stakes at tomorrow night's game if I'm going to take The Black Widow to Chez Bruno. Even the salads cost around twenty quid! She'd better thank me nicely.

Heavy Weather came over and cooked something she called 'cottage pie'. An accurate description, as it tasted exactly like a demolished cottage covered in bludgeoned potato. I refused to eat it and had a pork chop in Marsala sauce instead, ignoring her guilt-trip waterworks. Bored, bored, bored of this bullshit 'Let's try fooling a carnivore' bollocks. Direct result of sullen little Gaylord going vegan. Supercilious wanker. Lock all vegans in a smug hippie camp somewhere near Glastonbury so the rest of us can just get on with enjoying veal, foie gras and steak tartare without some face-like-a-smacked-arse passing judgement. God she pisses me off.

Sunday 3 June. Crippling hangover. Mason, will you ever learn? Never mix grape and grain. Managed to meet Bumble and Dopey for golf. Put the wind up them with a few hints about the new book and watched them sweat.

'Acerbic university satire. All names changed, no need for alarm.'

'Agent called it explosive, you know.'

'Editor wants a quote from Amis Junior on the front.'

Bumble called me after lunch, worried it might tarnish his wife's reputation. Told him I couldn't promise anything and rang off. One of these days, I intend to back his wife into a corner and give her reputation a damn good tarnishing.

Beatrice screwed up her face in disgust. Then she punched her fist into her palm and reminded herself of her purpose.

"Stop judging, starting working," she said in a sharp whisper.

The diary, as far as she'd seen, wholly vindicated her impression of an egotistical misanthrope. However, her job was not to validate her own opinions, but to glean any information about who might have poisoned him.

She made up her mind to start at Bonfire Night and the infamous row with Heather. She flicked through the messy book and stopped at a page near the end of October. Filled with excitable scribbles and underlined phrases, the page showed this must have been an exceptional day. Or night.

5am on The Day of the Dead and I am dead and the most alive I've been in years. Went to The Angel's fancy dress do as Death himself with white face paint and real scythe and got plastered but not as much as usual due to all the dancing. Almost pulled the girl from the BP garage – red devil with fantastic tits – until Rugby Boy muscled in. BUT THE BEST WAS YET TO COME! After upping the 'so drunk I cannot walk' performance, Lil S. drove me home. Not for the first time, but after I slipped over on the path, she helped me indoors. The opportunity I'd been waiting for. Then she never knew what hit her! Ooh la la!

Day of the Dead? November the first. The fancy dress do must have been a Halloween party. She turned the page.

Don't believe in luck or fortune as random happenstance. We make our own. Grab every opportunity and turn it to your advantage. Moron lost heavily last night and I dropped a hint he might be able to pay his debts another way. Lil S. is avoiding me, but I picked my moment when Moron was busy. Demanded a whisky chaser and slipped a letter into her hand along with a five-pound note. She gave me my change and made a big point of going over to the fire and chucking my letter onto it. Ha! I love it when they play hard to get. This little honey pot gets sweeter by the day.

Lil S. The Everly Brothers. 'Wake Up Little Susie'. Beatrice inhaled sharply, recalling her recent conversation with the landlady of The Angel. And that peculiar blush at the mention of Vaughan's conquests. A shadow in her peripheral vision made her snap her head around.

Dumpling padded into the living room, his expression curious. He sat beside her chair and gave a silent miaow. Beatrice patted the space beside her but he blinked, turned tail and leapt up to Matthew's chair. He circled once and curled himself into an elliptical mound of grey, his eyes yellow in the firelight.

Fireworks! Rockets and Catherine Wheels and sparklers and that was inside the pub! Tonight was no accident. I had every intention of breaking it off with Heavy Weather in public. Lil S. needs to know I'm serious so she can leave Moron. Mission accomplished. Free man bailing out – either women add value to my life or they can fuck off.

The next three entries were impossible to read. For all the sense the lopsided squiggles made, it could have been in Arabic. Finally there was a more coherent post, including a date reference.

Fuck them. Forget it. Stupid fucking gossipy bitches – I'm so arse-achingly bored of this female fucking ENTITLEMENT! 10 days after the row and everyone siding with Heavy Weather calling me a chauvinist pig or whatever hashtag trending term they're use to attack us this week. Can't win. They spread their legs, regret it, sling mud and suddenly all men are evil. Lil S. nowhere to be seen and I find out from Grimace she's gone to Bath to visit her dyke of a daughter. Sick of this small town mentality. Card Night tonight. More than one way to skin a cat.

Beatrice flicked back a few pages. The more lucid posts which included dates often fell on a Tuesday. So Vaughan stayed sober in order to fleece his friends at poker. She got up to find a pen and some paper. On the dining table, she found a discarded shopping list and took it back to her fireside spot to make some notes.

Heavy Weather – Heather Shaw
Gaylord – Gabriel Shaw
Lil S – Susie Hancock
Moron – Gordon Hancock
Bumble – Mungo
Dopey – Matthew
The Black Widow / Grimace – ??

She went back to the diary for more clues, stopping to shove another log on the fire and stroke Dumpling, whose purrs reverberated through his whole body.

27 Nov. Priceless! Lil S. turned up at my house this lunchtime. Warned me not to mess with her family or 'there would be consequences'. Seems she and Frenchkisser have been comparing notes. I took umbrage and said the bastard child of a Chinaman was not my type. Swore I'd never touched her and that the girl must have been fantasising. Can't actually be sure of that as I know I made a pass or two. She was sixteen, for God's sake, and what a doll! I do recall an incident on St Nicholas Day when I caught The Winter Queen coming across the green and bundled her up against a tree. Offered to warm her up the Mason way. Hard-faced little sow pressed her arm against my throat and told me never to touch her again. Her loss. Mummy was much more accommodating.

The floorboards overhead creaked. "Beatrice?"

She shoved both diary and envelope behind the cushion at her back. "Down here. Couldn't sleep. I'll just have a camomile tea and join you in a bit."

Matthew appeared in the doorway in his pyjamas, a rattle of claws in his wake. His hair stuck up in odd clumps, like a seascape, and Huggy Bear came wriggling past him, tail wagging, ready for whatever nocturnal adventures might be planned.

"Are you all right, Old Thing?"

"Yes, yes, just thoughtful. You go back to bed. I'll just put the fire guard on and I'll follow you up."

His tired eyes blinked and he shook his head. "I'll make us both tea. That always helps us sleep."

After he'd shuffled out of the room, Beatrice slipped her stash back into Rose's envelope and shoved it under the seat cushion. She gazed into Dumpling's flickering yellow orbs.

"What should I do, puss?" she whispered.

The cat yawned, showing ivory teeth and a spiky pink tongue, then curled back into a ball with his paw tucked over his face.

"Sleep on it? I think you might be right."

Chapter Twenty

At eight o'clock the next morning, snow was still falling and Matthew was still snoring. But both ladies of the house were wide awake. Sneaking once more out of bed, Beatrice took the terrier out into the forest, far from gritted lanes and salty paws. The dog dived and skipped and rolled in the white stuff while Beatrice's pace remained ponderous.

She was an amateur. Experienced detective work notwithstanding, she didn't know this village, its inhabitants, its history and personal loyalties, grievances or relationships. Everyone's opinion carried a taint of prejudice, even Matthew's.

How to get at the facts without the prism of prejudice? Who was honestly lying and who was deceiving her with the truth?

Spiders' webs encrusted with frost glistened like stage curtains, berries studded the hedgerows, prints criss-crossed the path, giving clues as to earlier visitors. Crows, foxes, rabbits all left their tracks and tiny funnels suggested mice had passed this way. Huggy Bear sniffed every single one of them.

The moth-like thought which kept escaping had woken her at half past seven. This time she netted it. Frankie. Twice she'd heard from mother and daughter that the girl hadn't been back to the village since the summer. Yet Gordon let slip she'd been home for her birthday. The seventh of December. The night someone poisoned Vaughan Mason.

That wasn't all he'd let slip. Francesca had received counselling.

'A few teenage problems' was how he described it. Of course, it could be anything: issues at school, confusion about her identity, an eating disorder, or quite possibly sexual harassment by an older man. She needed more information and knew exactly where to find it.

She pulled out her phone. *I'm a good client, returning her call. Responsive and respectful. No ulterior motives at all. Just being polite.*

The phone rang four times. It occurred to Beatrice it was Saturday morning and not all that polite to call just after half past eight.

"Hello?"

"Good morning, Gaia, this is Beatrice Stubbs. You left a message on my machine."

"Oh yes. Hello, Beatrice. How are you feeling?"

"I've been better. It's Christmas in two days, I have a wedding to organise and yesterday I set off the sprinklers after forgetting a coffee pot on the stove. How are you?"

"In a similar state. How could I leave marzipan off the shopping list? I cannot wait for Boxing Day when all I need do is lie on the sofa and eat leftovers."

Beatrice chuckled. A noise attracted her attention. Huggy Bear was furiously digging at a patch of ground, scattering clods of snow and earth in arcs behind her. Her progress was impressive. "I'm sorry to call so early on a Saturday, but just wondered if the offer is still open for a quick chat. I think I had a bit of a down-cycle over the last few days."

"I'd be very pleased to see you. No pressure, more a get-to-know-you meeting. What are you up to this morning?"

"Walking the dog, or to be precise, dragging the little bugger out of a rabbit hole. Would you have..."

"Come over, bring the dog, let's have coffee and flaunt every code of decency by having a mince pie for breakfast. I'm here until teatime so turn up when you're ready."

"Will do!" Beatrice would have offered a more elegant farewell but Huggy Bear was rapidly disappearing into the ground. She ended the call and rushed to grab hold of the terrier by her tail. It was only when she noticed breath clouds in the frosty air that she realised she was laughing.

"Morning, my love. Can you feed Huggy Bear? I just bagged a slot with my new counsellor this morning. I know there are a million things to do and I promise to be on duty all day. It's just I really want to meet this woman and see if she can help. The last few days have convinced me I need some professional kind of support. I'll only be gone a couple of hours. Do you mind?"

Matthew stood in his bathrobe, hair awry. "Not at all. I'm happy to hear it. Go, and good luck." He knelt to make a fuss of the filthy mess weaving in and out of his bare ankles. "What on earth happened to this dog?"

"She went rabbiting without official permission. I was lucky to catch her before she disappeared into a warren. Let her dry off and it will all brush out. See you later!"

The twenty-minute drive was precarious in the relentless weather and took closer to half an hour. Beatrice wished she'd spent an extra five minutes to make herself a coffee. Then she remembered the wrecked coffee pot and frowned. Gaia's house was right out in the sticks with nothing around but a few farms. At least that meant tractors, whose mighty tyres had driven great ruts through the lanes, creating passable roads. The track leading to Gaia's home, however, still had sufficient snow to give her pause. She drove on a hundred yards or so until she spotted a recess next to a five-bar gate. She parked the car, dragged on her wellies and trudged her way back along the lane to the track.

Stomping through the mud and slush up to the house, she saw no evidence of sundials, wind-chimes or one single esoteric talisman to ward off evil. The house was about as remarkable as a loaf of bread. She rang the bell, observing a lean-to to the right, under which a black Land Rover was parked along with an assortment of snow shovels and a wheelbarrow. Either Gaia was a poor driver or the car was a farm vehicle, as it was scratched and dented in several places. Perhaps Gaia's husband was one of the farmers. Surely she wouldn't be managing all on her own all the way out here. It wouldn't be Beatrice's idea of fun.

The woman who opened the door looked exactly like the sort of person who should live in such a house. She was in her early forties, with laughter lines around her dark eyes. Her shoulder-length dark hair was flecked with grey and she wore jeans with a zip-up top. Beatrice knew the sort. Women's magazines and Waitrose were full of them.

"Beatrice, hello!" She stretched out her hand. "We finally meet." It was warm and soft, as if she'd just been baking muffins. "Where's your dog?"

"At home. She got covered in mud so I left my partner to sort her out. I tried to send you a text but I only have your landline number."

"Come on through to the kitchen. It's very considerate of you to send a message but I'm afraid the landline's all I've got. No signal out here so a mobile is a waste of time. What breed is your dog? I used to have a Labrador."

Of course you did. Internally, she chastised herself for making assumptions, but continued to do so as Gaia chatted on while settling her in at the kitchen table (cosy), serving coffee from one of those Italian capsule machines (delicious) and offering her a plate of mince pies (home-made). Beatrice scoped the room but saw no childish drawings stuck to the fridge, no men's muddy boots or any other indication of family members. Just clean, glossy perfection. This woman could never be her counsellor. Beatrice would always feel inferior opposite this domestic goddess with her retro kitchen and cookery books and quilted cushions.

As if she'd been listening, Gaia said, "My practice is actually in Crediton, but as we're not having a formal session today, I thought we'd just sit in the kitchen and chat. It's the warmest room in the house and I've been baking so it smells nice and Christmassy."

"It definitely does," Beatrice replied, wondering how to keep up her end of the conversation. She was not comfortable with small talk when this woman knew everything about her. "On the phone, you said you would be here till teatime. Are you and your family going away for the festive season?"

"Yes, I'm going to join my mother and sisters in Cornwall. It's our tradition. We share all the duties and my job is to do all the baking."

Beatrice flailed around for a socially acceptable comment but could only come up with a limp observation. "That's nice. Everyone loves cake."

Instead of taking a chair on the other side of the table, directly opposite, Gaia sat at the end so she and Beatrice were at right angles to each other. The natural place to focus was the conservatory and beyond, the snow-covered garden. James used to do something very similar. Rather than looking at Beatrice as the problem, they focused on her issues together, objectifying them against the wall. She was grateful.

Gaia stirred her coffee. "If we decide to work together, we'll need to go into a bit of background and you might want to set some ground rules. But today, let's just deal with the here and now. You mentioned you'd had 'a bit of a down-cycle'. I couldn't help but notice you used the past tense. How would you describe the way you're feeling now?"

"Stressed. My to-do list is out of control because I've taken too much on. We adopted two animals just recently and I'm conducting an investigation on behalf of my partner. I'm matron of honour at a wedding on Sunday and I'm not ready, nor anywhere near prepared for Christmas." Beatrice stopped.

Gaia stirred her coffee. "You're giving me reasons for your feelings, past and future. I'd like you to stick to the present. Can you describe your current state of mind for me?"

On the bird table in the garden, a team of blue tits took turns to peck at the bag of nuts while blackbirds staged noisy raids on the scattered seeds.

"Panicky," said Beatrice. "Anxious and worried and stuck in fifth gear. But at the same time, I just want to crawl into a hole and lie down. My whole body is heavy, as if it will never have energy again and even if it did, there would never be enough. I want to please people but I just can't achieve a single thing. I already know I'm going to let them all down."

They watched the birds. "Are you describing how you feel now or how you felt when you were in a down-cycle?"

Beatrice was surprised by her insight and a little offended at being so transparent. She drank her coffee and considered. "Both, I suppose, but it was much worse a couple of days ago. Matthew made me take my mood stabilisers again, so I still feel panicked but not quite as wobbly. As if I might fall and there's nothing to catch me."

"Can I ask why you chose to stop taking the mood stabilisers?"

Gaia's voice was gentle but Beatrice grew defensive against any kind of judgement.

"It wasn't a choice. I just forget sometimes, particularly when all's going well and I'm excited about things. I don't do it on purpose."

"I see. You've described your down-cycling frame of mind very eloquently. Could I ask you to do the same about your up-cycles?" Her enquiry was innocent enough but Beatrice spotted the trap.

Beatrice turned to face her. "I don't need to describe my up-cycling because you already know after reading my files and you're going to tell me that's exactly when I'm most vulnerable and that's why I need to keep a mood diary and ensure I take my tablets because up-cycles are followed by down-cycles and being in a good mood does not mean I'm 'cured' and all the rest of it. You're just like James."

Gaia let the heated words hang in the pastry-scented air for a moment then gave a faint smile. "Thank you."

Beatrice rested her cheek on her fist and watched the fluttering around the bird table. This wasn't going the way she'd planned. She was here under false pretences and had to remember her intention.

Again, Gaia tuned into her train of thought. "Why did you call me, Beatrice?"

An opportunity opened up and Beatrice took it. "If you want me to be honest," she said, being precisely the opposite, "I resented James dumping me. I didn't want to change counsellor and decided I could do without. Then out of the flue, your name came up in conversation as being highly recommended. So I thought I might as well give it a shot. Especially after the last few days I've had."

Her conscience was shaking its head in disgust at her underhand tactics.

Gaia didn't bite. "I'm glad you did. I think we could be pretty effective at working together. James probably told you that I have a particular interest in complementary medicine."

"Homeopathy and that sort of thing?" said Beatrice, with no attempt to disguise her cynicism.

"Not exactly. More a holistic approach to your life and health, working with organic ingredients to maintain your natural balance. I'll need to know a lot more about you, behavioural patterns, diet, relationships and medical history in order to suggest how we achieve stability. I understand you're rushed off your feet at present but what do you think about scheduling an official session between Christmas and New Year?"

"Perhaps. Let me have a look at the calendar when I get home. I can't even see past the next few days at the moment. In the meantime, I'll take my stabilisers and keep a diary. That's always helped before." She hesitated. If she couldn't fish for information as a side issue, perhaps she could try the direct route. "Can I ask you a question?"

"Go ahead." Gaia's eyes, shaded by long lashes, were so dark one could barely distinguish pupil from iris. Her strong eyebrows lifted in enquiry.

"It's not about my mental health. I'm following a line of enquiry, on an informal basis, into the death of Vaughan Mason."

For the first time, Gaia's forehead creased just a fraction. "I see."

"Did you know him?"

Gaia shook her head. "Only by reputation. I read his book when I was at university. Didn't everyone?"

"Mason had two reputations – literary and predatory. Gordon Hancock, landlord of The Angel, mentioned you counselled his daughter, Francesca. Can I ask you if Mason's reputation ever came up?"

The head-shaking went on longer this time. "Mr Hancock really should not share that kind of information without his daughter's permission. I cannot discuss any of my other clients with you. How trusting would you feel if I blurted out what other people say in confidence? I understand as an ex-detective you want to pursue every lead but I could only break client confidentiality if instructed to do so by a serving police officer." Her eyes did not leave Beatrice's and something crackled in the air between them.

"Even for a murder enquiry?"

Her brow creased again. "I have the greatest respect for all you achieved as a detective for Scotland Yard, Beatrice. But the reality here is that you are not a police officer, there is no murder enquiry and I believe you might be testing my confidentiality."

Beatrice took a moment to consider. "That's very professional of you. Thanks for the coffee and the pie. You know, I think we could have a go at working together. I'll send you some dates and see if you're free. Thanks for making time for me, and happy Christmas!"

Before she even started the ignition, Beatrice tried to dial Will. There was no signal so she drove back towards Thoverton, occasionally stopping to check the bars on her phone. Finally, she pulled over and called him again.

"Beatrice? You OK?"

"Fine. I know you're busy, but I need your help. Can you spare me an hour or two?"

"Hang on. I'll just go outside."

She waited till he'd found a quiet place to talk.

"Beatrice, you still there? I'm driving Adrian and Catinca over to Silverwood Manor this morning. They need a couple of hours to decorate, so I'm free until they need to be picked up. Where do you want to meet?"

"That hairdresser's in Crediton. Get the name and number from Catinca. I know Tanya has an appointment there at midday and she can give us the information we need."

The Saturday before Christmas was ridiculous. More people than actually lived in the whole of Devon were invading shops, parking spaces and streets. Beatrice drove around the town three times before spotting a couple loading boxes and bags into the back of a Volvo. She indicated and sat there stubbornly until they finally vacated her spot.

Herr Kutz was on a back street, yet had the typical large windows of any hairdresser, exposing the poor creatures therein to gawping passers-by. Beatrice scanned every one of the dozen seats and spotted Tanya's patchwork holdall beside one of the indistinguishable figures. She shoved open the door, dismissing the receptionist and marched over to Tanya's chair.

"Beatrice! You having yours done here as well?"

"No. I need to ask you a few questions. In private."

Tanya's expression of pleasant surprise turned to puzzlement. "OK, just let Nadine finish my highlights and then we can talk while my head bakes. Why don't you get us both a coffee and come back in five?"

By the time Beatrice came back from the coffee shop with a three lattes and a doughnut, Will had arrived. Tanya sat under some kind of heat helmet and her interrogators drew up two stools to sit either side. Will took out his notebook.

Tanya in her tinfoil helmet looked at them in the mirror, laughing. "Come on then, Hot Fuzz, what do you want to know?"

"Can we record this? Just to save me taking notes?" asked Beatrice.

"Sure you don't want to take me down the station, guvnor?"

Beatrice set her phone to Voice Memo. "Nothing formal, just getting a bit of background. Recording the conversation just makes things easier. Tell us a bit about Frankie," said Beatrice.

"What? Why? You know who Frankie is."

"Will doesn't. In a nutshell, who is Frankie Hancock?"

Tanya tilted her head, her curiosity evident. "Well, for a start she's not called Frankie Hancock. Her name is Francesca Gwynne. She took Susie's maiden name as she was born years before Susie met Gordon. She doesn't know her father. Susie used to be a backing singer in a band and had a fling with the Japanese keyboard player in the 90s. Frankie was the result."

This much Beatrice knew, if not in quite as much detail, but chose not to hurry the girl for two reasons. One, she needed Will to have the full picture before proceeding. Two, if equal time and attention were given to all answers, Tanya would not guess which ones mattered most.

"Would you say she has a good relationship with her stepfather?"

"Yeah, most definitely. To all intents and purposes, he's her dad. She's got a great relationship with both her parents. Susie dashes off to visit her in Bath every chance she gets."

"I didn't know that," Beatrice lied. "When was the last time she went?"

Tanya boggled her eyes. "No idea! Ask Susie."

"Sorry, can't expect you to know all the details. I'll check with Susie and ask her the date of Frankie's birthday at the same time."

"That one I do know. Seventh of December, same day as Glynis Knox. I always send them both a card."

Beatrice did not answer, her mind scrolling Vaughan's diary. *Lil S. nowhere to be seen and I find out from Grimace she's gone to Bath to visit her dyke of a daughter.*

Will filled the gap. "Who's Glynis Knox and can you spell her name?"

A woman came over to check Tanya's hair and they all smiled politely while the woman peeled back a piece of foil, scraped it and put it back.

After she'd gone, Tanya resumed. "G-L-Y-N-I-S and Knox as in Fort. We were in the same class at school. She owns Dust Demons, you know, the cleaning company. They do most of the local businesses, including The Angel. Glynis often says she never built a career, just hoovered it up."

"Do you know if one of their clients was Vaughan Mason?" asked Beatrice.

"Oh yeah. Not one of their favourites, from what I heard. I couldn't swear to the details, but some of her staff complained about him wandering about in a bathrobe, making innuendoes and other randy old goat behaviour. Glynis used to pop in for a spot check every now and then. She said it was to keep the girls on their toes, but I think we all know who was under surveillance."

The corners of Will's mouth dropped in disgust.

Beatrice changed tack but kept her tone light. "Gordon mentioned that Frankie had seen a counsellor when she was a bit younger. Do you know anything about that?"

"Not much. She told me she went through a tough time in her teens and sought help, that's all. In those days, she was all grunge and attitude, spending every weekend and holiday with her grandmother. As soon as she left for art college in Exeter, all that fell away and she seemed to grow into herself. She still lived at the pub but had a whole new life and it suited her. That's when she started baby-sitting for Luke. We became friends even though she's a decade younger than me. She's one of those people I'd describe as a good soul."

"Any relationships?" asked Will.

"She brought some boyfriends back now and then, but I couldn't tell you their names. I know she had the hots for Gabriel

Shaw and practically offered herself to him on a plate. He wasn't interested. I asked him once why not. Beautiful, young, smart and smitten with him, where's the problem? He just said she's too young. Whether she has anyone in Bath, I don't know. But you've seen her. I'd say she's beating them away with a stick."

"Time you were rinsed off." The hairdresser stood with her hands on her hips.

Will and Beatrice did not stay for the unveiling of the highlights but said their goodbyes and went outside into the cold. The snow fell in fat flakes like communion wafers, the pavements were soggy and slippery and the walk back to Will's Audi was treacherous. Once in the car, they brushed themselves off and Beatrice explained what she wanted him to do.

Will listened, gnawing on his knuckle. Finally he spoke. "Why don't we share our theory with the local force and let them handle it? They have the authority to get this therapist woman to share what she knows."

"But they won't. They've already dismissed me once. If some old biddy brought you a diary and a bunch of gossip, how seriously would you take it? I think Gaia has something to say but wants to follow protocol. You don't need to lie, just omit the fact you're not part of the investigation."

Will chewed his lip. "The DI in charge could make the same enquiries which would be admissible as evidence in court."

"She could, I suppose, but I'm not sure these country forces have the same investigative rigour we do. My feeling is they're doing a half-hearted look around and then will record it as accidental death. It's up to us to find the truth, Will. Once we have evidence, they can't ignore us and will have to verify our findings. Then they can prepare a case for the CPS." She was pressing his buttons and she knew it.

He released a sigh. "All right. Here's the deal. If she answers my questions and we turn up anything useful, do you promise we hand everything over to the police? You and I have got to focus on the wedding. I've still got to collect Catinca and Adrian then drive down to Exeter for his wedding present this afternoon."

"Yes. Cross my heart. I just need some concrete evidence and all I've got so far is a rough suspicion. Just ask Gaia about the issues between Vaughan Mason and Frankie Gwynne, because I believe we're close to finding out why the man was poisoned. Motive is everything. Know why, know who."

Will raised his eyes to the roof. "Do I look like I just got out of training? Give me a break, I said I'll do it. Where did you park?"

Beatrice thought about that. "I have absolutely no idea. I'll get out and retrace my steps. Best you set off now, so you'll be all done and busted by two o'clock."

"Beatrice, please be careful," Will said.

She got out into the snowstorm once again. "You too. Take care and good luck!"

Chapter Twenty-One

"*The person you are calling is not available. Please try later.*"

Adrian slammed his phone onto the table, attracting the attention of two lunching ladies. Again. They'd done nothing but gawp at Catinca since she'd entered the restaurant and something told him they were not in awe of her style. To be fair, she was wearing painter's overalls and a headscarf knotted at her forehead like a woman from a World War II motivational poster.

"Where the hell has he got to? We agreed we'd call him to get picked up after lunch and it's now half past two!"

"Is after lunch. Stop stressing. You don't want them chips?"

"Crisps, not chips, we're not in America. No, I don't want them. Why would an upper-class restaurant such as this serve crisps with a gourmet sandwich?"

Catinca reached over and grabbed a handful from his plate. "People like 'em, is why. Chips go with everything. Look, we can't reach Will, so call someone else. Beatrice or Matthew or Marianne. They won't mind to collect us. We gotta get on, mate."

Just to be sure, Adrian rang Will again. Same message. He dialled Matthew's number, reluctant to add to Beatrice's stresses. Matthew was sympathetic but had no transport.

"I'd love to help but Beatrice has taken the Volkswagen. She's running a few errands. Why not give Rose a ring? Her Land Rover is the best thing for this weather. Tell the truth, I'll be relieved when Beatrice gets back in one piece. Those smallish cars are not the best in the snow."

Once Adrian rang off, a whole new scenario entered his head. Will's Audi, upturned in a gully, his husband freezing to death in a silent shroud of white.

Catinca kicked him under the table with some savagery. "Oi! Call someone else and stop the dramatics, I'm warning you!"

As it turned out, Rose and Maggie were just up the road at a garden centre. They rolled onto the forecourt fifteen minutes later, twittery and cheerful and glad to make themselves useful. Catinca and Adrian got in the back and sat beside something large wrapped in sacking. There was still no reply from Will.

Back at The Angel, Rose dropped them off at the door and drove her four-wheel drive round the back to the guests' car park. Catinca spotted Tanya and Marianne chatting to Frankie at the bar and went over to squeak about someone's hair. Adrian waved but continued upstairs, a genuine fear gripping him. What if Will had cut and run? What if he'd dropped them at the Manor, come back, packed his stuff and left? Running from all the ceremony and commitment, free in his Audi with the roof down and his future wide open, leaving Adrian jilted at the altar. He should have seen this coming. Will had always wanted a quiet private ceremony, not the three-ring circus of Adrian's dreams. His fingers were clumsy as he turned the key in the brass lock, already envisaging a bare room apart from a note on the pillowcase.

The room was exactly as they'd left it, apart from an absence of Will. He took off his jacket and sat on the bed, a sense of isolation and loneliness creeping over him like mist. There was so much to do! How come everyone always left him alone? Why was he the only person to worry about all the things that could go wrong? His cycle of self-pity was interrupted by a knock at the door.

He leapt to his feet and fumbled with the lock. "Will?"

"Ah, no, sorry. It's Matthew here."

Adrian wrenched open the door. "What is it? Where's Will?"

"I don't know his precise location but I do know he's with Beatrice. May I come in?"

A mixture of relief and fury exploded in Adrian's chest. He stood back, inhaling deeply in an effort to keep calm. It didn't work.

Matthew closed the door and sat on the small armchair, his hands dangling between his knees. "Tanya and Marianne called round about an hour ago. Beatrice left her phone in a Crediton hairdresser's earlier today. Apparently, she and Will arrived while Tanya was having her hair done and asked some questions. Beatrice recorded the answers but forgot to collect her phone when the conversation was over. Marianne drove Tanya over to our cottage to hand it back, but Beatrice is still not home. So I asked the girls to give me a lift over here, wondering if she and Will had turned up yet. I know you are worried and I cannot exactly offer reassurance, but wherever they are, they are together."

Adrian rubbed his face, pressing on his eye sockets. So Will had not got cold feet or been killed on black ice, but was detecting with Beatrice Stubbs, the day before his wedding.

"This is never going to stop, is it?" he asked, staring at his feet.

Matthew took a long time to reply. "Adrian, why do you love Will? Tell me his top five qualities, the ones that make you feel you can be together for the rest of your lives."

"He loves me." Adrian answered without thinking. "He puts up with all my weaknesses and supports my strengths, even though I've got more of the first than him. He's tenacious. He goes after what he wants with everything he's got and never gives up. I love Will because he's his own person. He doesn't accommodate me or expect me to do the same as him, we just fit. He's skilled and ambitious and talented and driven by an urge to do the right thing. He has other attributes but I guess they're not relevant here."

Neither man met the other's eyes.

Matthew spoke. "Your husband-to-be has a passion, much like my not-quite-wife. They will always do what they've been trained to do, whether retired or off-duty or on holiday or even asleep. Like collies to a shepherd's whistle, they are conditioned to respond and cannot do otherwise, because their minds are trained to investigate. They are unable to stop themselves and we shouldn't even expect them to try. You and I have to understand that their job will always come first. If you don't appreciate that now, your marriage will be far less happy that it should. So to answer your question, no, it's never going to stop. That said, this particular disappearing act is most likely my fault. I asked her to look into my friend's death and even after I called her off, she hurls herself into the fray, taking Will with her."

Adrian lifted his head. The dusk had descended, making Matthew a shadow silhouetted against the evening sky. "Which is why you love her. Thank you, Matthew. You've made me feel far better than I did an hour ago."

The professor heaved himself to his feet with a groan. "Mission accomplished. I'm off home, if I can cadge a lift. As soon as either of us has news..."

"Of course. Thank you."

Matthew patted his shoulder and opened the door to leave.

Adrian grabbed his jacket. "Hang on. I'll come downstairs with you. If I stay up here on my own, I'll just fret."

He locked the room and followed Matthew down the poky little staircase. As they reached the last flight, raised voices could be heard from the bar.

"...without asking me!"

"Just calm down, Tanya. She has a right to know."

"Why? What is the point of telling her now?"

"Because Beatrice knows we've been keeping them apart and she doesn't! We always play fair!"

"Does Dad know?"

"Does Dad know what?" asked Matthew, stooping as he ducked under the lintel to the public bar.

All heads snapped in their direction and Huggy Bear ran across the floorboards, tail wagging in greeting. Adrian took in the scene. In the centre of the room, two sisters stood opposite each other in a confrontational stance. Catinca perched on a bar stool, drinking something blue which matched her maxi dress. With her silvery hair curling over her shoulder, she looked like a mermaid. On the other side of the bar stood Frankie, her lovely face creased in concern.

The tension caught the interest of the clientele. The whole room was silent, all eyes on the family drama.

Matthew glanced behind him at the empty snug. "Tanya, Marianne, in the back, please. We do not air our differences over family business in the public bar. Catinca, Adrian, you too. Come this way, everyone. Frankie, could we have a pot of tea, please?"

Adrian closed the door after they had all trooped into the room, the two sisters' faces like granite. Frankie placed a tea tray on the bar and retreated.

"Am I to understand," said Matthew, in a quiet, moderate tone, "that Marianne has seen fit to inform your mother of who will be present at the wedding tomorrow?"

Marianne scowled. "Yes, Marianne has. Just like you saw fit to tell Beatrice why we'd been sneaking around."

"That's different!" Tanya exploded. "Beatrice caught us in the act. It was either hurt her feelings or tell her the truth. Mum didn't need to know and I can't help thinking you only told her to stir the shit. What *is* your problem?"

"Tanya, please keep your voice down." Matthew accepted his tea from Adrian. "I confess I don't really understand why you would share that information with Pam, especially now we have everything organised so their paths need not cross. Marianne?"

Catinca caught Adrian's eye and glanced at her watch. He blinked in acknowledgement. Buttonholes from florist, cake from bakery, cars to be confirmed, guests to be welcomed, gifts to be stored, groom to be found. *Gotta get on, mate.*

"I told Mum because we promised to treat them equally. She understood why we kept it quiet and why I was telling her now. She's not planning on coming to Silverwood tomorrow. Everything is fine. There's no risk of Mum turning up for some reason. So I have no idea why Tanya's making such a hysterical fuss about it."

"Because," hissed Tanya through clenched teeth, "we are trying to work as a team. As a family. One of us goes off to do her own thing and we all suffer."

Matthew nodded. "I understand your motivation, Marianne, but I think Tanya has a point. Best to talk to us before taking unilateral action. I intend to say the same thing to Beatrice when she and Will resurface. Now there's a substantial list of duties to be completed, so I suggest we all get back to work. Catinca, will you direct the troops? I would appreciate it if someone could drive me back to the cottage so I can find that Stubbs woman. Huggy Bear, come."

Chapter Twenty-Two

Despite the weather, traffic and rumbling stomach, Beatrice managed to tick off the majority of her errands by half past two. On her way back to the cottage, a large delivery van rounded the corner and blocked her route. There was a passing space a few hundred yards behind her so she reversed and allowed the van driver precedence. He gave her a wave of thanks as he manoeuvred his white truck past and carried on his way. Beatrice put the Volkswagen into first gear and attempted to get back on the tarmac.

The wheels spun, gaining no purchase. She twisted the wheel, backed up a little more and tried again. The engine whined but nothing moved. She closed her eyes, swore with considerable violence and turned off the engine. No traffic of any kind could be seen in either direction along the lane. She reached for her handbag, planning to call Matthew for some help in getting out. Her phone was missing. She emptied the entire contents onto the passenger seat but her mobile was absent. She was on her own.

Gloves on, coat buttoned, she got out of the car and examined the front wheels. Large grooves under the left and the right semi-buried in snow. She began gathering sticks, twigs, leaves, anything to shove under the tyres. With the snow still falling, it was hard to tell how much she'd need. She dug away at the sludge beneath her car with ever colder hands and finally decided she'd done enough. She got back in the VW and fired the engine.

"One, two, three!" she whispered and tried once more to drive out of the rut. There was a slide forwards but the wheels spun uselessly once more and she was going nowhere. She attempted to do the same in reverse but she just dug herself further into the mud.

"Right!" she yelled. "Stay there, you stubborn bastard! I'll bloody walk the rest."

She was shoving her purchases into a canvas bag when the sound of an engine reached her ears. She dropped the turkey onto the back seat and turned towards the lane. Round the corner came Rose's Land Rover, the word Defender emblazoned its bonnet. Beatrice imagined she could hear trumpets and almost cried with relief.

"Rose!" she called, waving her arms. "Rose! Over here!"

The huge beast pulled over and Beatrice saw the driver's profile. Not a little old lady, but the striking features of Gabriel Shaw. He put on his hazard lights, switched off the engine and jumped out.

"DI Stubbs! In a bit of bother?" he called, his smile warming her even at that distance.

"Gabriel. I'm so pleased to see you! That wretched van, I had to back up, got stuck and can't get this damn thing to move an inch, even after chucking half the hedge under the tyres."

He stooped to look under the car. "You need dragging out of there. I'll get the tow rope. Half a tick."

He sprang into action, moving the Land Rover forward, attaching a bright yellow strap to its underside and lying in the snow to fix the other end to something underneath her vehicle. She stood beside the car like a spare part.

"Get in now and let's take it slowly. Handbrake off, switch it on, put it into first and when you feel a bit of solid ground, give it some welly. Careful you don't spin too fast and bump into me."

Within thirty seconds, she was back on the road. Gabriel's brake lights came on and she stopped her car behind him, remembering to put on her hazard flashers.

"Gabriel, you are an ... umm ... absolute star. Can I give you something for your trouble?" she asked, as he set about detaching the tow strap.

"Don't be daft. What are neighbours for?" He looked up at her from the ground with that knee-melting smile.

"Let me buy you a pint, at least. Will you be in the pub on Christmas Day?"

He rolled up the strap. "I do like a pint before me Christmas dinner. Which pub?"

"I had The Angel in mind."

"Yeah, OK. I've been avoiding that place just lately but don't need to no more."

Beatrice threw him a sharp look but his smile was still in place, his face open and honest.

"Then it's settled. I am buying the drinks. Thank you so much and merry Christmas!"

"Same to you, DI Stubbs. Take care now."

The rest of the journey back to the cottage, although alarming at several points after Gabriel had driven off with a friendly toot of the horn, was precarious and snow-clogged. But once she pulled into their short driveway, she saw it had been cleared and the parking spot swept. Bless Matthew and his 'rugged manly tasks in the garden'. There was no sign of him or Huggy Bear, so she put the turkey in the fridge and spotted the remains of a chilli con carne in a pot on the newly cleaned hob. But before satisfying her hunger, she took her purchases upstairs, wrapped and packed them away, ready for the morning.

When she'd finished, she came downstairs with every intention of stuffing herself while reading some more of Vaughan's diary. Sending grateful thoughts to Matthew, she warmed the chilli and tore off a chunk of crusty bread. The diary was still in its hiding place under her chair cushion so Beatrice settled down at the kitchen table to read the remaining few entries before Vaughan Mason's unpleasant death.

Publishing is so fucking PREDICTABLE! Some trust-fund twat – Simple Simon's replacement at Carson Chambers – called me today with 'a few comments' on the outline I sent. In honeyed tones, Priscilla, Ariadne, Nectarine, whatever she calls herself, told me that 'certain themes might hit an OFF note in the current environment' (she pronounced it 'orf') and that the editorial team 'expressed some discomfort at the portrayal of women'. If I am willing to rework the central narrative as a story of gradual male enlightenment, CC might reconsider in the New Year. I told her to Fuck Orf and opened a bottle of claret. Tomorrow I'm going to phone that Coat-tails Johnny of an agent and have him offer it to the highest bidder. Carson fucking Chambers are emasculated crowd-pleasers and they can stick their feel-good chick-lit up their prissy pink arses.

4 Dec. New face at the game tonight. App developer, whatever that is. I don't have a clue what the hell he's talking about most of the time but his wallet speaks for itself. Reeled him in like a red snapper. Best of all, you could see it in his face. Next time, he was thinking, I'll get him next time. Ha!

Dumpling appeared like a dustball from beside the Aga and rubbed his head against her leg.

"Am I forgiven?" She stroked him and went to the fridge. "Have a slice of ham and let's never speak of it again."

The cat accepted the peace offering and with calm grace, leapt onto Matthew's chair and turned to observe her, licking his lips.

Weds 5. Stroke of luck this morning. One of the hideously unattractive cleaners with verbal diarrhoea let slip she also works at The Angel. Five minutes of sophistry later, I gained the mobile number of Lil S. Spent all morning sending her romantic text messages. Try tossing those on the fire, light of my life.

Thursday. Bloody awful hangover after golf club party. Bumble and Dopey brought their wives, both of whom pulled faces like a smacked arse as soon as they saw me. I wear it as a badge of pride. Those career shrews mistrust a man who does exactly as he pleases and gives their browbeaten husbands a glimpse of what fun life can be.

Crossed paths with The Black Widow just as I came out of the butcher's. First time since I dumped her. She's still sulking. Shame really. The fact is, even if I hadn't got my heart set on Lil S, I couldn't afford her. Professionally or privately. She said she wanted to give me a Christmas gift with THAT look in her eyes. Almost turned her down but I haven't had a decent shag in weeks. One last time can't hurt. Agreed to pop into the practice tomorrow for one last session on the couch. Champagne and caviar and Mason rides again! Tally ho!

December 7: Christmas card from G along with classic corporate gift of port and cigars. When the fuck has she ever seen me smoke a cigar?! Complete absence of invitation to New York, which I suppose is not surprising after that fracas two years ago. Or was it three? Who gives a shit?

That was the final entry. To all intents and purposes, those were the last words of literary giant Vaughan Mason. *Who gives a shit?* Beatrice closed the book, slipped it back in its envelope and thrust it into her handbag. *Face like a smacked arse.* She let out a short laugh and took another bite of bread.

Two minutes later, Dumpling lifted his head and turned his absinthe eyes to the window. They listened to the front door opening and Huggy Bear barrelled into the room, jumping up at Beatrice.

"Hello, pooch, did you have fun? Down now, good girl, I'm eating. Matthew, you are such a darling for leaving me some lunch. I was starved!"

Matthew stood in the doorway, blinking with the same kind of bewilderment as the cat. "You're here. Where's Will?"

Beatrice swallowed a mouthful of chilli. "No idea. I've not seen him since lunchtime. Surely he'll be at the pub with Adrian or maybe at the hotel welcoming guests? Have you two been for a walk?"

"No. Frankie gave me a lift home from The Angel. Adrian is terribly worried. Apparently Will went off to join you this morning and still has not returned. None of us can get a reply from his phone and you left yours in the hairdresser's in Crediton. We thought you'd both had an accident." He lifted up her mobile.

Beatrice stopped chewing. "Oh that's where it is. I'm sorry. I must have left it there this morning. Will should have been back hours ago. The signal's not great where he was going, which explains why you couldn't get through. Though why he's taking so long, I have no idea."

Matthew didn't answer but handed over her mobile. "Check your messages. And if you know where he is, please call Adrian. It's getting dark, the weather's getting worse and everyone apart from you is extremely concerned."

He stomped back into the hallway to take off his boots. As she entered her pass code, she distinctly heard him mutter, "Bloody woman," before the messages began.

Beatrice abandoned her food to listen. Messages from Adrian, Tanya, Matthew and one from the florist about the buttonholes, but no feedback from DS Quinn on his unofficial interview.

Matthew stood over her, hands on hips.

"There's not a single message from Will and I can't say I'm surprised. He's busy. I know he was going shopping after he finished doing a favour for me. Let me make a quick call and see what time he left there. Hold on."

"Hullo? Anyone home?" Mungo stood on the threshold, bearing a large Harrods bag. Whatever it contained caused Huggy Bear great excitement.

"Come on in, Mungo!" called Beatrice, pressing Gaia's number. "You look like Santa Claus with that sack. Huggy Bear, get your nose out, that's very rude."

She led the way into the kitchen, listening to the ring tone from Gaia's landline, but she didn't pick up. Beatrice considered her next move and ate another forkful of chilli.

"Tea?" Matthew asked his friend.

"Don't mind if I do. After the day I've had, I jolly well deserve a cuppa." Mungo dumped his bag on the kitchen table. "Santa Claus doesn't work half as hard as me, Beatrice. My dear wife had me delivering presents all over Devon. Those are yours, by the way, and she's even added a little something for the new arrivals. I am utterly exhausted, I tell you. Driving is no joke in this weather. Damn and hell blast, but those roads are treacherous."

"That's very kind of you," said Matthew. "Perhaps I might let the dog have hers now. Otherwise I fear we'll have no peace."

He selected a substantial chew from Mungo's bag and handed it to Huggy Bear. She sniffed once, grabbed it and scampered off to her bed.

Beatrice swallowed. "You're right about the roads. I got stuck in a rut and would still be there now had it not been for Gabriel Shaw towing me out."

Matthew glanced over. "You didn't mention that."

"You didn't give me a chance."

Mungo, with classic diplomacy, continued. "Ah yes, the Shaw boy has the right kind of vehicle for these conditions. The military use them, you know. Deserts, mountains, all sorts. Tough as old boots, a Land Rover. Whatever are you eating, Beatrice?"

"Chilli con carne. There's some left if you're hungry. It's not just the military. Favourites with police forces all over the world."

"Thank you, I'll pass. Spicy food plays havoc with the gout. Yes, I had one once, you know, when I was working on the farm. That was a magnificent workhorse. None of this new soft-edged business. Mine was a boxy old-school Defender in classic army green."

"Gabriel's is black. But yes, it is a Defender."

"I think you'll find his is a Discovery. The newer model. It is black, though, I grant you. Ah, tea and biscuits, just what a body needs."

Matthew placed the teapot, three mugs and a plate of mini Christmas cookies in front of them. "Enough of the petrol head talk. What are we going to do about Will?"

Beatrice put down her fork. "Just a minute. Mungo, the car outside Vaughan's house on the Friday before he died. You told the police it was Gabriel's."

"Indeed it was! Muddy, scraped and bashed up with some kind of hippie sticker on the rear window. He's a vegan, you know. Anyway, yes, I recognised it straight off."

"What was the number plate?"

"No idea. Police asked me the same thing. Can't be sure I even looked. Just spotted a vehicle I recognised and said to myself, there's Gabriel Shaw's Land Rover. That's queer."

"Do you remember which word was on the bonnet?"

Mungo rolled his eyes. "Land Rover?"

Beatrice's thought processes began making connections and joining the dots while her stomach filled with a cold dread.

Need to up the stakes at tomorrow night's game if I'm going to take The Black Widow to Chez Bruno.

"Did you know him?"

"Only by reputation. I read his book when I was at university."
I couldn't afford her. Professionally or privately.

Agreed to pop into the practice for one last session on the couch.
Gaia Dee?

Matthew was staring at her. "What is it, Old Thing?"

"I met my counsellor this morning, mostly to try and get some information about why she'd counselled Frankie. I suspected it may have had something to do with Vaughan. She wouldn't share client info with me but said she would with the police. So I asked Will to go and speak to her, as a police officer. What concerns me now is that she drives a large black SUV with a No GM Food sticker in the back. Secondly, I have reason to believe she and Vaughan may have been closer than I thought. And Will has not returned."

"What is your counsellor's name?" Mungo asked.

"She's called Gaia Dee. She lives out towards..."

"...Appleford," Matthew finished her sentence, shooting a look of consternation at Mungo.

Mungo's eyes widened. "Lady D! I remember. He couldn't stop crowing about having an affair with his shrink. Good God!"

Beatrice snatched up her phone. "I'm calling the police. This time they'll have to listen to me. Matthew, will you please call Rose? We're going to need her Land Rover."

Chapter Twenty-Three

Once again, Rose's driving left Beatrice speechless, which was not ideal as she was supposed to be giving directions. In the back of the vehicle, Maggie and Matthew clutched their seats and each other as the elderly lady hurled the Land Rover through the swirling, shifting whiteness.

The vehicle sped along the country roads, occasionally pulling in for a similar four-wheel drive travelling in the opposite direction, a constant snowflake starscape creating a hypnotic effect on the silent passengers. When Rose turned on the radio, it took no longer than two minutes for a severe weather warning to interrupt some forgettable pop music.

Beatrice strained to catch the forecaster's words. "Yellow warning ... only travel if absolutely necessary ... stay off roads ... check on elderly neighbours ...conditions treacherous ... take no risks."

After the second repetition, Rose switched it off.

Finally, once they had crossed the motorway, Beatrice shuffled round to address Maggie. She had to raise her voice over the sound of the engine.

"I'm so grateful to you both. And I am sorry to drag you out on a night like this. We're worried about Will. I was following a lead and asked him for help. You see, when assessing who had both the expertise and motive for poisoning Vaughan Mason, I suspected Susie Hancock and her daughter of acting in tandem. I can't say why, but I promise you I did have good cause.

"On a completely unrelated note, my counsellor in London found me a local person whom I met this morning. She seemed very nice. After doing the usual client-counsellor thing, I asked her a couple of questions because I happen to know she also counselled Frankie, or Francesca as she was then. I suspected a link between Vaughan, Frankie and Susie. She gave me nothing. Very professional, she refused to break client confidentiality. She hinted she would be able to offer more information to someone currently employed as a serving police officer. Hence my asking Will if he would pop round and see what he could glean."

The road grew rougher and each invisible pothole tossed them about in the back of the Land Rover. No one spoke for several moments as one would need to shout to be heard. After a particularly violent bounce drew a furious bellow from Maggie, Rose changed gear and the vehicle slowed to a less terrifying pace.

"But he should have been back hours ago," Beatrice continued, no longer forced to shout. "And I assumed he was. Then this afternoon, two pieces of the puzzle fell into place. Vaughan Mason was having an affair with someone he referred to as The Black Widow. He broke that off sometime in November. And outside his house on the Friday afternoon before he died was a large black SUV. A witness identified it as belonging to Gabriel Shaw. But Gabriel drives a Defender, just like this one. Gaia on the other hand..."

Rose didn't take her eyes off the road. "So where is Will now?"

"He must be still at the property," said Beatrice. "It's off the beaten track which is why we need your Land Rover. We're not doing this alone, don't worry, the police are on their way."

No one spoke.

Beatrice craned her neck, squinting into the darkness and checking her phone for guidance. "Rose, take the next turning on the right, then straight on for about a mile."

They all peered out into the night but the hedgerows either side of the headlights gave little away. Beyond the bend in the lane, Beatrice spotted a blue flashing light reflecting off the fields. She frowned. The police had got there before them? Rose indicated and pulled the wheel to the right, onto a narrower lane, which seemed to be surprisingly popular, judging by the amount of tyre tracks on the ground. Then she stopped.

In the middle of the road stood a blue sign. TRAFFIC INCIDENT. ROAD CLOSED.

A cold sense of dread sank to the pit of Beatrice's stomach. She opened the door, jumped out and moved the sign to one side. Clambering back in, she said, "Take it very slowly but let's keep moving."

Everyone leaned forward, eyes on the road. Rose rounded the corner, doing around five miles an hour, and slammed on the brakes. An ambulance was heading towards them, with no siren or flashing lights. Rose reversed to a wider section of the road to let the vehicle pass. She wound down the window to hear the driver.

"The road's closed. Traffic incident up ahead. Turn around and find another route!"

"Oh dear. I hope no one was hurt?"

The driver gave a grim nod. "Not a night to be on the roads." His window rolled up and he drove away.

Rose looked at Beatrice. "What now?"

"Put it in first gear and keep going."

The Land Rover moved on at a cautious crawl, blue lights getting brighter as the approached. Around the next corner, a police car and reflective barriers blocked their path, emergency floodlights illuminating the scene. Several other vehicles were parked ahead, including a tow truck, and in the glare of the lights, first responders worked in high visibility jackets. Beatrice could see the underside of a car up against a stone wall, the front third crushed like a tin can. Even at this distance she recognised it. A silver Audi.

"No. Please no. Oh God." She got out, her breath shallow and skin icy, and walked closer, her hands in her armpits to stop them from shaking.

A uniformed officer came towards her. "Sorry, madam, the road's closed."

"What happened?"

"Traffic collision. I need you to move away, please. The scene is not secure and your Land Rover is blocking the entry for emergency vehicles."

Beatrice pointed, her voice shaking. "I think that's my friend's car."

The officer looked behind him at the crumpled metal. "I see. I'll ... er ... get someone to come and talk to you. Just wait there."

She sensed Matthew come up behind her to place an arm around her shoulders. "Beatrice? Is that Will's?"

"Not sure yet," she said. It wasn't true. She could see the twisted cabriolet and she knew.

Footsteps sounded behind them and Beatrice turned to see two figures silhouetted in Rose's headlights walking towards them. DI Axe and DS Perowne.

Axe took in the situation in one searching glance and looked from Beatrice to the mangled metal. "Is that his car?" she asked, her voice gentle.

"Yes." Beatrice's whole body was trembling.

A man in a hi-vis tabard over his coat came across and seemed surprised to see DI Axe. "Hello, Caroline. They told me it was a relative after information."

"Hello, Gerry. We're looking for an individual in connection with a case." She pulled out her notebook. "Last known to have visited a house half a mile up the road earlier this afternoon in a silver Audi cabriolet. We passed an ambulance just now. The occupants...?" She indicated the crash scene.

Gerry pressed his lips together. "Just the driver. A fatality, I'm sorry to say. The body's gone to the morgue already if you want to do an official ID."

Beatrice knees buckled and the only thing that kept her from falling into the snow was Matthew, gripping her shoulder like a vice.

Chapter Twenty-Four

The raucous laughter and occasional outbursts of song from the bar were unbearable to Adrian, as were Catinca and Tanya's frequent reassurances and concerned looks. His room, which had once felt so charming and spacious, now seemed oppressive and stuffy. In fact, it was pointless trying to sit in one place until he had news of Will.

He put on his coat and slunk down the stairs, mobile in pocket, intent on walking and clearing his head. But before he'd got to the landing, he heard familiar voices. His sister, his mother and most voluble cousin were in the hallway, looking for him. Of course they were. All excited and keen to meet the grooms before the wedding, they must have got a taxi here from the hotel.

He couldn't stand it. There was no way he could sit with friends and family, chatting about plans for tomorrow when he didn't even know if there would be a tomorrow. He couldn't go back upstairs to his room because that was the first place they would look for him, so he took a left along the first floor corridor, wondering if there was a fire escape. Halfway along, he noticed a door marked Function Room and tried the handle. The door opened without a sound and he saw a dozen tables covered in holly-printed tablecloths in semi-darkness. Exactly what he needed. He threaded his way through the room and sat on a window seat, looking out over the green.

His phone rang and he checked Caller Display. Jared.

"Jared, hi," he said, trying to keep his voice upbeat. "How's Alejandro?"

"He's home. It was a virus and he's still sick but I just wanted to tell you it isn't meningitis and your godson going to be fine."

"Oh that is wonderful news! Thank you so much for letting me know. You and Peter must have been distraught."

"Pretty much. We're relieved but so really disappointed we couldn't make your big day. We both wish you all the happiness and luck in the world. You're good people and we love you."

Adrian couldn't speak.

"Hey, you must be crazy busy, so have a wonderful wedding and call me when you get back from honeymoon. OK?"

Adrian swallowed. "We will. Love to Alejandro!" He ended the call and switched his phone to silent.

The only call he wanted was from Will.

Detective Sergeant William Quinn. Adrian's mind floated back to that cold wintry night when he'd arrived home to find two detectives standing in the hallway, asking him to come in for questioning. Someone had maliciously accused him of possessing indecent images of children. After hours of answering the same questions, he had permission to go. They kept his computer overnight and one of the detectives took it upon himself to return it in person. DS Quinn left his card, suggesting if Adrian experienced any other forms of harassment, he'd be willing to listen.

The detective got fed up of waiting and called him for a date. They went out for some food and wine and said they should do it again. Adrian called him the very next day and they had been together ever since. Will moved in, met Beatrice and introduced Adrian to his friends. They went on holidays, spent weekends with each other's families and discussed kids (no), dogs (yes). Will sold his motorbike and bought a car. And on one beautiful summer's evening in Portugal, Will brought out a ring and said, "Will you marry me?"

Tears were flowing freely now and Adrian wiped his face with his sleeve. *Will, where are you? Please, please come back!*

The door burst open and Adrian blinked, half-expecting his plea to have been answered. Instead, Susie stood in the doorway, peering into the gloomy room.

"Here you are!" she exclaimed and turned to call over her shoulder. "He's in the Function Room!"

"Susie, please, I just need a minute ... oh no."

Running footsteps came down the corridor. Catinca, Tanya and Frankie shoved themselves in and shut the door.

Catinca held up her tablet and tapped a few buttons. "Susie just saw this on news. Listen to end, mate. Then we call Beatrice."

A poor quality video from a local TV station began to play. *Extreme weather conditions have already claimed several lives in the region. A two-vehicle collision on the M5 near Tiverton resulted in three deaths. Two children have been taken to intensive care. A fatal accident occurred just off the A396, killing the driver, a 43-year-old woman from Appleford. No other vehicles involved. Heavy snow caused the roof of an old people's home to collapse in the Swilly area of Plymouth. No residents or staff were injured.*

Catinca rewound and played one section again. *A fatal accident occurred just off the A396, killing the driver, a 43-year-old woman from Appleford.* She paused and pointed at the screen.

It took a moment but when he saw it, he caught his breath. "That's Will's car!"

Catinca clutched his arm. "Will's car but driver is a woman. Call Beatrice, mate. We got to know what's going on."

Tearing his eyes from the horrible wreck of Will's car, Adrian shook his head. "I want to keep my line clear in case he calls. You phone Beatrice and put her on speakerphone."

The phone rang three times.

"Hello, Catinca. Can I call you back later?"

"NO!" yelled the little Romanian. "Just seen Will's car smashed up on telly but news says driver is woman. Where's Will? Adrian and me want to know what's going on. Not later, mate, now!"

There was a muffled conversation then Beatrice's voice came on the line. "Who else is there with you?"

"Susie, Tanya and Frankie. All worried sick."

Beatrice exhaled. "OK, OK. Will was not in his car when it crashed. That said, we still don't know where he is. Adrian, I'm so sorry about all this. I was following a lead and asked Will for help. I went to see a counsellor this morning and asked her a couple of questions because I had very good reason to suspect a link between her and Vaughan. She wouldn't speak to me, a civilian, but said she could be able to offer more information to the police. Will agreed to go round and make enquiries. Now he's disappeared and it was the counsellor who crashed his car into a wall."

Adrian's head was so hot it must be letting off steam. "I couldn't give a shit about your case, Beatrice. Where is Will?"

"I'm with the police right now. We've searched the counsellor's house and we're now checking the grounds. It's an uphill struggle in this weather and in the dark, but we'll find him. I promise we'll find him."

"Beatrice?" Frankie stepped forward to speak into the phone. "The counsellor who died in the car crash? Can you tell me her name?"

There was a pause. "Yes, all right. Her family's been informed so it'll be on the news soon enough. Her name was Gaia Dee."

In the silence after Beatrice rang off, the sounds of Slade floated up from the public bar below. Adrian's phone vibrated again. Not Will. He declined.

"This can't be happening. My fiancé goes missing the night before my wedding?"

Catinca squeezed his arm. "This time is OK."

"This time *what* is OK?"

"Dramatics. I always tell you don't be drama queen. Today, you can."

"Thank you," said Adrian, but could do nothing more than clench his fists and try not to cry. A thought occurred and he lifted his face to the waiting women. "We should help. We should get to wherever it is and help them search!"

"Yes!" said Tanya. "We have to do something. If he's out there in the snow, he'll be dead by morning. I just have no idea where to start."

Frankie's expression changed from concern to conviction and she rotated her head to look at her mother. "I know where to start."

Everyone turned to Susie, whose frightened stare switched between Adrian and her daughter. She and Frankie locked eyes and Adrian sensed a battle of wills.

"There is one place you could look," said Susie, her voice defeated. "You're going to need a driver. Tanya, go downstairs and drag Gabriel away from his beer. Tell him to take you to the hunters' hide in Appleford Woods. Because of that crash, he'll have to go the long way round."

Temperatures had dropped and Arctic winds broadsided the small party waiting outside the Land Rover. Catinca hunched her shoulders to her ears and Adrian put up his hood. The forest, silent and menacing, seemed impossible to negotiate. Yet Gabriel switched on his torch and picked up his first aid kit.

"Won't risk driving any further. We'll walk the last bit." He offered an arm to Tanya.

"No thanks, I'll only pull you over. You go ahead and I'll follow. How far is this thing?"

"Couple of hundred yards. You can see it from here on a clear night."

"What we looking for? Apart from Will," asked Catinca.

"It's a viewing platform with a hide. Forest workers and hunters use it to observe wildlife. This is one of the highest in the region at fifteen foot," Gabriel answered, setting off at a surefooted pace. "Watch your feet, it's easy to trip. Try to walk in my tracks."

The mismatched party followed in single file. Snowflakes

blew into Adrian's eyes and his ears hurt from the icy wind, but all he could think of was Will out there, alone. He heaved freezing air into his lungs and marched ahead.

Somewhere across the fields came a sudden screech and Catinca grabbed his arm.

"That's only an owl," said Tanya. "Don't panic."

Adrian was still processing the forester's words, struggling to make sense of what the hell they were doing in a forest in the middle of a snowstorm. "Hang on, how do you get up fifteen feet?"

"Ladder. The place is pretty well maintained from spring to autumn, but no one uses it in winter. Perfect place to hide something you don't want found."

"But why would Susie think he's there? How would a woman carry Will up a ladder? He's six foot one and weighs a hundred and eighty pounds."

Gabriel shone his torch ahead and Adrian could see the solid wooden legs of a structure emerging from the snow. "There's a pulley system for lifting equipment to the top. I thought Susie was off her head suggesting this place, but somebody's been up here today. Look." He pointed to a pattern on the ground. Snow had fallen into the grooves, but the marks of a car's wheels turning and reversing made an almost perfect pair of heart shapes.

"You wait here and I'll climb up." He zipped the first aid kit inside his coat and started his ascent of the ladder with the torch in his right hand. It looked dangerous and slippery and utterly terrifying. Adrian held his breath as the torchlight bobbed upwards and Gabriel disappeared into the dark. Each second stretched as three upturned faces waited for a sound. Catinca's gloved hand slipped into Adrian's and his heartbeat boomed in his ears.

Snow fell from the platform in a clump to land at their feet, making them all start. A canvas panel unzipped and Gabriel leaned out, shone his torch at them and then aimed the light at himself as he called down.

"There's a man up here! He's unconscious but breathing and has a strong pulse. He's freezing and in real danger of hypothermia. I've wrapped him in a thermal blanket for now, but we have to get him down and take him to a hospital. Tanya, go round to that end," he flicked the torch to the left, "and grab a hold of the pulley rope. Pull until the basket gets up here. I'm going to secure this guy in it, then when I say so, I want all three of you to hold on and bring him slowly down."

Adrian stumbled after Tanya and while she looped the pulley rope off its pegs, he knocked all the snow off the folded canvas basket, which unfolded to the size of a child's dinghy. He and Catinca manhandled it onto position and Tanya began to pull, backing away across the clearing. Its upward progress was rapid and Gabriel shouted for her to stop.

Several minutes passed as they strained to see what was happening high above them. Finally, the torch flashed back to their faces.

"I'll keep the light on him and you release the rope, slow and steady, one hand over another, till he's safely down. Adrian, tie the end of the rope around your waist, just in case there's a slip. Tell me when you're ready."

Adrian did as he was told and called up to the blackness where Gabriel should be.

The weight of the basket came as a surprise and Adrian leaned back to take the strain as Catinca struggled to get a foothold in the snow. Gabriel kept up a running stream of instructions and inch by inch, they fed the rope out until the basket touched the ground.

Adrian ran towards it, forgetting he was still attached to the end and a sudden tug at his middle caused him to fall headlong into the snow. Catinca helped him up and untied him, by which time Gabriel was scrambling down the ladder.

Inside the basket, a figure was wrapped in a silver blanket, blond hair poking out of the top. Adrian peered to look closer and let out an involuntary gasp. Will's skin was candle wax pale and his lips a violet blue.

Gabriel handed his torch to Tanya and detached the pulley clip. "Adrian, can you and I carry him back to the Land Rover, you reckon? We'll be faster taking him to hospital ourselves than calling an ambulance. Catinca, give him your hat."

Catinca covered Will's blond hair with her trapper hat and tucked the flaps over his ears.

The two men got a grip on the canvas and in a stumbling, awkward shuffle, they bumped, wobbled and sometimes dropped the basket along the path. Eventually, Gabriel gave up. He hoisted Will into a fireman's lift and heaved him into the back of the Land Rover.

"Get in with him," he motioned impatiently. "Take off his clothes because they're frozen and will get wet as he heats up. Cover him with a couple of them fleeces and put the thermal blanket over the top. Don't rub his hands, just cover them up. I'm going to take him to Tiverton. Catinca, as soon as you get a signal, call DI Stubbs." He slammed the door and they got to work.

Chapter Twenty-Five

How many times had Beatrice's notebook proved a lifesaver? She had lost count. She sat in a police interview room on the line to Tiverton Community Hospital, waiting for someone to locate the doctor treating Will. Finally, Dr Wade came to the phone. The second Beatrice said the words *Amanita virosa*, he understood the seriousness of the situation.

"I can put your mind at ease on that score. The people who presented him mentioned a possible connection. My assessment at this stage is that DS Quinn has ingested no poison. Nor are there any indications of amatoxins in his system. He is merely under the influence of a large dose of benzodiazepine. It's a tranquilliser that..."

"I know what it is," Beatrice gave a little laugh to counter her sharp tone. "I've come across them before. What effect will it have?"

"Very little. He's been sedated, that's all. Had it not been for the cold and resulting hypothermia, he would not need to be in hospital and could sleep it off at home. He should wake up in a few hours, feeling a little disorientated and with little memory of what happened. These drugs are designed to make people forget traumatic events such as seizures. Even so, we want to keep an eye on him over the next few hours."

"How did it get into his system?"

Wade cleared his throat. "As I told DI Axe earlier, Mr Quinn ingested a large amount of a prescription drug. Whether he took the medication voluntarily or not, I cannot possibly say. Although why he would take such an amount the day before his wedding is beyond me. We'll just have to wait till he wakes up to find out more."

"In your professional opinion, when might that be? He's getting married today."

"You are the seventh person to tell me that. I don't know exactly when he'll come round, but his future husband will be the first to know. He's sleeping in a chair right next to him. Goodnight."

Beatrice thanked the testy doctor and hung up. Her mouth was dry, she had a headache and her stomach was empty. She was just about to go and find a coffee machine when DI Axe stuck her head round the door. "Any luck?" she asked.

Beatrice nodded. "Just spoken to the doctor. As far as poisons are concerned, he's clean as a thistle. But it's going to be a while before we ... I mean you ... can interview him. Wade said it might take a few hours and even then he may not remember much."

"In that case, could I have a word? Fancy a cuppa?"

"You read my mind."

Axe sat at a corner table in the police canteen while Beatrice bought the tea. When she returned with a tray bearing five cups, DI Axe raised her eyebrows.

"Are we expecting guests?"

"No. Four of them are for me." She took a swallow from the first cup and shut her eyes to appreciate the bliss. Strong, sweet and warm, it was the most welcome thing she had ever drunk.

Axe took a cup for herself. "Fair enough. I have an update. A family member made a positive ID of Gaia Dee's body. She also confirmed there had been several conversations between her and her family yesterday afternoon, letting them know she'd be later than expected. You know what I think? She planned to brazen it out."

Beatrice shook her head. "I don't get it. Why would she tell me she would talk to the police and then when a detective turns up, she tries to get rid of him? It doesn't make sense. Why did she drug him? How the hell did she get him right up that tree where Gabriel found him? If she sedated him in her house, how did she even get a man that size out of her house and into her car?" Beatrice started on her second cup.

"I'm pretty sure that was misinterpretation on your part. Like certain other people, she was reminding you that you are no longer an officer of the law. But you took it as a hint. When DS Quinn turned up, she panicked. She made him tea or coffee laced with a strong tranquilliser, answered his questions and waited till it took effect. Maybe she offered him a lift back down to his car – he parked at the end of the lane like you did – or waited till he keeled over and put him in a wheelbarrow."

Neither spoke for a moment, both imagining alternate scenarios.

"What was Gaia doing in his Audi? Did she drive into that wall on purpose?" Beatrice wondered, half to herself.

"My theory is that she drugged him, dumped him in her car, drove to that hunters' hide, and winched him up there, expecting him to die overnight. Then she had to get rid of the Audi by leaving it somewhere which would throw us off the scent. Experience tells me she was heading for Devil's Bridge. It's about a mile from her house and a well-known suicide spot. She could have walked home from there, and the search for DS Quinn could have taken days. Everything appears to make sense apart from one factor. How did the people who found Quinn know where he would be?"

"You'd have to ask them. But Gabriel Shaw is a forester. He uses those places for his work. He probably realised how close it was to her house and sounded the alarm. Was Gaia Dee a suspect in the Vaughan Mason investigation?"

"She was certainly a person of interest. Her name had cropped up in connection with another case. But we checked out her social media and found an alibi. She attended a medical conference in

Bristol from Friday afternoon to Sunday lunchtime. If you had brought your evidence to me rather than involving DS Quinn, that would have convinced me to interview her."

"That was the whole point. I didn't have any evidence, just some strong suspicions. She wasn't even in the frame," said Beatrice, opening another packet of sugar. "Anyway, your instructions to me were to keep away from the enquiry."

"Which you obviously obeyed to the letter."

Beatrice didn't argue, just drank her tea and accepted the rebuke. Then something Axe had said struck her. "Do you know what time she checked into the conference?"

"Around four. Confirmed by the hotel."

"So after Vaughan met Gaia at the practice in Crediton for sex, she must have driven directly to Bristol. It couldn't have been her car outside Vaughan's on Friday afternoon."

"To be honest, it could have been anyone's. Mr Mungo Digby's memory is not entirely reliable. What concerns me is that he has a key to the house. There were no signs of a break-in, more signs of a break-out."

"A break-out?" asked Beatrice, confused.

"Damage around both front and back door frames leads us to believe Mr Mason tried to get out of the house, but whatever reason, he couldn't. Someone locked him in."

"His house is right on the street and is a semi-detached. If he'd wanted to attract attention, he could have banged on the windows or the connecting wall."

DI Axe rotated a teaspoon between index finger and thumb, her expression pensive. "But on Saturday afternoon, when his symptoms returned, there was some kind of village fête going on. Would anyone have noticed him?"

Beatrice rested her forehead on her palm and replayed the events around St Nicholas Day.

Thursday. Vaughan Mason goes to the butcher's to buy ingredients for his famous cassoulet. There he meets Gaia Dee. She invites him to her practice the next day, ensuring his guaranteed absence for a couple of hours.

Friday. Vaughan makes his cassoulet in the morning and leaves to meet Gaia. A vehicle is seen outside his house. He returns and leaves for the pub. Around midnight, he staggers home and eats a portion. He is violently sick in the night but feels better by Saturday morning. Perhaps he recovers his appetite and eats some more. When the poison attacks him again on Saturday afternoon, he is weakened and unable to open the door. Because it is locked from the outside.

There was only one conclusion. If Gaia Dee was behind Vaughan's murder, she did not work alone.

Beatrice's head snapped up. "What do you mean, her name cropped up in another case?"

Axe looked around the cafeteria, almost empty at half past midnight. "As you know from experience, it is unprofessional to discuss ongoing investigations. Let's just say we may have good grounds for revisiting a cold case. Eight years ago, Mr Richard Dee died suddenly, while his wife was away visiting family in Cornwall. The cause of death was a heart attack. Some questions were raised about the condition of his body, but tests were inconclusive."

Beatrice stared at her. "My God. She poisoned her own husband?"

Axe stood up, her face impassive. "I'm ready to call it a night. Shall I get someone to drive you home?"

"Yes please. I just need to pop to the ladies. One can have too much tea."

A hand on his shoulder woke Adrian from an uncomfortable doze in the hospital visitor's chair. His eyes flicked open to see a nurse's face.

"Mr Harvey? Sorry to disturb, but I thought you'd want to know. Your friend is awake now." She indicated behind her and left the room.

Will was sitting up in bed, sipping water through a straw. His eyes met Adrian's and his face performed contortions. In a second, Adrian rushed across the room and held him, so all emotions could be poured onto each other's shoulders.

They stayed that way in silence for several minutes, all communication conveyed through breath, kisses, squeezes and strokes.

Finally, Adrian drew back, holding Will's shoulders. "How do you feel?

"Groggy. Confused. What the hell happened? The nurse didn't tell me anything apart from the fact I had mild hypothermia."

Adrian related the events of the previous evening, playing down his fear.

"She left me there to die." Will closed his eyes and opened them again. "You must have been out of your mind with worry."

"I was terrified. I thought you'd got cold feet."

Will's eyes widened and Adrian realised what he'd just said, then laughter at the ridiculousness of the situation overtook them.

"I mean I thought you'd left me."

Will reached for his hand. "That will never happen, I promise. Remind me, who was it that proposed?"

"I know, but after total silence all afternoon. I could only think of accidents or you'd changed your mind."

"Adrian, I didn't want to get into this. I asked Beatrice to take it to the police. She convinced me otherwise and I gave in, just to humour her. I thought it would take no more than an hour. The counsellor was perfectly civil and answered all my questions. Even offered me a mince pie. Next thing, I wake up in hospital. My mind is a complete blank and I keep fighting sleep. I don't remember anything."

"You have no idea how you got up in the forest?"

"None. I think I woke up once because I was so cold and tried to stay awake. Someone had to come eventually because Beatrice knew where I was." Will's eyelids drooped, as if reliving the battle with sleep.

"Except you weren't. You were freezing to death in some

bloody tree house. I could strangle our matron of honour for putting you in this position. Today, of all days."

"She wasn't to know the woman was a psycho. Don't beat her up about it. Where is she now?"

"At the police station, I believe. Matthew's coming to collect me but you're staying here. Don't look like that. I would like a couple of hours' sleep before we get married and you're going nowhere until the doctor says you're fit to get up and marry me. Nothing is more important."

The friendly nurse entered with a tray. "Mr Quinn, please eat some soup now. A doctor will see you at eight o'clock and if all is well, you can go home. Mr Harvey, your friend is here. You should get some rest. Big day today." Her smile was infectious.

Adrian couldn't bear to leave and watched Will devour a bowl of soup. He stood, dithering, until a tentative knock at the door interrupted his indecision.

"Hello, Will, so relieved to see you back in the land of the living. How are you feeling?"

"Matthew! I'm fine, or soon will be. Sounds like you had an eventful night. Why don't you knock off and get some sleep?"

"Because I am determined to ensure both grooms turn up at the wedding. I'm taking Adrian back to The Angel now so he can get some rest. Once the doctors discharge you, I shall come by and we can repair to my cottage. There you can change, freshen up and prepare yourself. A car shall take us to the Manor where we'll greet the guests and await the groom, bridesmaid and matron of honour."

Will saluted with his spoon. "Sounds perfectly organised."

"Sleep well and I'll see you in a few hours."

With a last embrace of his husband-to-be, Adrian followed Matthew down the stairs and out into the little car park. The snow had stopped.

"Have you heard from Beatrice?"

Matthew unlocked the car. "Yes, the police brought her home and she's now fast asleep, thank the Lord. Sometimes she's like

Huggy Bear. She runs around until she's exhausted herself then sleeps like a log. If there is such a thing as a snoring log." He waited till Adrian had fastened his seatbelt then reversed out of the car park. "On that subject, you two have a hatchet to bury. What do you say to Will spending the morning with me? You stay at the pub with Catinca, the guests and sort things out with Beatrice."

"I'd rather keep an eye on Will."

"That's my job. He will be in safe hands. Anyway, some might say it's romantic, arriving at the ceremony separately."

Adrian allowed his head to fall back onto the cushioned headrest. "You are such a decent person, Matthew. Not to mention incredibly tolerant. Have you and Beatrice never thought of making it official?"

"It's taken a quarter of a century to get her to live with me. One step at a time."

Chapter Twenty-Six

After all the tension and drama of the day, Beatrice had expected sleep to elude her. When she opened her eyes and saw it was already half past nine, she was appalled. Why had no one sounded the alarm? Matthew's side of the bed was empty, as was the dog's basket. She pulled on her dressing gown and opened the bedroom door, only to hear the most glorious sound. From the bathroom, an off-key voice singing 'Oh What a Beautiful Morning' could be heard over the splashes of the shower. Will!

The smell of frying bacon floated up from the kitchen and she realised she'd eaten nothing since that chilli yesterday afternoon. Dragging on a jumper and jeans, she hurried downstairs to find Matthew at the Aga, creating a full English breakfast for three.

"Good morning. How are you? How is he?" she asked, crouching to greet Huggy Bear.

He looked up from the sausages. "I'm in fine form, if a little peckish. As for our guest, you can ask him yourself."

Will stood in the doorway, fresh and fragrant in T-shirt and jeans, with a broad smile. "Morning! Something smells good."

Beatrice burst into tears.

"Hey!" Will eased her up from her squatting position and folded her in his arms. "You're not to cry on my wedding day. Everything's fine. Ssh, now, ssh." He patted and stroked her back just as she had done to the dog.

"I'm so sorry," she snuffled into his T-shirt. "You could have died."

"But I didn't. You weren't to know what she was capable of and anyway, it's all over now. If you must cry, save it for the wedding. Because I'm getting married today!"

Matthew placed a piece of kitchen roll into her hand and she let go of Will to blow her nose and dab her eyes. "Thank you. I just feel so terrible about putting you in that situation. If I were you, I'd never forgive me. I should have listened to you and gone to the police."

"Of course I forgive you. Neither of us could have predicted..."

"Sit please, breakfast is served," said Matthew, placing three plates on the table.

"This looks fantastic," said Will, choosing another chair after finding Dumpling asleep on the first. "I don't remember ever being so hungry. Matthew, you should have a knighthood."

"I think so too. Not everyone suits a 'Sir' before their name, but I think I'd sound quite magnificent. Toast?"

Will attacked his breakfast with gusto while he and Matthew discussed the Audi's insurance. Beatrice was only half-listening, buffeted between swells of relief, affection, guilt and the demands of her own growling stomach.

"After the shock of hearing she'd totalled it, I wasn't surprised. You'd have to be an exceptional driver or extremely lucky to handle my car under those conditions."

"Judging by her own knocked-about vehicle, she was definitely not a good driver," said Beatrice. "It all fitted with the ditzy earth mother persona. At least I'm not the only one to get it wrong. James told me she was highly recommended."

"You didn't get it wrong, though." Will mopped up egg with a piece of toast. "She answered my questions. Even if I can't find my notebook or phone or remember anything about what happened after that, I know what she said. You were right. Aged sixteen years old, Francesca Gwynne was referred to her for counselling. She was Dee's client for over a year. What started off as an assumption of bullying turned out to be a case of sexual harassment. An older man hounded her, groped her, tried to lure her back to his house and on one occasion, he attempted rape."

"Mason?"

"Francesca refused to identify him, but I'd say that's more than likely."

"So Dee should have reported him!" exclaimed Beatrice. "And if she already knew what kind of man he was but still accepted him as a client *and* embarked on an affair! Why on earth..."

"Perhaps she didn't know it was the same guy," Will said. "Mason sought her services for anger management issues, she told me. As for the affair, he was rich and influential, or at least pretended to be."

"Maybe she found out and that's what triggered her to..."

"STOP!" Matthew's voice startled everyone, including the dog. He placed his knife and fork on his plate. "Today of all days, please stop being detectives. Forget the case and focus on what is important. For the next twenty-four hours, Adrian should be our only concern. Beatrice, you need to make your apologies. I'm not sure he will be quite as forgiving as his fiancé. Go and get into your wedding togs and I'll drive you to The Angel. Will and I shall join you at Silverwood Manor at midday. Please. If only for today, just let it go."

At eleven o'clock, a Volkswagen drew up outside The Angel. Out hopped Beatrice Stubbs in a calf-length silver dress with matching jacket and a pair of wellies.

Catinca, waiting in the hallway in a leopardskin onesie, dashed out to hand over a bag to Matthew. She paused to gaze at Beatrice and put a hand to her mouth.

"You look gorgeous! Wish I thought of wellies!" she said, her face creasing into laughter. "Here. His buttonhole. Good luck, mate."

Beatrice hitched up her dress to cross the road, ducking behind a black SUV parked right outside the front door. The back window bore a logo: *Dust Demons*, with an image of a little devil holding a feather duster. She would have thought Glynis Knox would delegate Sundays to one of her staff. Cleaning the pub after a Saturday night was no one's idea of fun.

The bar was empty and the door to the snug closed. A bucket held open the ladies' toilets where waitress Amanda was mopping the floor. Beatrice kicked off her wellies and wrinkled her nose at the smell of disinfectant. She was just about to pad up the stairs in stockinged feet when she stopped. Amanda was The Angel's long-suffering waitress, not a cleaner. Where were the Dust Demons?

A low murmur of voices came from the snug. Beatrice crept closer and eased open the door. Five women sat in an arc around the fire, holding mugs. Glynis Knox, Heather Shaw, Susie Hancock, Demelza Price and Frankie Gwynne looked over their shoulders, wide-eyed, as if she'd disturbed a nest of baby owls.

Susie broke the tension. "Good morning, Beatrice! Just having a coffee and a chinwag. Can I get you anything? That dress looks lovely on you! We're all excited about Catinca's outfit. She could teach us all a thing or two about fashion. How's Will?"

"He's fine," Beatrice replied, her antennae twitching to the atmosphere in the room. "Everyone is incredibly relieved we found him before things got worse. I wanted to thank you personally, Susie, for pointing us in the right direction. We're deeply grateful. The police asked me how you knew about the hide and I realised I had no idea. Why did you tell Gabriel to look there?"

Scant shafts of sunlight threw spotlights on dancing dust motes, the smell of stale beer and filter coffee overpowered the acrid stench of toilet cleaner and in the air, something else hovered. Tension. Everyone was holding their breath.

"It won't make no sense to a Londoner, I'm sure," Susie began. "To this village, St Nicholas Day is bigger than Christmas, bigger than Easter, Bonfire Night, Halloween and everything else. It's ours. The day we all come together and celebrate our community. It's also fierce competitive. Floats, music, stalls, decor and ambience are planned months in advance. Most groups prepare their floats in secret. Spies are everywhere!" she laughed.

The women joined in and Beatrice smiled, despite the lie-detector alarms in her ears.

Frankie took over, her face open and innocent. "When we prepare our float, we meet in secret. Up in the hide, no one can hear or see you. It's never used in the winter so we could conceal our creations up there, have meetings, prepare our costumes and plan our strategy. Gaia was a part of our committee, so Mum and I had a feeling. If she was going to hide something, or someone, that's where she'd do it."

The fire spat and a shower of glowing sparks landed on the carpet. Susie jumped up to stamp on them and the women made a big fuss of assisting.

Heather tilted her head in an expression of concern. "Do you think it was a cry for help? The young man went to Gaia in desperation, looking for a way out. Out of compassion, she gave him what he needed and a place to hide. Maybe he didn't want to be found. Why else would he drive all the way out to Appleford the day before his wedding?"

Anger roiled in Beatrice's gut and the urge to spit out exactly what Will was doing burned in her throat. Instead, she shook her head, her eyes resting on each face as she looked around the room.

Susie Hancock, the object of Vaughan's desire, succumbed or was forced into a one-night stand. Desperate to rid herself of this threat to her marriage, had she connected the dots to her own daughter's distress?

Frankie Gwynne, profoundly affected by harassment by an unknown older male, had been educated by her grandmother as to the power of the forest.

Glynis Knox, whose Dust Demons vehicle was a large black SUV with a devil logo on the back, had a key to Vaughan's house.

Heather, rejected, mistreated and bent on revenge, knew his habits of making a cassoulet on Friday lunchtime to last him the weekend and spending Friday evening in the pub.

Demelza Price, next door neighbour, could slip between

the properties through her own garden, locking his doors and blocking her ears.

And Gaia Dee, the Black Widow, who ensured Vaughan was otherwise engaged on Friday afternoon.

Each had an alibi.

Not one of them had means, motive and opportunity

But together?

"No, I don't think anything of the sort. That sort of speculation is not helpful and could hurt people's feelings. Will is the opposite of suicidal. He is bursting with joy for life and cannot wait to get married. He loves Adrian and vice versa. They are a wonderful, perfectly matched couple who deserve to be happy. Now, I'm sorry for the interruption and I really must get on."

"Thank you."

She wheeled around to see Adrian standing in the doorway.

In his Dries Van Noten suit, ice-blue tie and matching pocket handkerchief, his eyes were full of tears. "I knew we should have made you best man."

Chapter Twenty-Seven

In Adrian and Will's bedroom, Beatrice repaired her make-up while Adrian attached his buttonhole in the mirror.

"I cried when I saw Will, too."

"Well you can stop it now or you'll set me off again."

"It's going to be very hard. I keep getting these big emotional bursts of pride. You're both so handsome."

"Thank you. And you look stunning in that colour. Working that Helen Mirren silvery vixen vibe. You and Catinca are going to be such kick-ass bridesmaids. How's this?" He twisted to show her his flower.

She shook her head and fiddled with his lapel. Neither spoke, reluctant to address the elephant in the room.

Eventually, Beatrice took a deep breath. "I want to apologise for yesterday."

"Me too. I shouldn't have shouted like that."

"Yes, you should. I deserved it. Putting Will at risk was unacceptable and I'm truly sorry. I can't bear to think..."

"Nor can I, so let's not. Listen to me, Beatrice. I had a chat with Matthew. You and Will are always going to chase after justice, endangering yourselves and frightening the wits out of us. It's not going to change. I have to accept that before I say my vows. I've forgiven you both already. Just for the next few hours, please can you be bridesmaid first and detective second?"

"I promise. There. You're all done." She stood beside him as he appraised himself in the mirror and gave a huge hiccupping sigh. "I don't know why I'm so tearful today. It's not as if I'm the mother of either groom. Maybe I'm just tired and overexcited."

"So at four o'clock, we'd better put you and Luke down for a nap. Come on. Let's get downstairs. Will and I have an extra present for you and Catinca."

"I don't deserve it," she sniffed.

"I'll be the judge of that. Now stop crying or you'll go all blotchy."

She held it together, mostly. When Catinca made her entrance, she took Beatrice's breath away. The girl had made her own dress, a white strapless fitted gown with crystal-studded bodice and full skirt, accessorised with a white faux-fur shrug. Catinca had dip-dyed the dress so that it changed colour from brilliant white at the top to ice-blue at the bottom. She totally upstaged the groom and got a round of applause as she walked into the bar.

Adrian gave both bridesmaids a beautiful silver charm bracelet as a thank-you present. Each charm related to *The Chronicles of Narnia*. Catinca's were a ship, a horn, a snowflake and a lamp, while Beatrice had a lion, a snake, a horse and a faun. They were still exclaiming over the delicate craftsmanship and how well they complemented their outfits when the silver MK2 Jaguar arrived, complete with white ribbons tied to the bonnet.

Groom and bridesmaids got into the vintage car and waved goodbye to the crowd outside The Angel. On arrival at Silverwood Manor, Matthew and Will stood waiting, all spruced up and shiny and although she had to swallow several times at the expression on Will's face when he saw Adrian emerge, she still didn't weep.

Thanks to their rehearsals, the ceremony went without a hitch. All through the vows and the emotion on the faces of those very dear men, Beatrice clutched at her tissues but held on to her tears. The dam broke only when Luke walked up the aisle carrying a cushion bearing two rings. The delight on his little face as he offered them up to Will and Adrian was too much and Beatrice dissolved, sniffing and blowing her nose loudly. Then it was all over and they were being bossed about by Catinca and Rose, herding everyone into position for the photographs.

In the dining room, Beatrice and Matthew could not find their seats until Catinca pointed out their code names. Colonel Mustard and Lady Lavender found they were seated at the top table which came as a surprise to them both. Matthew struck up a conversation with Adrian's mother and sister so Beatrice turned to the man on her right. Without glancing at his name card, she could see the resemblance.

"Mr Quinn, I'm Beatrice Stubbs."

He shook her hand. "I know. I've heard all about you."

"Ah. Most of it is wild exaggeration so take it with an inch of salt. I apologise for blubbing in the ceremony. It's just these boys are rather important to me and seeing them so happy tipped me over the edge, you see."

"I understand completely. I've never seen Will so ... I don't know how to put it. Happy, of course, but also, balanced. Adrian is a steadying influence on my son, who if left unchecked would let police work take over his life."

"Happens to the best of us. What do you do, Mr Quinn?"

"Please call me Mick."

A waitress moved around the table pouring white wine. Another placed bowls of chestnut soup in front of each guest.

"Thank you very much, that smells delicious!" Beatrice smiled up at her and turned her attention back to Adrian's father-in-law. "All right, Mick, but only if you call me Beatrice. So, what line are you in?"

Mick Quinn looked over at his son. "The lad's a chip off the old block, Beatrice. Like you, I'm an ex-copper. Cheers!"

Beatrice beamed. "Cheers! I knew I would enjoy this wedding but not quite this much. Now tell me, which force were you with?"

After the speeches, Beatrice began to feel the slightest bit squiffy. So many toasts, so much champagne and that was on top of all the wine. She decided to visit the ladies before enjoying her slice of wedding cake. The party had got to the stage where people were leaving their seats to chat with groups at other tables, swapping places, loosening ties and generally letting their hair down.

She excused herself and left the dining room. The foyer was quiet, cool and something of a relief after the reception, tempting her to sit down on one of the leather sofas and have a few minutes to herself. Yesterday's emotional ups and downs combined with lack of sleep had drained her. But a horde of small children came screeching across the hall, on the hunt for something terribly important. She laughed to see Luke in their midst, red-faced and sweaty. She continued to the ladies' toilet, all piped Vivaldi and fresh flowers. It reminded her just a touch of James's practice.

After washing her hands, she took her time freshening up her make-up and sat on the little banquette to check her messages.

"Hello, Ms Stubbs, DI Axe speaking. I know you have a lot on today, but just to let you know we've opened a new enquiry into more than one suspicious death connected to Gaia Dee. One of those is Vaughan Mason. I can give no more details at present, but out of courtesy for your ... erm ... assistance, I wanted you to know. What I would say is that we have this under control and further participation from your side is not required. If we need your help, we'll ask for it. We will be speaking to DS Quinn in the New Year in the hope he's recovered some memory of last night's events, although I'm not optimistic. Unlikely as it sounds, we might have a better chance with the cold cases. If so, I'll let you know. Have a good wedding, wish them both my best and merry Christmas to you all."

Beatrice stared at the hand dryer. So Gaia Dee had done it more than once before. An all-too-familiar heat of righteous anger surged in her stomach. Mainly for Will. She imagined his body lying in the cold and dark, face pale, lips blue and eyes closed. Leaving him there could have ended in tragedy and Gaia Dee must have known that. Now she would never face justice for what she had done. But there was still the question of her possible collaborators. Her nails were digging into her palms so she forced herself to take a deep breath and relax.

Bridesmaid first, detective second.

If only for today, just let it go.

Gaia was dead. Will was alive. She herself had done what Matthew asked and passed her information to the correct authorities. It was pointless and self-destructive to get upset because the outcome was unsatisfactory. It was over.

The thought occurred to her that she would need to address the counselling situation. Part of her was itching to call James but she had to wait till after Christmas. Her urgency was less driven by her mental stability and more by gleeful vindication. *I did try, James, but since the counsellor you chose for me was a murderous sociopath, I have no choice but to continue my treatment with you.*

No need to be petty, said her conscience. She ignored it.

Time to get back to the party. She picked up her handbag, checked her hair and sighed. No hairdresser in living memory had managed to make it behave for more than a few hours and today was no exception. She opened the door and came face to face with a short blonde woman her own age.

"Hello, Beatrice."

"Hello, Pam."

Chapter Twenty-Eight

It was hard not to stare. Pam's features, as familiar to Beatrice as a sister's, had aged and sagged over the decades. As had her own. Looking into each other's eyes was a curiously powerful experience.

Pam gave a tight smile. "I knew you'd be here today. Thought I'd come and say hello," said Pam. "Do you have a minute? I know you're busy." She indicated the Chesterfield Beatrice had fancied earlier.

"Yes, of course. As a matter of fact, I could do with a break."

Pam led the way and they seated themselves on the sofa, knees angled towards each other. Beatrice placed her handbag on her lap, changed her mind and placed it on the floor.

"How are you?" Pam asked, folding her hands on her knees.

"Very well, generally speaking. Today's been quite emotional on top of an exhausting week. What about yourself?"

"I'm fine. Usual pre-Christmas stress, but nothing out of the ordinary."

The silence expanded, somehow intensified by the hum of happy chatter from the wedding guests in the opposite room.

Beatrice swallowed. She was awfully thirsty. "I understand you manage events here. It's a lovely place."

"It is. I count myself lucky every morning when I come to work. And you? From what I hear, you have retired?"

"Yes. The Met got its money's worth out of me. In the last few years, I came to see I was no longer up to the job. Too old, tired and jaded."

Pam gave her the once-over. "You don't look it to me. You still seem full of vim and vinegar."

Wondering if she'd misheard, Beatrice didn't reply for a moment. When she did, she chose her words carefully. "Believe me, in the last few cases I investigated, I simply didn't pass mustard."

Pam's lips twitched. "It must be such a stressful job. With the whole world going to hell in a handbag, I often wonder how police officers cope."

"Sometimes they don't. You can only make a pig's rear of it so many times before handing over to the next generation."

The front doors opened and a pack of children came running across the foyer, making for the dining room. Luke skidded to a halt in front of them. "Hello-Beatrice-hello-Grandma-can-I-go-in-the-maze?"

Pam reached out to smooth back his fringe. "Hello, Luke. I think Beatrice and I would say you should ask your mum. You look very hot to be running about in the snow."

"I *am* hot. Can I take this off?" He tugged at his tie.

"Give it to me. You look very smart today. Doesn't he, Beatrice?"

"Dashing, I'd say. His performance as ring-bearer was terrific."

Luke looked over his shoulder in impatience. "So can I go in the maze or what?"

"It's not up to us," said Beatrice. "If your mum says it's OK, you can go."

Luke dashed away, colliding with one of Adrian's cousins on her way to the bathroom. She was none too steady on her pins to begin with and clutched the door jamb for support after the small whirlwind had passed.

Pam rolled up his tie and handed it to Beatrice. "That's what I wanted to talk to you about. That boy should be able to have his extended family present at birthdays and school plays and so on. Trying to keep the pair of us apart is a strain on the girls as well. Time we forgot our differences and behaved like grown-ups. What do you think?"

"I think that would make the lives of our loved ones a great deal easier. Shall we shake on it? To civilised behaviour."

Pam took her hand and gave it a quick squeeze. Their eyes met for a moment. Then the door to the dining room opened as another guest walked towards the entrance with a packet of cigarettes in hand.

"I must go." Pam stood up. "Have fun today."

"Thank you, Pam. It was good to see you. Merry Christmas."

"Merry Christmas, Beatrice."

Chapter Twenty-Nine

Tanya was a touch dishevelled, her hair coming out of its pins and her face flushed. She wandered over to their table, a happy grin on her face, and flung her arms around Adrian and Will's shoulders.

"Best wedding ever. Best grooms ever. I've had such a lovely day and you two gave the best speeches. So did your best man." She looked over at Will's brother, who was explaining something to Catinca with the aid of a pepper pot and flower arrangement. "Is he single?" she asked.

"This week, yes. So make your move now," said Will. "It has been a perfect day, I agree. Everyone played their parts perfectly. Both mothers cried..."

Adrian interrupted, "Not to mention Beatrice."

"OK, so all our 'mothers' cried. Luke was a little star, the food was excellent and it stopped snowing long enough for us to get the photographs. The cake was on the heavy side, but I'll be working that off on the dance floor later tonight."

"See, I usually hate weddings, but this one? Gorgeous!" Tanya sighed.

"Mum?" Luke ran up to their table, equally flushed as Tanya but not for the same reasons, Adrian hoped.

Tanya hadn't heard her son's urgent appeal. "You're going to make each other very happy, I can see that already. Hark at me, getting all sentimental."

"Mum!" Luke insisted.

"Hello, my darling boy. You did a brilliant job today. Not a foot wrong."

Will agreed. "For a first-time ring-bearer, you knocked it out of the park."

"Good job, Luke and thank you," said Adrian. "We'll bring you a present back from the Caribbean."

Luke nodded but his attention was elsewhere. "Can I go with the others into the maze? Mum? Can I?"

"It's freezing out there, Lukey. You'll have to put a coat on. And where's your tie? I'm not sure it's safe for kids to go into the maze. Who are the others, anyway?"

"Them!" He pointed across the room. Four children of various ages waited by the door. "That's Jason and Hadley and ... the other two. We won't be long. Come on, Mum!"

"They're my cousins' kids," said Adrian. "I trust them."

"Oh OK then. But put your coat on and if you're longer than fifteen minutes, I'm coming to fetch you." Tanya ran her hand through his damp hair. "Where have you done with your tie?"

"I gave it to Grandma." Luke was straining to get out of his mother's grasp.

Tanya frowned. "Grandma?"

"He probably means Beatrice," offered Adrian. "That's the role she's playing today."

Luke tugged away from Tanya. "Grandma's got it. I was too hot and she said I could take my tie off. So I did and gave it to her."

Will leant his forearms on his knees to talk to Luke. "Do you mean Beatrice? Because your grandma isn't here today."

"She is!" Luke was indignant. He poked a finger in the direction of the foyer. "Us lot were out there playing and I saw her talking to Beatrice. That's when I gave her my tie."

Adrian scanned the room. Matthew, now seated next to Marianne, was chatting to one of Will's police colleagues. There was no sign of Beatrice Stubbs.

"Can I go, Mum, please, can I?" asked Luke.

Tanya released his hand and he peeled off towards the waiting children, doing a fist pump all the way across the room.

The tension at the top table had caught attention from other tables. Marianne laid a hand on Matthew's arm and they both stared at the two grooms. Conversations ground to a halt as Adrian, Will and Tanya glanced wide-eyed at one another and back to the double doors. Catinca leant past Will's brother to hiss, "What is it?"

Adrian was about to open his mouth to reply when the double doors opened. A figure stood back to allow a pack of children to rush outside. Facing the silent, curious crowd stood Beatrice Stubbs. Alone.

"What? Did I miss the cake?"

Chapter Thirty

At half past eight on Christmas Day, Beatrice Stubbs was wide awake. A gap in the curtains allowed a shaft of sunshine to creep across the room, along the carpet, over the sleeping dog and onto the bed, where a large snoring heap showed no signs of rousing. Slipping out of bed, she pulled back the curtains. The snow had finally stopped, the day was crisp and bright as fresh bread and blue skies glowed with promise.

She turned back to the bed. Huggy Bear sat up in her basket and stretched, her toothy grin already in place. Beatrice pulled something from the bedside cabinet, got back into bed and blew in Matthew's ear till he opened his eyes.

"What? Why are you bothering me at this godforsaken hour? Close those curtains and go back to sleep."

"Merry Christmas!!!"

"Hmmph." He rolled away from her and pulled the duvet up over his head.

"Matthew, it's practically nine o'clock and I'm awake."

"That much is obvious. Take the dog out and leave me in peace."

"Open your stocking first."

Matthew squinted at her over his shoulder. "Presents after breakfast. That is the rule."

"This is not a present, it's your Christmas stocking, to be opened in bed."

With a groan, Matthew sat up, rubbing his eyes. Beatrice handed him an oversized sock in garish colours. The weight of it clunked against his knee.

"Why do I..."

"Just open it!" Beatrice hugged her arms.

Several seconds later, and far more slowly than Beatrice would have liked, Matthew tore away the brown paper to reveal a brand-new Moka coffee pot. He kissed her with a laugh. "Thank you, Old Thing. I shall put this to use in the very near future."

"I rather hoped you might." Beatrice flung back the covers. "Come on, Huggy Bear, I've got something for you too and it's just your colour. Walkies!"

Every Christmas, Bailey and Stubbs maintained their own favourite traditions. A large and indulgent breakfast (Matthew), personal present-giving (Beatrice) and a brisk walk into the village for a pint at the pub (both), before lunch with all the trimmings (mostly Matthew). Whether the girls could join them or not – alternate years for each parent – Matthew and Beatrice always made the most of December the 25th. Somehow this year had an extra significance.

They now had the animals, of course. And it was their year to host the girls and Luke, which made it more of an occasion. But the biggest difference was that Beatrice was not joining in as a mere guest, but a permanent resident. A local.

After an hour scampering in the snow, woman and dog returned, exhilarated, wet and hungry. The scent of kippers and fresh coffee wafted into the hall as Beatrice took off her boots and dried the terrier. She went into the conservatory to water Will and Adrian's white rosebush, a wedding gift from Rose and Maggie, which was still in its sacking container till the ground thawed outside. The happy couple, lacking a garden, had decided to plant it at Beatrice and Matthew's cottage, just beside the back door. Beatrice was delighted. She would be able to see it through the kitchen window and every time she did, she would be reminded of the boys and their wonderful wedding.

The strains of *St John's Passion* filled the kitchen and the sun shone from a sky so blue it could be Greek. Even though it was Christmas, Beatrice observed her rituals. She fed the dog, trotted upstairs, wrote in her diary and took her stabiliser. Then she thundered downstairs for coffee and kedgeree.

On Beatrice's insistence, Matthew wore his new jumper to the pub for their lunchtime drink. It was a cable knit with leather elbows, precisely the sort Vaughan would have deemed 'Old Fart'. But Vaughan wasn't here to judge and Matthew looked most distinguished in royal blue. The public bar at The Angel was crowded and good-humoured, largely due to Gordon's Christmas Cup. Frankie and Susie managed the bar while the merry landlord offered a free glass of punch to each guest.

Beatrice greeted various villagers as she wove her way through the throng, on her mission to find Gabriel Shaw. Something clamped onto her leg and she looked down to see Luke, in an elf hat. He reached up for her hand and dragged her to the fireside, where Tanya sat in conversation with the very man she'd been looking for.

"Merry Christmas!" Tanya jumped up for a hug and a kiss.

Beatrice turned to Gabriel. "My knight in shining Land Rover! I want to buy you a drink and you may not refuse me. What are you drinking?"

"Merry Christmas, DI Stubbs. That's very kind. I'll have a pint of Tanglefoot."

"I'm not buying you a drink unless you call me Beatrice."

He laughed, his face even better looking as he relaxed. "All right, Beatrice it is. I'll call you anything you like so long as I get my beer. How's the dog settling in?"

"To be honest, I don't know what we did without her. She's over there somewhere with Matthew. Luke, you want some more juice? And I don't need to ask Tanya what she's drinking on Christmas morning."

"At least I'm consistent. Gabriel even gave me a bottle as a

Christmas present. Hey, there's Marianne." Tanya waved at her sister to join them.

Assisted by Luke, Beatrice went to the bar and waited till Frankie had finished serving Demelza Price and her sisters their gin and tonics before giving her order.

"You're not trying Dad's Christmas punch, Beatrice?"

"No fear. I've not forgotten what happened last time he persuaded me to try a glass. I'll stick to Prosecco with the girls." She felt a tug on her arm and looked down into a pair of hopeful blue eyes. "Oh and a packet of cheese and onion, please."

Frankie handed the crisps over to Luke. "Here you go, Santa's Little Helper!"

Mission accomplished, Luke gave them both the thumbs-up and opened the packet.

"Did the boys get away OK?" asked Frankie, pulling the draught pump towards her and filling a pint glass with a golden liquid Beatrice quite fancied.

"Last thing I heard they were in the First Class Lounge at Gatwick. I'm not sure either of them had any sleep. They were both buzzing with excitement and Adrian was still issuing orders."

"I miss them. Without those two and Catinca, the place feels empty. Especially after Rose and Maggie left yesterday afternoon." Frankie placed the drinks on the bar. "You take these and I'll bring the rest over to you. I want to come and say hello to Tanya."

Beatrice stopped to greet Heather Shaw and pointed out one very happy terrier sitting at Matthew's heel as he chatted to Mungo.

"Makes my day to see them rehomed and happy. Thank you; Beatrice, you're very good. How did the wedding go on Sunday? I heard it was quite the spectacle."

"It was beautiful. A day I'll never forget. Everything was as we'd imagined and I cried more times than I can count." She looked at her watch. "If my time zones are correct, they should be landing in the Caribbean for their honeymoon about now."

"Aw, bless them. I wish them every happiness. Has Will remembered anything about the incident in Appleford?"

"No. I don't think we'll ever get to the bottom of that. I just thank our lucky stars Susie knew where to look."

Heather didn't reply, her focus on the landlady behind the bar. Susie caught her eye and a look passed between the two women Beatrice could not interpret. There was a defiance in Susie's jaw as Heather's stare bored into her. Then Frankie broke the moment by calling her mother to fetch more ice. Heather recovered herself and raised her glass of punch.

"Have a lovely Yuletide, Beatrice!"

Beatrice chinked her glass with the schoolteacher and returned to the fireside. When she got back to their little group, Frankie was sitting on the arm of Gabriel's chair, laughing at one of Tanya's stories. Beatrice poured the fizz and observed their body language. Frankie was leaning in, her leg touching Gabriel's, her lovely face lit up by her smile. But Gabriel's attention was one hundred percent on Tanya and the look in his eyes was quite unmistakeable.

"Here we are. Proseccos all round and one pint of Tanglefoot."

Gabriel gave her his slow smile. "Thanks, Beatrice. Merry Christmas to you."

"Merry Christmas!" They chinked glasses and drank. Beatrice spotted the red liquid in Marianne's glass. "You're not on Gordon's Christmas Cup, are you? That stuff is rocket fuel."

Marianne's cheeks were already glowing and she giggled. "Can't deny it's got a kick to it. What does he put in it, Frankie?"

"You don't want to know. Mind, I think he toned it down this time after what happened on St Nicholas Day."

Tanya shrieked with laughter. "That was priceless! Remember the Morris dancers? They got absolutely plastered!"

"They weren't the only ones. Didn't certain people join in the dancing?" Gabriel grinned at Beatrice.

"Don't remind me. Flailing around on the village green with a hanky in each hand at my age? I still can't believe I did that," Beatrice groaned.

"I can. It was hilarious!" Frankie laughed. "And St Nicholas himself threw up on his fake beard. It was like Armageddon!"

Beatrice joined in the laughter but spotted an opportunity. "It was a day we won't forget, that's for sure. But I don't remember seeing you there, Frankie. I thought you hadn't been back since the summer."

Frankie clapped her hand over her mouth. "Me and my big mouth. Should have remembered I'm talking to an ex-copper." She dropped her voice. "I was here that weekend, but I didn't tell anyone. I always come home for my birthday, but because it falls on or around St Nicholas Day, they keep voting for me to play The Winter Queen again and again. It isn't fair, specially as I don't even live here anymore. It was time for someone else to have a go, so I told a white lie and said I wouldn't be here that weekend."

"That was a nice gesture," said Gabriel. "We voted for Kimberley Damerel this year and she did a grand job."

"She did," said Frankie, nodding. "Her hair looked gorgeous against that dress."

Marianne put down her glass of punch. "Maybe I should stick to Prosecco. I'm a bit of a lightweight at the best of times."

"Luke, pass me that glass so I can give your Auntie Marianne some Prosecco. Who said you could have crisps?"

Luke handed over the glass and pointed at Beatrice.

"Sorry, I should have asked, but it *is* Christmas."

"Yes, it *is* Christmas," echoed Luke and with childlike cunning, changed the subject. "Frankie, when are you going to babysit for me again?"

"Whenever you like, my little superhero."

"How about tomorrow night?" asked Gabriel. "Because I'd like to take Tanya out for dinner. If you're free?" he asked.

Tanya looked taken aback but not displeased. "Er ... OK, why not!"

"Yes!" Luke did his little fist pump and it was all Beatrice could do not to join him.

Matthew wandered over to join them, his personal tankard in hand.

"Merry Christmas, everybody! I just got this and thought you'd like to see." He passed his mobile phone to Beatrice. The screen showed a photo message.

The image showed two men on a beach in swimming trunks, carrying snorkels and each wearing a synthetic silver beard.

Beneath the picture there was a caption.

"Merry Christmas, St Nicholas! Love from St Barts! xx"

There was a collective 'aww' and the buzz of conversation continued. Frankie went to collect empty glasses, Matthew sat down to chat to Gabriel and the sisters were arguing over whether St Barts was French or English speaking. A roar of laughter erupted from the bar and she saw Gordon in the middle of it all, holding a piece of mistletoe over his head. Her attention was drawn to Frankie, who had bent down to whisper in Heather's ear. The schoolteacher was listening intently, her expression severe and her eyes on Susie. When Frankie had finished, she straightened and walked back the bar, passing her mother with a reassuring smile. Both women glanced over at the corner table by the door, where Glynis Knox sat with Demelza Price and her sisters.

Her observations were interrupted by Luke, who wanted to tell Beatrice all about the mobile phone he had been given for Christmas. She devoted her attention to the small boy and his device, just occasionally allowing her gaze to drift over his head. For all the frivolity and good cheer in the room, a tension like an invisible spider's web connected five women.

"...a selfie?"

"Sorry, Luke, what was that?"

"A selfie. Can I send Will and Adrian a selfie? So they can see my elf hat."

"That's a great idea! Why don't you do it outside in the snow, to make it look like Greenland? Get Grandpa to take a photo of you and Huggy Bear, your ersatz reindeer."

Luke needed no more encouragement. He tapped Matthew's arm and began explaining his mission.

In the noisy bar, Beatrice focused on the fire and zoned out from her surroundings to make a decision.

A bell rang. "Last orders, ladies and gents!"

Susie held the bell in her hand, smiling at the punters crowding the bar, but her eyes sought Beatrice. She waggled a glass and raised her eyebrows.

Beatrice sensed five pairs of eyes watching her reaction. She lifted her glass. "No more for me, thanks. I've had quite enough. Merry Christmas, everyone!"

Chapter Thirty-One

"Are you awake?"

"I wasn't. I am now."

"I just wanted to ask you something."

"What is it? I'm hog tired."

"Today was just perfect."

"It was. My ideal Christmas."

Pause.

"Are you ever going to tell me what happened between you and Pam?"

Pause.

"Nothing to tell. We're just keeping the peas."

Pause.

"You are a bloody awkward female, but I love you, Beatrice Stubbs."

Snores.

Chapter Thirty-Two

On the true Day of St Nicholas, Thursday the sixth of December, the village which bears his name does not rejoice. All rejoicing is postponed for two days till Saturday's festival, when saintly celebrations happen at a time that suits everyone. Feverish sewing of costumes, decorations of tractors, last-minute music rehearsals, labelling of jams, allocation of stall space and car parking demarcation has worn everyone out. After the pub closes, the villagers make their way home through fallen leaves and the promise of a frost, each to dream of the festival, the biggest day of their year.

In the distance, a church clock strikes twelve, its sonorous bells echoing across the river, over the fields and into the woods. The village sleeps, not one window still lit. But for the occasional street lamps to give its presence away, a traveller might pass Upton St Nicholas without even knowing it was there.

Above, the cloudless sky deepens to a crow-black, with the new moon invisible to the naked eye. Without its dominant glow, stars sparkle all the brighter, like crystals of salt on Cornish slate. A stillness settles over the landscape. An owl screeches. In the undergrowth, leaves rustle. A fox padding past stops to listen, head cocked, only the tip of his brush visible as his rust-coloured coat blends into the forest floor.

Yet on this night of St Nicholas, nocturnal predators are not alone. At the edge of Appleford Woods, where the road widens to accommodate picnickers in summer, three figures walk single file into the midnight-black forest. Only once they are out of sight of the road does the leader switch on a torch to illuminate their path.

Without hesitation, they head for the clearing and the tall wooden platform at its centre. Now the two followers switch on their beams and all three make a steady sweep of their surroundings. Apparently satisfied, they kill all lights and lift their gaze upwards.

A dim glow from the platform above tells them they are expected. They begin to climb.

In the black canvas hide, three others await their arrival, seated in a semi-circle on the floor around a lantern, their faces lit by the steady flame.

The trio completes the ring and all six women push back their hoods.

Eyes flicker with uncertainty until one person withdraws a box. Everyone is transfixed as gloved hands open the lid. Instinctively, they all lean back.

Inside lies a mushroom. White, innocent and perfect.

The clock strikes one.

Message from JJ Marsh

I hope you enjoyed SNOW ANGEL. If you're interested in a taste of AN EMPTY VESSEL, by Vaughan Mason, the first chapter is included at the end of this book.

Also in The Beatrice Stubbs Series:

BEHIND CLOSED DOORS
RAW MATERIAL
TREAD SOFTLY
COLD PRESSED
HUMAN RITES
BAD APPLES

For more information, visit jjmarshauthor.com

For occasional updates, news, deals and a
FREE exclusive prequel: *Black Dogs, Yellow Butterflies*,
subscribe to my newsletter.

If you would recommend *The Beatrice Stubbs Series* to a friend, please do so by writing a review. Your tip helps other readers discover their next favourite book. Thank you.

Acknowledgements

Snow Angel owes much to editors Catriona Troth, Liza Perrat, Jane Dixon Smith and Gillian Hamer, aka Triskele Books. Input from Florian Bielmann proved invaluable and many thanks to Julia Gibbs (proofreader) and JD Smith (cover design).

Also by Triskele Books

TRISKELE BOOKS

*The Charter, Closure, Complicit, Crimson Shore,
False Lights* and *Sacred Lake*
by Gillian Hamer

*Tristan and Iseult, The Rise of Zenobia, The Fate of an Emperor,
The Better of Two Men, The Rebel Queen* and *The Love of Julius*
by JD Smith

*Spirit of Lost Angels, Wolfsangel, Blood Rose Angel,
The Silent Kookaburra* and *The Swooping Magpie*
by Liza Perrat

Gift of the Raven and *Ghost Town*
by Catriona Troth

http://www.triskelebooks.co.uk

AN
EMPTY
VESSEL

A novel by

VAUGHAN MASON

1

Nancy

They do like to lay it on a bit thick. That whole rigmarole. Black cap, which was more of a black cloth if you're calling a spade a spade, the not-quite-silence of the courtroom and the deep, theatrical breath. He had to have his moment. And the language he used. '*Hanged by the neck until you are dead*'. I would have got it first time if he'd just said 'hanged'. Don't think anybody would have had their doubts, would they?

"What's he mean by that then? Hanged a bit, or the whole hog?"

"Is she really going to swing?"

Is she?

Am I?

Nancy Maidstone, I will not seek to add further hardship to yourself or others in this courtroom by repetition of the details of this most distressing murder. I will content myself now with passing the sentence of the law, which is, that you be taken hence to the jail of Holloway; to a place of execution and be there hanged by the neck until you are dead; and that your body be afterwards buried within the precincts of the prison in which you shall be last confined after your conviction; and may the Lord have mercy upon your soul! Amen.

It's quiet now. I'm sat on the cot, looking at me hands. Funny, how your hands show more about you than your face. These hands are all right. I couldn't say they look like mine. They look older, harder, more capable than the rest of me. They look like my mother's hands.

When Ma died, I remembered her hands. I can still picture the graceful scar right across the base of her thumb, a white arc like a crescent moon. That was from the biscuit tin when we had the bus crash. I can recall my mother's hands far better than her face.

My fingernails are filthy. *You could grow taters under there, my girl.* Never used to let them get like that when I had my white coat on. Clean nails, tidy hair, it was all part of the job. What would be the point of a clean pair of hands now? I got what I expected. Got what I wanted and it won't be long before I can bow out. Goodbye, then. And thanks, for my life.

What did I do? I killed. Mostly I killed kindly. It was what I wanted to do; it's what I was trained to do. If killing is to be done, best 'tis done kindly. Now it's my turn. I'm sure they'll do the same for me. If you have to go, they'll try to make it painless. Nan, it's almost done now. All you got to do is face it and take your medicine like a big girl. No bawling and snivelling, no dramatics nor hysterics. Don't let yourself down. Deep breaths now, can't get dizzy again.

I hit me own head on the basin when I came over a bit woozy earlier. At least it cheered the warders up. If I was to go base over apex again, they'd be delighted with that, wouldn't they just? Wonder if they'll be worse or better now I'm getting my 'just desserts'? Or will they spit twice? Tell the truth, I'm past caring. This lot in here are different. You can tell they feel superior because they are in charge of the 'condemned suite'. I'm in a suite now, don't you know. It is and all. Three rooms, if you count the visitors' cell. The one who brought me in said they'd be watching me all night. I was only under observation in the hospital wing, which means they have a look in every now and then. Wonder why? Is it in case I do away with myself? We wouldn't want that now, would we? That would be a sin.

In my time, I've spent many hours with creatures breathing and bleeding their last. You have no idea how much they really suffer or if your presence is any use. Stroking and patting, trying to ease the pain. I heard once that fear is worse than pain for animals. That's why I spoke soothing words to a condemned cow. Wonder who I was really helping? Poor old cow can't tell me how she feels. Maybe the only one I helped feel better was meself.

I know about death, about the long old walk to the exit. But those creatures didn't know it was coming. I do.

How do I prepare for something like that? Something like this.

Who's looking after this poor old cow?

What happens? Is that it, lights out, thank you and good-night? See, this is the trouble with religion. They go on at you for so long about heaven and hell and purgatory and afterlife and all, that even when you do give it a good hard look and realise that it don't hold up, you can't let go.

There's got to be something, you say to yourself, even if I don't go along with what the clergy tries to stuff down our throats. Good job I don't believe in all the angels and harps business. Because think about it. If you believe in One, that means there's the Other. Downstairs with Old Nick and his merry games. After all they said about me, what have I got to hope for?

No idea what time it is but I just woke up with a right start. Might be gone midnight. That means I'm due to die today.

I'm glad. I tell you, I am glad. Half of me wants to get up off this blanket and do a jig. Here and now in this bare and echoing cell. But what with my giddy head and all, I'd just as well give it a rest. I can't help but smile, though. No more of it. No one can get at me any more. No fellas in wigs, asking me over and over the same old story. No police, no doctors, no guards nor no relatives. No vicars, no priests. And nobody out there is allowed anywhere near me.

The prison officers did a funny stunt with the Black Marias and an Army van, so that the people outside didn't know it was me. We went out far too early and had to drive all over the shop, so the guard said. Not to me, of course. They won't hardly talk to me no more. She told one of the courtroom girls while we were waiting. She said to Marlene (that was her name and they knew each other from way back) the Army van was the decoy and the two paddywagons were supposed to be full of coppers. That guard was proud as punch, she was. Fooled old Joe Public. I couldn't hear what was going on, but apparently the crowd gave the Army van a right battering. Because they thought I was in there. What they really wanted to do was to batter me.

Can't tell if this is the shivers or the shakes. The first is all right. Shivers is natural, because I am cold, haven't slept properly in weeks and all I've got is this blanket, which smells sour and mouldy. Shivers I'm used to. But the shakes aren't really to do with here and now. Shakes are to do with before, what happened before and what's going to happen after. If this is the shakes, well, I have to say it's a first. This is the first time I have had the shakes about after.

Before today, there wasn't a future, just the next day. I could never have got through the court case if I'd thought about the future. All I could manage was the next twenty-four hours. Get up, try to clean up as best I could, eat up my rations such as they were and go to court. Listen, try to understand; try to care.

Trouble is, it was lovely and warm in the courtroom and all those voices went on and on. I had the hardest job staying awake. I could feel, even with my eyes forced wide open, my head lolling a bit. If I closed my eyes for a second, it would be all over. It happened, more than once. Usually, the lawyer lady spotted it and nudged me awake. Good Lord and Peggy Martin, but it was hard.

See, with all the thoughts and worries to think and worry about, not to mention the blinking awful dreams, I could hardly sleep nights. Leave alone them vindictive guards who loved to bang and clatter enough to scare the living daylights out of you, just when you'd dropped off. I wasn't sleeping much.

But the courtroom, and I know how daft this sounds, was a safe place. All I had to do was sit in the warm, listen, look at people and answer questions. No-one could hurt me, they weren't allowed. I saw the judge frown once, as my head jerked upright and my eyes flew open. Head lolling about.

You will be hanged from the neck until you are dead.

Can't sleep tonight, although I ought to try. And why would that be, Miss Maidstone? Going somewhere, are we? Got plans for later in the week? Don't matter whether I sleep or stare at the patch of reflected sodium light in the corner. This is no longer my room. I shall be checking out in the morning. Could you make up my bill, there's a good chap? I am on my way out, and don't bother yourself about my bags.

and that your body be afterwards buried within the precincts of the prison in which you shall be last confined after your conviction; and may the Lord have mercy upon your soul! Amen.

Amen.

I wonder if they let anyone in at all. No, they wouldn't, would they? That horrible woman said that in America, they let the family of the victim watch the execution. Sometimes the condemned person's family comes along too. What a thought. What must they see in one another's eyes in a situation like that? Still, we're not in America, so I should be grateful for small mercies. Not that I'd have anyone from my side to watch. Not any more. Frank wouldn't come. He's washed his hands of me. Changed his name, so they said. I can't blame him.

When they first brought me in here, that must have been three or four months back, the first visitor I had was Frank. I was surprised by that. I wasn't expecting anyone at all. They only allow close family and Frank was all I had left. Frank coming to a women's nick. Poor beggar. What a thing to have to deal with for a man.

Frank was here. Funny to think of it now. He didn't stay long at all. He didn't have a clue what to say and I still wonder why he bothered. He never knew what to say to me on an ordinary day, never mind when I'd just been arrested for murder. Just sitting there, shaking his head, looking at me again and back to the floor, shaking his head.

He hadn't said a word when he first arrived.

Well, just the one.

Nancy.

"Nancy," he said, as he walked in. All formal, with a nod, like as if he was a neighbour and we happened to meet in the doctor's surgery. Nancy. Same tone he would use with a distant nephew, one he didn't like all that much.

I think the silence and head-shaking was supposed to let me know that he couldn't believe it. Not of me. Not his own flesh and blood. Not Nancy. But Frank was not one to let gestures speak louder than words.

"I can't believe this. I cannot believe I am here".

He looked at me, incredulous. I tried a weak smile and raised my eyebrows.

"Oh, that's right, you grin away, girl. You have yourself a laugh. They ain't mucking about, Nancy, this ain't a bit of a slip-up what will get you a slap on the wrist. This is Holloway, girl. You're in the nick!"

I blinked. Frank was telling me that I was in prison. Perhaps he thought I hadn't twigged yet.

"Good God Almighty, Nance, what the hell is this?"

His face got redder then, which was reassuring. He was quite pale when they let him in and I thought he looked proper peaky. Mind, I was used to seeing him near puce most of the time.

Always in a fury, is our Frank. They're all out to get him. Everyone lies in wait to make our Frank's life a misery. If you're in the car with Frank and you pull up to a junction, a stream of cars comes round the bend and he has to wait for ages till he can pull out. He always says the same thing. 'Those blighters were waiting for me, see! Just bloody marvellous, innit, as soon as I want to get out, they all bloody queue up to stop me getting where it is I want to go'. Poor old Frank. But he was off again.

"They tell me you ain't said a word, Nancy. Well, I'll tell you what, my girl, you going to say a word or two to me. We'll get to the bottom of this and sort it all out. Right? Right, Nance?"

I met his eyes, but I could not think for the life of me what expression I should have, so I just didn't. No expression. I looked away.

"I don't know what went on there and to tell the truth, I don't want to know. But I know it can't be what they're saying. That weren't you. I know that much, I ain't daft. Thing is, Nance, you got yourself mixed up in something very nasty. You got to come clean, so we can sort it out, innit?"

Pressure built behind my eyes. I rubbed my face with my hands. I wished he'd give over. But he was working up quite a head of steam. Thing with Frank is, he can't half talk. Ooh, what? Our mother used to say he'd have the hind leg off a donkey. Charlie was quieter. He'd whisper to Frank and Frank would do the foghorn bit. Sitting there in the visiting cell, he shook his head and got himself into a right muck sweat. I could see why. He was out of his depth. In the normal course of events, if I'd spilt a pan full of greens or knocked over a basket of clean shirts or couldn't open the coal house door, he'd barge me out the way and sort it out. All the while calling me a 'daft cat' or 'great heifer' or mostly 'useless mare'. This time, he was stuck. I wanted to tell him not to bother himself, just to go on home. It ain't going to work, Frank, and it don't matter how many blood vessels you pop.

"You shamed me, Nancy! Do you realise, have you got the foggiest of how shamed I am? Not just me, all of us! Can't look anyone in the eye. You know what, you have taken away my pride in my family name, that's what you've gone and done. Taken away my pride, one of the worst things you can do to a man. Thank God our Ma and Dad ain't here to see this. Thank God Charlie is dead and gone. Never thought I'd hear myself say them words but as God is my witness … "

He never thought he'd hear himself say them words. *Thank God Charlie is dead and gone.* Well, I been saying them ever since he died. The real queer part is that I never thought I'd hear Frank say that. Not the bit about Charlie. The bit about talking. All I can remember from when I was a nipper is being told to shut it.

Quiet, girl, you'll wake your father. Hush. Sssh. Will you put a sock in it? Can't you shut her up, Mum? Hush now. Little girls should be seen and not heard. Shut up, Nancy. No-one's interested. Don't tell. Sssh. You better not open your mouth. If you say any-thing about this, we'll call you a liar. And who're they going to believe? Keep your trap shut, girl, if you know what's good for you. Sssh, not a whisper. There's only one thing your mouth is good for and it ain't talking. Nancy, would you please shut your bleeding cake-hole! Hush, sweetheart, hush now.

Seems Frank changed his mind. He wanted me to talk.

"What the hell was it all about, eh? Why the hell Gerry Murray? That lad was only twenty-one. What the bloody hell was going on, Nan, what the firing bloody hell? All right, all right. You don't like the language. I know, I can see it on your face. Thing is, I'm in the dark, see? I don't know what to think. You're in shock, your brief told me, but ain't we all? Ain't we all smacked sideways by this one? Nan, you saw what happened. I can't believe it was you, don't ask me to get that into me skull. Tell the coppers who done it or we ain't never gonna know, innit?"

He looked old, did Frank. Funny how you add up all the little changes and it comes to one great big one. He'd gone old. Don't get me wrong, I wasn't thinking that was anything to do with me and all of this business. He did look a bit drained and tired, but there could be a lot of wherefores as to that why. His suit was shiny, like it had been ironed too often. Not shiny all over, like

Mr Harmsworth. He has his done in a shop up West and they're supposed to be like that. Frank's was shiny in patches. I could feel that old itch. I wanted to take it off of him, give it a decent hand wash, then press it while still damp, covering the suit with an old cloth. It'd come up lovely then. But I didn't. Come to that, I couldn't.

"Gawd, I don't know if I'm talking to a brick wall or what. You can't just keep schtum, girl. You don't want to talk to the Old Bill, and nor don't I, but you got to say something. Innit? I'll tell you something for nothing. What's it been? Two days, well three, if you're counting the Monday. People are singing a song about you. Famous, that's what you are, girl. Do you want to hear it? No, I don't expect you do. Well, I have to hear this, day in, day out, so it's time you done too.

Who's sorry now, who's sorry now
Who took a gun to shoot poor Gerry down
She heard him groan, she watched him moan
'Cos she's got a heart made of stone."

I hope I die before hearing my brother sing again. I've never heard him sing before and going by the sound of it, he didn't practise much. It was the worst thing I ever heard in my life. His voice was weak and creaky, like an old man's, and his embarrassment contagious. He sat opposite me, in that cold light, with the warder watching expressionless, opened his mouth and sang. It was ugly, painful and raw as a grazed knee. I was mortified and my face burned as if I'd opened the door to a furnace. I looked away, up and down, like a cornered creature, but there was no way to escape. I was so horrified by Frank's singing I don't think I paid all that much mind to the words. It lasted a few agonising, eternal seconds.

Frank spoke. "See? Nice. Lovely. 'Maid of Stone'. I just cannot wait to show my face in my place of work come next Monday. The reception will be royal. ROYAL! For crying out loud, you silly bitch, will you tell us what the hell happened?"

I stared at my hands and waited till my face cooled.

"I got sweet Fanny Adams to go on. The papers say it looks like you done it and you ain't arguing. But it don't add up, not to my mind, it don't. What was he to you? Far as I know, you was just working with the bloke before, but he could have been your weekend fancy man for all that I know. I just don't know.

"He wasn't, was he? Was he, Nan? Nah, nah, he weren't. Give me strength. What I do know is that you will get yourself nowhere by keeping your gob shut. What did he do, Nan? If he tried to hurt you, well, that's self-defence. Your brief will be banging on about that one, but only if you help. She says you are 'uncooperative'. Know what that means? It means you are a stubborn little cow, that's what it means. I don't think she likes you. Who can blame the woman, eh? If you won't help yourself, why should anyone else?

"RIGHT! I am sick to the back teeth of this! You will tell me what the bloody hell went on in that place or I swear on my lites, I will do for you!"

The warder took a step towards us. "Mr Maidstone, would you take your seat, sir?"

"All right, I got the point. I'm sitting, see? It's enough to drive you round the bend, though. It would try the patience of a saint. She's gone simple on me. Can't get a word out of the dozy mare. Thank you, miss, I'll keep seated now.

"See? See what you are dragging me down to? Your level, that's what. Have I ever had a brush with any area of the law before now? No, I have not. Not on my life. But no apology. No, sorry I am dragging you into all this, Frank. I am deeply ashamed of the disgrace I have brought on our entire family, Frank. No. Not a bleeding word. The silent treatment. Nancy, I don't know if you thought this through or what, but I got to tell you, you could get the death penalty for this. They ain't used it for a while, true, but that's only 'cos the soft soapers created such a three-ring circus over that last one. It's still in place. You could face the noose, girl."

An electric shock charged through me. The second time

Frank had shocked me, but this time with hope. They wouldn't, would they? They wouldn't actually let me go? That was the first time I dared to entertain the thought. Up to then, I'd been convinced that they'd punish me forever, by keeping me in that place, with those women, till I died of old age. Make me live with myself. I didn't dare believe that they might let me leave early. I couldn't think about it. If I did, it would never happen. I never got anything I wanted.

"No, no. Don't look like that. I'm only putting the wind up. Oi, Nance, it's all right, I said. They ain't going to do you in, girl. Honest to God, though, you got to talk. You can't go all blank like that. Makes everyone a bit jumpy. Tell the truth and shame the devil, innit? If you can't rely on your own family, who can you ... are you yawning? Am I boring you? Oh, I do apologise. I shouldn't keep you. After all, I am only trying to keep you from swinging from the bleeding gallows, you daft cow!"

I blinked a few times, trying to concentrate. Frank got up, making a right show of biting his lip.

"Goodbye, Nancy. I can't wish you good luck because that would be stupid. About half as stupid as you are. All I can say is that from now on, I am an only child. I never had a sister and my name is not, at least no longer, Frank Maidstone. I'll keep the Frank, but you have spoiled the rest of it. Who knows, I could always call myself Murray. Excuse me, miss? If you don't mind, I'll be leaving now. Ta-ra, Nance."

The warder opened the door. His last glance was a mixture of puzzled, angry and hurt. As if I was a well-trained dog which had just bitten him. I wouldn't see him again. My heart went out to him, it really did. Odd how personal it was. He really thought I was doing it to hurt him. Funny, in a way. If I'd known what it would take to make him care.

Poor old Frank. I cared for him. He got in the firing line, did Frank, in a manner of speaking. Charlie, God rest his soul, started the fire, but Frank was the smoke. He was the one who got caught and copped it. Charlie would stand, wide-eyed and shocked, saying, 'Oh, Frank!', like he couldn't believe it. His face was always pale, not like Frank, who used to flush beetroot when they got caught. No matter what the punishment, Frank never told on him. Never dobbed his brother in and just took the clip round the ear like a good 'un. No wonder Frank thinks the world's out to get him. He took the blame for them both. Charlie never copped it, not once. Tell a lie, he's copped it now.

How can you think things like that, eh? Your own brother, flesh and blood. God, just thinking about the funeral makes a lump in me throat. Mum's face, cracked, wrecked, drained of all she had. Frank, white and lost without his navigator. Charlie's girl, the glamorous Lana, powder, mascara, foundation, all gone to the dogs.

Dearly beloved …

Dearly beloved, my foot. He wasn't, not by me, leastways. He might have been beloved by the rest of them, and judging by the floods of tears at the crem, he probably was. The golden boy. Tall, fair and handsome, if you go for thin lips, a beaky nose and the cruellest mouth you can imagine.

Shakes are getting worse now. Calm yourself, girl, there's no-one what can hear you. All right to tell the truth when it's just between you and your Maker. *You what? You can't have it both ways! All right then, just between you and the mattress. That'll do.*

Charlie was hateful, cruel and a master manipulator. There. Not just to me, mind, don't get me wrong. This is not just a little sister's old, cold resentment. He did it to Frank, too. The difference was Frank was grateful, just to be let in, to be talked to, included and overjoyed to do all Charlie's dirty work. Don't know how happy he was to take the rap for it all, but he never let out a whisper of complaint. Stupid bloody fool. *Oh, good gracious, what is it with you today, Nan? May as well be hanged for a sheep as a lamb? How to follow up getting charged with murder: not content with bad-mouthing your poor dead brother? Why not finish off with a bit of foul language?*

Charlie makes me think of foul language. I don't care how big a war hero he was in Italy. At home, he was a coward, a sneaky little weasel and a bully. I hated every hair on his golden head. Funny enough, I didn't hate Frank quite as much. More like a bit sorry for him. He was one of Charlie's victims, just didn't know he was.

I knew I was. They would plant the seeds for days, even weeks before, sometimes. They would whisper together, mouths and ears towards each other, but eyes trained on me. I knew. Message received. They were planning how to get me. I could not escape. Never. I could try and tell Mum, but sobbing and crying and saying 'They're looking at me' was never going to get me much sympathy. They always chose humiliation. Fear over pain. Showing me who was boss. There was never a serious mark, apart from the thing in the greenhouse. And that was explained away in no time. My role was the victim, they were going to get me and it was only a matter of time. I spent all my life until they left home in a state of fear. Never a happy-go-lucky moment, never blithe or gay, always waiting and watching. That way, they could hurt me for one day, but make sure they blighted my life for weeks.

One of their favourite targets was my hair. I had lovely hair, the only thing about me that you could call pretty. I had a very plain face, with a big jaw like both the boys. It suited them. My eyes were the palest blue-grey, like dishwater, my Mum used to say. And ever since I can remember, I was big. Big face, big head, broad shoulders, wide hands, as clumsy and awkward a child as you ever met. Dad would call me a blunderbuss when I came pounding down the stairs or knocked into the table and set everything toppling. He used to smile and shake his head. So I didn't mind. I minded a bit when the other kids at school called me sausage-fingers or moon-face, but soon learned to ignore it. My brothers called me Desperate Dan, even in front of my mother. She chided them for that, but even she used to say I should try to be a bit more feminine. Act a bit more like a lady.

My hair was feminine, ladylike and beautiful. Thick as you like, in long ringlets down my back. Mum used to put it in rags for me. The boys laughed themselves soft when they saw me with my hair in rags. Scared the dog, too. He came wandering in, took one look and shot back out again with his tail between his legs. I didn't give a fig for them or the dog. I loved the way my hair came out. Shiny fat curls, looping down my back. Mum never said too much, as she said people who thought a lot of themselves were heading for a fall. Still, she'd comb it through for me, using her fingers very gently and you could see she was proud. When we brushed it at night; one hundred strokes, no more, no less; we were peaceful. We were happy then. Charlie knew I loved my hair and that's why he kept telling me he'd destroy it.

Cowboys and Indians. Tied up to a lamp-post, as trees were a bit thin on the ground. They showed me the matches, built a fire round my feet. Tipped a bottle of brown ale over the broken sticks and told me that pouring alcohol on the fire makes it burn all the wilder. Lit matches, held them to my face and behind my head. I could smell my hair singeing. My throat was hoarse for days after from the screaming.

Scientists. Tied to the table in the greenhouse when Mum had gone on the bus to town. All kinds of chemicals in small jars. Planning to turn me into a peroxide blonde. Pouring liquids onto my skin with so much ceremony and glee that I shrieked fit to wake the dead whether I could feel anything or not. I still have scars on the back of my neck from some chemical or other and on my wrists from the twine holding me onto the Formica.

Barbarian tribes. Sharpening knives, talking about cutting, scarring, scalping and watching my face. I tried pleading, appealing to their sweet sides, threatening to tell, asking, begging them to let me go. Screaming again. That was before they discovered gags.

Then it was Doctors and Patients. Most children's games include nurses, but I was only an 'im-patient'. They found themselves very droll. I once saw Frank damp his shorts through laughing. They wanted to see what was different. They wanted to see how it all fitted together. Innocent enough, kids experimenting. Except I had no choice. They opened the door without knocking.

Of course, they were left to themselves mostly, that was part of the problem. Mum was either out at work or in at work. The boys were her pride and joy. When we went shopping '*I need an extra pair of hands*', she would tell people about them. Both sharp as tacks, oh, she had high hopes for those boys. They were clever, they were running rings round her; they were into everything, especially trouble. She would laugh with the ladies in the shop and shake her head fondly. Charlie and Frank were good looking and badly behaved. Just as a lad ought to be.

I was neither.

She was always exasperated with me. If I wasn't under her feet, then I was making myself useful. When I got a bit bigger, I went with her to her cleaning jobs and tried to help where I could. I was a hard worker and I think she was pleased with me. Although she never said much. Life was so much happier when Mum was home. She would find something for me to do, which got me away from the boys, kept me in her sight. I liked being useful. She had a lot to do, what with Dad being the way he was. I was a good girl.

I was a good girl the day of the bus crash. We'd been round at the Timtons' big old house in Blackheath. I liked the house and the heath with the kiddies flying kites, but not the long walk from the bus stop. That afternoon, Mrs Timton came out as Mum was putting on her coat. She had a small brown envelope in her hand and a biscuit tin under her arm.

"Mary, your wages, dear. One other thing, I'd like you to have these for Nancy. She's a little trouper and she deserves to be paid." She smiled a lovely smile and gave me a little wink. I smiled back, but at the same time hid my face behind Mum's hand.

She handed Mum the biscuit tin. My eyes widened and my mouth began watering.

"Thank you very much, Mrs Timton. That's very decent of you. Say thank you, Nancy."

"Thank you."

"Don't mention it, my dear. You have earned it."

Mum was chuffed, I could tell. She clutched the tin to her chest on the walk to the stop and placed it on her lap as we settled in for the bus ride. I stared at the pictures on the lid, imagining how each biscuit would taste and deciding which one to eat first.

We were on the top deck, as a treat for me, so we never saw the car coming. They told us later a driver took a chance at the lights in Deptford, rushing through as amber changed to red. A motorbike waiting for the change was quick off the mark and pulled away just a touch early. The car saw him, over-corrected and swung straight into the path of our double-decker. I heard the squeal of brakes a second before my mother's forearm slammed across my chest.

The force made my bottom slide forward, knees smacking into the seat in front. I began to cry, more through frightened surprise than pain. Mum's protective gesture towards me left her with one hand to brace herself. Her instinct was to throw her right arm across me and use her left elbow to prevent herself being thrown forward. Her left hand clutched the biscuit tin, which bent, parted and presented a knife-like edge to my mother's thumb.

That was the first time I saw real blood. My tears and snuffles dried instantly as I watched dark surges of my mother's blood pour from her hand. Mum's face was white as she too gazed at the phenomenon. Shouts of anger and outrage came through the windows, as other passengers began to cry or comfort one another. When we bled, Mum stopped it. Now it was my turn.

I reached into her pocket for her handkerchief, the spit-and-polish for dirty faces handkerchief. I took her hand and wrapped it around the base of the thumb, careful to hold it as tight as my small chubby fingers would allow. It must have hurt, because Mum flinched and her eyes sharpened.

"Right, Nance, we may as well walk to the next stop, 'cos this old heap's not going anywhere."

"What about your hand?"

"I'll see to that when I'm home. You've done a good job and it'll hold for now. Up you get."

It took us another hour to get home, by which time the hanky was soaked through. She went into the bathroom, telling me to make us all a cup of tea. I did as I was told, took Dad's into the front room and waited for her to come downstairs. She was waxy pale as I passed her a cup of tea with half a sugar. Her hand was neatly bandaged and there was no more blood.

"Well done, Nance. You kept your head. Just knuckled down and got on with it. You're a good girl, Nancy. Let's give the boys a shout and tell them we've got biscuits, shall we?"

Mum was wrong. I wasn't a good girl. Those biscuits were for me and I didn't want to share them with my greedy selfish brothers. I wasn't good at all.

The front room was for Dad. We were quieter when walking past the door and respectful once inside. We never stayed long because we wore him out, he said. He didn't seem to mind me so much, because I didn't like to talk. It was hard for Dad to talk on account of his lungs. Hearing him make conversation would pain you, it sounded such a struggle. The boys, though, couldn't stay quiet for long. Dad preferred to hear of their achievements and exploits through Mum. Trouble was, when Mum was out and Dad shut up in the front room, the boys had the place to themselves. Sometimes they played on their own, generally something involving shouting and banging. The danger was they'd get bored. If they got bored, they'd come looking for me.

Charlie was the mastermind and Frank always did the dirty work. If ever there was a visible result of their handiwork, Frank copped it. Charlie always appeared distressed about it and would often comfort his trembling little sister. Who would have trembled far less with some distance between me and him. As time passed, Frank grew out of it, found other people to bully. Charlie never stopped.

When they grew older, my big, brave brothers both left home to join the Forces. Frank went into the Army, like our dad, but Charlie was in the RAF. I was happy as a sand-boy, gay all day, singing around the house, as long as Mum was out of earshot. For the first time in my life, I was not terrified and I will always remember those times as pure, perfect happiness.

They came home on leave, throwing my Mother into an enormous panic, using up the whole of our rations in preparation for a banquet. They both behaved like returning heroes, even though neither of them had seen a stroke of action. Frank ignored me, apart from to comment on my beefy arms. *Only way she'll get a decent fella is with an arm-wrestle! Ha ha ha.* The rest of the time, I was barely visible, apart from my maid duties. Tea. Ironing. Dinner. Sandwich. Wireless on. Tea. Wireless off. Bottle of beer. And another. Bag to be packed. He wrote to Mum and Dad. I never got a mention. The dog did, once or twice, but not me.

Charlie though. Charlie used to do what he did with Frank. With the eyes. Except he wasn't whispering to Frank anymore, he'd be talking to our neighbours, telling them about his training routine. Or with Uncle Brian, talking about tactics. Didn't matter who it was, he'd be watching me, with those eyes. I knew. He knew I knew. I tried asking Mum if I could sleep in with her as I was feeling poorly, but she told me not to be so daft. If you're going to be sick, you can do it on your own sheets. I just had to wait there, in my own bed, till it was all quiet. Waiting, as I always had, in fear.

He never did it again. Always threatened to, but never did. I don't know if he was because he was too scared, drunk or cowardly without Frank. I hated him anyway. For the fear. For the shame. For the knowledge that he could, he might, one day.

I did cry when we got the telegram. Mum's face changed as she read it. She went white as gauze. I thought it was Frank. Not for one second did I think it could be Charlie, the golden boy. Mum sat down heavily on the arm of the good settee, her eyes closed. As gently as I could, I took the telegram and read it slowly. That's when I started to sob. I slid down to the floor, put my arms round my knees and sobbed. I cried huge, hot tears and said, 'Oh God, oh God' over and over again in a cracked, clogged voice. What I meant was, 'Thank God, thank God'.

Not till a lot later did I realise how badly Charlie's death affected my mother and father. At the age of about twelve, I was listening to the wireless with Dad and half-watching Mum doing the ironing in the kitchen. Dad started to cough, those creaky heaving coughs which were so painful to hear. I stood to pat him on the back and noticed Mum, head tilted to the ironing board, hands rhythmically removing the creases, tears rolling silently down her face. She hid her sniffs and reached up her sleeve for a hanky. That was when I realised that some people had really loved Charlie.

Not me. I hated him and I am glad he's dead and buried. Selfish. I know I'm a bad person. No joke, the world will be better off without me.

The sky's getting lighter. It's today. My last day. Looks like we'll have nice weather for it.

The complete novel of
An Empty Vessel by Vaughan Mason
will be available in spring 2019.

Made in the USA
Monee, IL
29 March 2021